THE CONTROL
CENTER

THE CONTROL CENTER

THE CHINA AFFAIRS

BOOK 1

BRAD GOOD

CHAPTER 1

Even after all these years living in China, Jack Gold still wasn't used to it.

The spitting, that is.

He inwardly recoiled when his driver stopped at a red light, opened his door, and hocked what sounded like the dredges from the deepest part of his lungs onto the road, before shutting the door and sighing loudly. Spitting was common in Shanghai, but Jack still wasn't accustomed to it. If he thought back far enough, he could recall a day when he and his younger brother, Paul, had been about to go into a restaurant, and Jack spit—just a little bit—right before they went in. He was around eight years old at the time, and the look of disgust that crossed his father's face remained vivid in Jack's mind. It was almost involuntary, it seemed, because the look vanished a moment later and his father simply said, "Jack, I don't ever want to see you do something like that again."

But now, here he was, his Didi driver expectorating onto a road that had seen countless loogies, Jack was certain. He thought of saying something—a few days ago, in fact, an older gentleman had been walking in front of him and spit an impressive glob of phlegm onto the sidewalk, and Jack couldn't help but snap in Chinese, "What are you doing?" The man ignored him, but nearly everyone else in earshot had given him an enthusiastic thumb's up, which Jack took as a good sign. Despite its popularity, many people in China didn't like spitting, though they seldom said anything—not just about spitting, but anything in general. It was not the way of the Chinese to speak up, which was exactly how the government wanted it to be. Even still, Jack hoped to see things in China go the way they did in Hong Kong, which had eradicated spitting in public by imposing fines. Sounded like a great idea to him.

The light turned green and the car moved forward. Didi was the Chinese equivalent of Uber, though, unlike Uber, Didi had no competition—there was no Chinese equivalent to Lyft. The ride-hailing service in China was manned by Chinese drivers—the variety of different ethnicities that Jack was accustomed to in his native Los Angeles was simply not present here, a fact that made complete sense but also would, occasionally, give Jack a pang of homesickness.

Or perhaps it wasn't quite being *homesick*—he wasn't sure what it was. Loneliness? That wasn't quite right—he was surrounded by people. No, lately he'd been feeling what could best be described as a vague discontentment. Was it work? There were some issues there—particularly with one certain coworker—but overall, he enjoyed his job as "first vice president" at Global China Banking Group. It seemed like ages ago now that he had graduated from the University of Chicago Booth School of Business and made his way to China. *Why China?* his father had asked him skeptically, not needing to say anything for Jack to know his choice of place to start a career was not aligned with what his father thought he should be doing.

Jack had tried to explain. *If China, with its massive population, would truly open up, the business opportunities would be endless. I want to be there and be ready to take advantage of those opportunities.*

His father had regarded him without saying anything for a moment, then let out a deep, disappointed breath and waved him off. "Always trying to be three steps ahead," he'd said, as though it was a bad thing.

Jack pushed the thoughts from his mind. If he wanted to show up to this date in a good mood, thinking about his father's disappointment or this vague discontentment was not the way to go.

The car pulled up to the Congressman's Saloon, a 1920s style American whiskey bar.

"Thanks," Jack said in Chinese, as he stepped out of the car. Before he shut the door—"Maybe get yourself some cough drops."

The driver looked at him in confusion, so Jack just shook his head. "Never mind," he said. "It was a joke."

He walked into the bar, one of his favorites. The low lights, the red interior, the booths separated by tall wooden partitions; it made Jack feel as if he'd stepped back in time, into the age of speakeasies, glamor, and gangsters. As usual, the majority of the patrons were white, as few local people could afford to go to such a bar. Jack easily spotted his date, a woman named Kaili, sitting at the bar.

They'd been corresponding on LoveChina.com; in an effort to ease his discontentment, he'd finally got around to setting up a profile and inputting his preferences for a potential date. There'd been many matches, and he contacted several, but the conversation seemed to flow most effortlessly with Kaili, so he suggested meeting in person. He also appreciated the simplicity of her profile pictures; it was clear she wasn't trying too hard to impress anyone with glamour shots. Her profile stated she was looking for "a serious but playful relationship" and if Jack had to whittle his desire into five words, those seemed pretty accurate.

He took a deep breath before walking over, keeping his nerves in check. He was realistic about these things, knowing that, more often than not, it didn't work out, but at the very least, he could hope for a decent evening with good conversation and old-time American drinks.

Recognition lit up her face as he approached, and Jack realized she was older than she looked in her posted photos. Not by decades, but enough that it was obvious her photos were not current. She was still slim and attractive, in her little black dress and black pumps, her dark hair flowing down her back. He didn't mind that she was older; he minded the fact that she hadn't been completely truthful. For a moment, he considered leaving, but that would be rude.

He stopped at the empty barstool next to Kaili. A heavyset man sat on the next stool, drinking what looked to Jack like a gin rickey. He was scrolling through something on his phone, though he must've felt Jack's gaze on him because he turned his phone over and cast a look Jack's way.

Jack just gave him a brief smile before turning his attention to Kaili. "Hello," he said in Chinese.

She smiled, color rising on her cheeks. "Your Chinese is so good."

He bit back the urge to laugh. He hadn't even said two words! "Hi," he said, holding out his hand. "I'm Jack."

Her hand felt slim, cool, in his own. "I'm Kaili."

They both laughed; introductions like this were not necessary since they'd been chatting for a week online, but it seemed like a good way to break the ice now that they were meeting in person.

"I hope you haven't been waiting for me for too long," Jack said, sliding onto the stool. The heavyset man had gone back to scrolling through whatever was on his phone, though he was holding it in such a way that Jack couldn't see the screen.

"No, I just arrived," she said.

"Should we get a drink?" Jack glanced at the bartender, who had been wiping up a spot on the bar with a small towel. He tossed the towel over his shoulder and came over.

"Do you know what you'd like?" Jack asked. "They have good cocktails here."

Kaili started to say something but then stopped, shook her head, laughing. "I'm not sure."

Jack looked at the bartender. "Do you have a recommendation for my lady friend?"

"I think I have just the thing."

"Great," Jack said. "And I'll take a Dead Guy."

"A Dead Guy?" Kaili had a puzzled expression on her face.

"It's a beer," Jack said. "And I love the name. That's why I drink it."

The bartender retrieved Jack his beer and then started mixing up a special concoction for Kaili, a frothy, orange-y pink drink in an oversize wine glass that he slid across the bar to her.

"A Mary Pickford," the bartender said.

"A who?" Kaili asked.

"She was a very famous actress," Jack said. "In the 1920s."

Kaili picked up the drink with two hands and took a tentative sip. "It's good!" she exclaimed. She took another sip. "Mmm. It's *very* good. So sweet!"

Jack refrained from mentioning the sweetness masked the strong alcohol. So long as she indulged in maybe one or two drinks, she should be okay. He took a sip of his beer. "So," he said. "You mentioned you work at the duty-free shop at Pudong Airport. How's that going?"

"It's all right." Kaili took another sip of her drink. "I like getting to see different people from all over. It's so interesting. The only bad part is the dormitory."

"What's that like?"

"It's not that comfortable. Six people to a room, we have bunk beds. No privacy or place to put our things."

Jack nodded sympathetically. It was common for companies to provide dormitories for people working in such positions; really, it was because of the government, who had created an environment that did not encourage other companies to enter the country. This meant there was less labor demand and lower wages, which worked out fine for the government and the companies—it was the regular people like Kaili who paid the price.

She told him she had signed an agreement to work there for two years, the only way she'd be able to remain in Shanghai. There were many people like her in this city of twenty-six million; it was a city made up of *wàidìrén*, or foreigners from other cities, like Kaili. So while she might have felt she was seeing people from all over, the reality was China was a closed society with very few people living there from other countries—Jack himself was in a very, very small minority. China did not let foreigners immigrate to the country, even if they married a native.

"Have you ever thought of traveling?" Jack asked as Kaili drained the last of her drink. She set the empty glass on the bar, and when the bartender appeared and asked if she wanted another, she nodded. Then she looked at Jack.

"No," she said. "Where would I go? Everywhere seems so dangerous. Especially America. So many people with guns!"

There was color on her cheeks, and her eyes seemed bright; Jack could tell the alcohol was already affecting her, but he wasn't sure how well it would be received if he suggested she slow down with the second drink. He took another sip of his beer, which was still mostly full.

"This drink is so good!" Kaili said. "I could probably drink ten of them!"

Jack laughed. "I don't think so."

She raised an eyebrow. "You don't think I can handle my alcohol?"

He could hear in her voice she was already tipsy; if she finished this drink and had another, she'd be tanked. And if she drank ten? Hello, alcohol poisoning.

"I don't think I could handle more than four," he said.

"So *you* can't handle *your* alcohol."

She was trying to be funny, or flirty—or both—but it wasn't working, at least not for him. "The alcohol content is pretty high; it's just hard to tell because the drink's so sweet."

"Besides," Kaili continued, "the more of these I have, the more fun I'll be later!"

"More like, the more hungover you'll be," he said. "And, I have to make a call to America in thirty minutes. I might have forgotten to mention that."

She gave him a pouty look. Jack felt his irritation flare, but he pushed it aside and they continued to chat. She asked him if he had a Weibo account, which was China's equivalent to Facebook. He did not, and wasn't interested in setting one up, either, despite her encouragement.

It wasn't that Kaili was a bad person—their personalities just weren't meshing the way they had online. Jack waited until Kaili had finished her second drink before saying he was going to step outside to make his phone call. He paid the tab and thanked the bartender, and as he turned, the heavyset man caught his eye and gave him the tiniest of smiles, like he was commiserating in the awkwardness of having to end a date where one person was clearly way more into the other.

"Is it actually time to go?" Kaili asked.

"You can stay," Jack said, "but I have to make this phone call." There was actually no phone call to make, which he supposed was, in its own way, a deception, though not as bad as posting outdated photos of yourself on a dating app.

"No, I guess I should get going, too."

"How are you going to get back to the dorm?"

"The subway."

He didn't like the idea of her on the subway, alone, after she'd had those drinks. "Let me call a Didi for you."

He opened the app on his phone and handed it to her so she could type in her address. Then, he escorted her outside, right as the car showed up.

"Thank you for a pleasant evening," he said as he opened the door for her. "You have a good night."

She got in and maybe was about to say something, but Jack gently pushed the door shut, gave her a smile and a wave before the car pulled away, and that was that.

He could've requested his own Didi, but he instead decided to go back into the bar. He'd only had the one beer, and he wanted to drown out his disappointment. It was mild but it was still an annoyance that he'd rather not be feeling right now. He took the seat he'd previously occupied, right next to the heavyset man, who had again been looking at something on his phone but quickly set it aside when Jack sat down.

The bartender looked at Jack, seemed to be hiding a smirk, and Jack gave him a little nod, to which the bartender slid another bottle of Dead Guy to him.

"You put an end to things pretty quick," the heavyset guy said as Jack took his first sip of his second beer. "She would've let you have your way with her."

Jack raised an eyebrow. "Excuse me?"

The guy smiled and held out a hand. "That was inappropriate. Where have my manners gone? I'm Ari."

Jack took his hand. "Jack Gold."

"I wasn't eavesdropping," he said. "Your date was just . . . very good at projecting her voice, shall we say."

"The alcohol helped with that."

"But you're a gentleman."

"Sometimes."

Ari was scrutinizing him, but in a nonthreatening way, almost like he was trying to figure out if he and Jack had met somewhere before.

"No," Ari said, "you're a gentleman all of the time, I can tell. I'm a very good judge of character. So. You're from America?"

"Guilty. What about you? Israel?"

Ari grinned. "What gave it away? The nose? The abundance of hair?"

Jack tried not to laugh but wasn't entirely successful. "The accent," he finally said. "What brings you to Shanghai?"

"Oh, lots of things. I import and distribute liquor to restaurants all over the place. I do other things, too, but that's my main gig. I travel a lot. I like to move around. Meet people. Like I said, I'm an excellent judge of character. What about you?"

"I think I'm a pretty good judge of character. Except maybe when it comes to dating."

"Dating is not for the faint of heart, that's true. What is it that you do? Why are you here?"

"I actually first landed in Hong Kong and then went to Singapore, before ending up here. I've done various things within the financial sector. Business development. Consulting. I'm first vice president at Global China Banking Group currently. And why am I here?" He shrugged. "It seemed like a good place to be, if you were someone who wanted to take advantage of the potential business opportunities if China opened up."

Ari looked at him with interest. "Which hasn't happened."

"Right," Jack said. "Which I suppose should not be surprising. Disappointing, but not surprising."

"It almost makes you wish someone would just hurry up and *do* something about it."

Jack shrugged. "Yeah, of course. But what can be done? I've been living here for years and I still can't believe, sometimes, how much control the government has."

"That's just the Westerner in you."

"I know. And I'm sure if it was something I'd grown up with, I'd feel differently. But . . ." Jack shrugged again. "What, is any one person going to do to change things? It's an impossible challenge."

"Is it, though?"

Ari was about to say something else when his phone began to ring. "I have to take this," he said. "But let's stay in touch, yeah?" He snatched one of the cocktail napkins from its holder and stretched his impressive girth over the bar to the other side, where he seemed to know exactly where a cup of pens would be. He grabbed one and scribbled out his phone number.

"Call me anytime," he said, handing the napkin to Jack. "I mean it."

Ari slid off his bar stool as he answered the phone. He walked out of the bar, though not before giving Jack a warm smile.

Jack waved and then looked at the napkin, the scrawled number. There was something intriguing about the man, though Jack wasn't quite sure what.

He pocketed the napkin and finished his beer. His date with Kaili might not have been a success, but clearly, the evening had not been an entire failure, either, and that, at least, was something to feel good about.

CHAPTER 2

The following week, Jack tried to keep his focus on work, but his thoughts kept drifting back to Ari. He hadn't called him yet, though he kept it in the back of his mind that he would; maybe he'd ask him if to meet up for drinks again.

Kaili had been in touch a few times, so he had, in the nicest way possible, told her that he wouldn't be able to get together, and when she hadn't bothered to respond, he felt relieved.

At work, he had plenty to keep him focused—he was involved in a variety of projects, including a business plan he would present to the bank's chairman in a few days. He was pleased with the draft he had, but he wanted to talk to Priscilla Tan, head of consumer loans and private banking.

She had a corner office that faced the river below; Jack wouldn't have minded such a view. She sat behind a large desk, surrounded by stacks of folders.

"Hi Priscilla," Jack said.

She finished typing something on her computer and looked at him, adjusting her black-rimmed glasses.

"Hi, Jack. Have a seat."

He sat down in one of the chairs in front of her desk. "Thanks for seeing me."

"Not a problem," she said briskly. "How can I help you?"

He took a deep breath and smiled, a gesture that usually elicited a positive response in return, though no such luck with Priscilla. It wasn't so much that he was trying to win her over; her demeanor with him had always been cool, calculated, which he wouldn't have thought twice about if that's how she was with everyone, but the times he'd witnessed her interacting with their other co-workers, she seemed a different person: smiling, friendly, warm.

"As I'm sure you're well aware," he started, "I have a draft of the business plan I'll be presenting to Chairman."

"I am aware."

"Right. And I think it's critical that I have your input."

If his request for her help pleased her at all, she certainly didn't show it; she looked put off, as though he were purposefully adding to her workload. "I have the draft right here," he said, holding up the spiral-bound presentation slides. "We can run through it pretty fast. It won't take long, I promise."

She gave the slightest of nods and leaned forward a few inches, so he placed the document on her desk and began to go through it. Despite the fact she only nodded and murmured here and there, she seemed impressed with his work, which pleased him. Priscilla had a reputation for being both strong-willed and very bright, as well as ambitious.

"So?" he asked. "What do you think?"

"It's adequate." Probably the nicest thing she'd ever said to him. "A few of the branches have quite a few high-net-worth individuals. We should think about having a private banker at those branches."

"Great idea," Jack said. "Can you give me a sense of how many clients warrant a private banker? Then I can work with the branches to figure out exactly how many we're talking about."

"I'll have someone get that information to you."

"Anything else you felt was lacking?"

She held his gaze for several seconds without saying a single word, as though she was considering whether or not she should take him up on his query and inform him of all the ways she found *him* lacking, but then she looked away, shaking her head.

"No. As I said—you've done an adequate job." She turned her attention back to her computer. "That's all."

"Okay, well . . ." Jack stood, taking the document off of Priscilla's desk. "Thank you for your time. I appreciate it."

She gave him another almost imperceptible nod, and that was that. Jack left her office and returned to his cubicle. When he'd first been promoted to first vice president, he assumed that he'd have his own office. He actually did, for a few weeks, but then someone higher up than him decided that his office was needed for another purpose, and so Jack found himself back in his cubicle. He'd seriously considered leaving when that happened, but decided to stick it out, and hopefully position himself for an office at some point in the near future. Acing this presentation could certainly help with that.

By the time the end of the workday rolled around, Jack was more than ready to take off. Normally, he had no problem staying well past his scheduled work time, but today, he was eager to get out of the office. He didn't want to blame Priscilla, but after their meeting, that feeling of discontentment that he'd been hoping to assuage by going on a date had returned, full force. This confused him; all this time he'd assumed this discontentment had been because his personal life was lacking, but now he was wondering if it was, perhaps, his professional life, too.

Outside, his stress began to dissipate. It was August in Shanghai, and though to many, China was synonymous with smog and pollution, this time of year, the skies in Shanghai were relatively clear, since there was no need to use coal for heating. It was hot and humid, but Jack didn't mind it, and especially enjoyed getting to see the spectacular sunsets. Living in the financial capital of China suited Jack, and he knew to anyone observing from the outside, he appeared to be doing just fine for himself. He wanted to put this feeling of unrest to bed.

He pulled his phone out of his pocket and called Ari.

"Ari, it's Jack Gold," he said when Ari picked up. "We met at—"

"I had a feeling it was going to be you!" Ari exclaimed. "Good to hear from you, Jack. What are you up to? You hungry? I'm always hungry, you can probably tell. Just heading over to Cheese Co., if you care to join."

Jack perked up. He'd been to Cheese Co. before and knew the owner, Greg, an Australian who had a simple formula for resounding success: good melted cheese sandwiches and reasonably priced beer.

"That's perfect," Jack said. "I'm just leaving work now and can head right over."

"Great. See you soon."

Jack slipped his phone back in his pocket and began to walk toward the restaurant. It took him about five minutes to get there, and Ari was just settling in at one of the outdoor tables when Jack arrived.

"Perfect timing," he said. Jack smiled and they shook hands. Though this was only the second time they'd interacted, for some reason, Jack felt as if Ari was a long-lost friend.

"How are you?" Jack asked, taking his own seat.

"Busy, as usual. Busy for me, busy for girlfriend, Mary. I mean, wife."

Jack laughed. "Which is it? Girlfriend or wife?"

"It was girlfriend for a long time. We recently married, though. So, I'm still getting used to the new title. I mean, me, a husband! Who would've thought. But, everyone who told me that married life was some downward spiral into monotony was wrong—things seem pretty much the same. She just received a very lucrative offer from Nike, so that's exciting. I told Mary about you—she'd like us all to get together some time."

"Sure," Jack said. He caught the eye of one of the waiters and signaled him over so he and Ari could order beer.

"And what about you?" Ari asked. "You seem like the sort of man who keeps his plate very full."

"There's always things going on at work. It can be a bit of a headache sometimes." There was something about Ari that made him feel completely comfortable to open up and vent his frustrations, but it also seemed a bit strange, seeing as they had just met.

"Gone on anymore bad first dates?" Ari asked with a grin. The waiter returned with their beer and took their orders—a grilled cheese with pork and chili peppers for Jack and a grilled cheese with duck and onion marmalade for Ari. "Can't wait till the weather cools down," Ari said. "Then it's time to add some soup to that order!" He took a sip of his beer. "Unfortunately, I can't suggest that my girl—I mean, wife—might be able to help you out and set you up on a blind date, as she is categorically against such things. She knows they usually go wrong, and doesn't want to be to blame!"

"I held off on creating an account on LoveChina.com, but then I finally caved. That date I was on last week was my first real online dating experience. Maybe my last."

"Aw, come on. You don't seem like the sort of person to give up so easily."

"I'm not, it just . . . it doesn't always seem authentic. Like with Kaili."

"Good-looking woman."

"Yeah, she was, and our online correspondence was pretty great. Unfortunately, it didn't translate when we met in person. I might just try to do things the old-fashioned way. You know, meet someone when I'm out and about. That way, we'll know beforehand if we get along in person."

"I confess I am relieved—more than relieved, endlessly thankful—that I am now a married man and never had to participate in the horror that is online dating. I don't envy anyone that. But, I wouldn't get too discouraged, Jack—a man like you won't be single for long if you decide you don't want to be."

Jack took a long sip of his ice-cold beer. He set it down on the table and stretched. "We can talk about my love life another time. I have a question for you: What do you think about the current relationship between China and Israel?"

Ari raised his eyebrows and grinned. "You don't waste any time, do you?" The grin slowly disappeared. "You want the truth? I'm worried." He sighed. "You probably know that China's buying oil from Iran?"

"I'd heard something along those lines."

"Well, it's true. And it gives Iran money they can use for all sorts of things. You know, like buying weapons and funding terrorism. That sort of thing. The situation can't continue. It's blatantly wrong. For so many reasons."

"I agree," Jack said. "But what can be done?"

There was something familiar about the question, and he realized a similar thing was said the night he and Ari first met.

Ari looked at Jack with a level of seriousness that Jack might not have thought he was capable of, based on what he knew of him thus far. "I think it's fairly obvious what needs to be done," Ari said. "People need to know what's going on with China and Iran. The news needs to get out there. That would motivate the politicians to act. You want to know how things are going to get done? That's how."

Jack took a sip of his beer and mulled what Ari just said. "While that's all well and good," he said, "and, I do agree with you—how do you propose someone does that? I'd imagine it would have to be more than some*one*—it'd be a huge undertaking."

"I know," Ari said. "And to be honest—I really *don't* know how such a task would get accomplished." He leaned forward and waited until Jack did the same before he started speaking in a lower voice. "I've talked to a few friends in the Israeli Defense Forces and they're also worried. It's not just us. But Israel's too small to do much on its own. It'll need American support in whatever it decides to do."

Jack nodded. "I agree, but again—what can be done?"

Ari gave him a long look and then opened his mouth but stopped before he actually said anything. Jack waited, sensing there was something more he wanted to add, but then Ari shook his head and asked, "I'm assuming you are Jewish?"

Jack was somewhat taken aback by the question. "Yes . . . I am."

"You should join our WeChat group. Shanghai Synagogue. There's about three hundred of us and we do many different activities. I'll send you an invitation. Now that I have your number, Jack, expect to hear more from me. Like I told you when we first met—I'm a good judge of character, and there's just something about you—you're a good guy to have around!"

He clapped Jack on the back, and Jack had to admit—there was something about Ari, too, something mysterious and intriguing and even if it turned out to be nothing, it was clear the man knew how to have a good time.

It seemed an abrupt departure from what they were just discussing, but then their food arrived, and Jack let himself be swept up in the delicious aroma and the crisp texture of the grilled bread giving way underneath his teeth to the gooey, melted cheese, the pork and the chili peppers providing a burst of salt and heat. He sighed in contentment as he chewed; grilled cheese, the all-American food, yet the best one he'd ever had was right here in Shanghai. They could continue the discussion of this topic another time; it wasn't like there was going to be a resolution any time soon.

CHAPTER 3

The day of his big presentation, Jack arrived to work early to give everything one final look-over before making his way to the big boardroom at the end of the hallway. The chairman was there, and several of Jack's colleagues, including Priscilla, which Jack had not been expecting. But he didn't let his surprise show and instead gave her a reassuring look, to which she simply looked at him icily.

Standing at the lectern, Jack said, "All right, thank you for–"

"Chairman," Priscilla interrupted. "I'd like to first share some slides about the retail branch network, if I may?"

Jack realized his mouth was still open, as he'd been in the middle of saying something when Priscilla jumped in like that. He'd never been interrupted like that before, right as he was about to start a presentation. But he wasn't about to be rude back by talking over Priscilla, or insisting that he be able to go first, and the chairman had nodded when Priscilla stood up, so Jack sat back down and let her share her slides.

He tried not to stew about it, but he was irked by how unprofessional it was. Still, he paid attention to what Priscilla was saying, and he had to admit, she knew her stuff. She was a capable, more than competent employee, and it frustrated him that she clearly felt there was some sort of competition between them.

Finally, it was his turn, and he went through his presentation without any hiccups. Every so often, he'd let his gaze settle on Priscilla, and she was sitting attentively, at least appearing to pay attention to what he said.

At least there's that, he thought, still annoyed with the way she'd interrupted him.

Later that afternoon, Jack received a call from the company's executive secretary that Ernest Pang, the president, wanted to meet with him.

Jack had met with him once before, when he'd been promoted to first vice president, but he assumed this meeting had something to do with his presentation—it had been so well received, perhaps Pang wanted to commend him personally? Jack did have a bit of a spring in his step as he entered Pang's office, but any good feelings quickly evaporated when he saw that Priscilla was also there.

"Hi Jack, come on in," Pang said. "Have a seat. Would you like a beer?"

Jack nodded as he took a seat, even though he wasn't at all thirsty, especially not for beer. Pang filled two glasses, one of which he handed to Jack, the other to Priscilla. He poured himself some before taking his seat back behind his desk. Jack held the glass of beer but did not take a sip. His mind spun.

"So," Pang said. "I called you both here because . . . well, I'll just come out and say it. There's been a bit of talk the past week."

"About the presentation?" Jack asked. Something wasn't adding up.

"It's not about the presentation," Pang said. He slowly took a sip of beer, and then looked at Priscilla and then at Jack. Then back to Priscilla. And suddenly, Jack knew.

"No," he started to say, right as Pang said, "There is speculation that the two of you are having an affair."

If he hadn't been so shocked, Jack might've taken a little offense at the look of genuine disgust that lit up Priscilla's face when Pang made his woefully misguided observation.

"People are talking," Pang said.

"Like who?" Jack demanded. He set his glass on Pang's desk because he didn't want to end up throwing it across the room. He knew people talked and liked to gossip, but he never thought *he* would be the target of it, because all he did each and every day he came into work was exactly that: work. He did not engage in the petty office politics that some of his co-workers did, and because of that, he assumed he was immune to this sort of ridiculous chatter. And yet.

"It doesn't matter," Pang said.

"Actually, it *does* . . ." Jack stopped, realizing that Pang was right. Still, it did nothing to quell this quiet fury that was building in his chest. He looked at Priscilla. "This is ridiculous, right?"

"Absolutely!" She looked at Pang. "I thought the conversation was going to be about my promotion." Jack's jaw dropped as Priscilla started to cry. "I've been working so hard, hoping to be named executive vice president. I certainly thought it would have happened by now, yet it hasn't. And now, not only has it not happened, I'm being accused of having an affair with someone I wouldn't sleep with if he was the last man on the planet!"

She started bawling then, and Jack and Pang exchanged uneasy glances.

"Let's stop that now," Pang said gently. "No one's . . . no one's trying to make anyone cry. It's okay, Priscilla. Really, you don't have to . . ."

Jack stared as Priscilla's sobbing got louder. Was this some sort of joke? Pang handed Priscilla some tissues. Did she think this was the way to get promoted? Jack was so horrified that she would conduct herself like this that he couldn't even muster an ounce of offense at her "last man on the planet" comment.

He sat there uncomfortably until Priscilla's sobs finally subsided. What a silly thing to be crying about, anyway. Jack knew of at least a few people with important titles who simply used it as a buffer to keep from doing any real work.

"You've been doing a great job," Pang was saying to Priscilla. "Don't think it hasn't gone unnoticed."

Jack tried not to roll his eyes. He reached over and took a big sip of his beer, noisily downing about half of it. He didn't care if an observer might've viewed it as rude; it wasn't like Pang or Priscilla would've been able to hear his noises anyway, not over Pang's coddling. It was clear Jack was no longer needed here, so he made his exit quickly, though the frustration with everything kept spinning around his brain, wouldn't leave him alone no matter how hard he tried to focus on other things.

* * *

After work, Jack went home to his apartment. Located in the former French Concession, the four-story granite building, built in 1890, was heavily influenced by European architecture. There was a spacious, airy living room and a kitchen with a real oven—a luxury that many typical apartments in China did not possess. Jack took a beer from the fridge and leaned against the counter as he took his first sip. He felt unsettled. The whole situation with Priscilla was unbelievable, yet what could be done?

As the evening wore on, his irritation persisted. He glanced at the clock. A little after ten p.m. It would be morning in Montana, where his dad lived, so Jack picked up his phone and called.

He had a complicated relationship with his father, and it wasn't because that's how Jack wanted it. It frustrated him that his brother, Paul, seemed to have no problem cultivating a smooth father/son relationship, when it was so challenging for Jack. It wasn't like Paul had followed exactly in their physician-father's footsteps, either—Paul was out living in Sedona, designing and manufacturing furniture and art.

"Jack," his father said brightly when he answered. "I was just starting to wonder when I might hear from you again."

"Hi, Dad," Jack said. "Things have been pretty busy over here with work and everything."

"Things opening up over there, the way you want?"

"Err . . . Not really."

"Maybe it's time to come back, then. You've gained plenty of experience over there, I'm sure. Experience you could put to good use."

Jack sighed. No conversation with his father would be complete without the helpful suggestion that Jack return to the U.S.. "I'm not ready to make any big moves just yet. I do have this rather unfortunate situation happening at my job, though."

"What's going on?"

Jack told his father about the presentation he gave and then the situation with Priscilla, how it all culminated in being called into the president's office.

"Did you?" his father asked.

"Did I what?"

"Have an affair with her?"

Jack recoiled—Did his father really think he would do something like that with a co-worker?

"No," he snapped. "I certainly did not. I've been respectful and professional in my dealings with her. And all she's clearly concerned with is climbing the ladder. I even went to speak with her and get her input before the presentation."

"Maybe that wasn't a wise idea."

"Apparently not."

"Jack, this is an imperfect world and you're a big boy. By now, I hope you realize that there are assholes everywhere. Some people will do just about anything they can to get ahead. I have to admit, though, I'm a little surprised that *you're* so surprised. You've always been a good two or three steps ahead of everyone else—put that skill to good use! I know you think I give you a hard time, but it's just because I don't want to see your natural abilities going to waste."

"I'm doing the best I can. Not all of us can be a preeminent physician *and* have worked for the CIA."

Jack's father chuckled. "Yes, well, the CIA thing was a long time ago. And I'm not a physician anymore, either. Retired life suits me just fine. Turns out, being a surgeon really helped with my fly knot tying skills. Even the guys at the bait and tackle store were impressed."

"What did you do for them, anyway?" Jack asked.

"Just making fishing flies."

"No, I mean the CIA. How'd you get involved with that?"

"Like I said, it was a long time ago. They approached me, because they needed help. Don't get too excited though; I just transported some documents. Nothing glamorous."

Jack gave his father another moment or two to decide if he wanted to elaborate, which, unsurprisingly, he did not. He didn't have a military background or anything, so Jack had always assumed there was more to the story, but his father never elaborated.

"You've been fortunate," Jack said finally. "You knew early on what you wanted to do, you were one of the top in the field, *and* you get recruited to do . . . well, I don't know exactly, but I'm sure it was something important. Believe me when I say that I'd like nothing more than the chance to do something similar, but I'm no surgeon."

"You don't need to be a surgeon to make an impact," his father said.

"Well, it's not like I know anyone in the CIA, either."

"That's not how it works. If they need something, they'll find you." His father cleared his throat. "Enough about that, though. Those days are long over. You think you might make it down to Cabo this winter? Your brother's going to visit at some point."

Jack rubbed his eyes, finally feeling the day catch up to him. He stifled a yawn. "Is he? Well, Paul's always been able to just get up and go."

"You could, too. It's not like you have all this stuff holding you up in China."

"I know, but . . ." Jack let his voice trail off. There was a part of him that would enjoy taking a week or two off this winter and fly down to Cabo. But there was another part of him that knew it would devolve into what it usually did when he was together with his dad: His father trying to encourage him to "do something meaningful with his life," which generally meant making Jack feel bad about the choices he had thus far made.

Jack's mother had been more understanding, had gotten him in a way that Jack did not feel could be said of his father. But his parents divorced, and then, years later, his mother died. She had been an artist and a typical free spirit, the sort of person who encouraged people to *follow their hearts* no matter how small or large the impact on others. Jack's father, on the other hand, felt that things should be done with the idea to help as many people as possible. Natural abilities and god-given talents should not be wasted.

"I know you're so busy," his father said. "Well, the offer's always on the table, you know that. And maybe, once you've decided you've had enough of living over there, you'll decide that you want to come back here and really do something with yourself."

His tone was completely good-natured, yet it still stung. "Okay, Dad," Jack said. "I'll see what I can do."

"Sounds good. Love you, Jack. Take care."

"Thanks, Dad. Love you too."

When the call was over, Jack tossed his phone down and stifled a yawn. It was time for bed, even though he still felt a current of frustration coursing through him. He hadn't been planning on getting up early and going to the gym tomorrow, but he could tell that's exactly what he needed to do.

CHAPTER 4

Jack had time the next morning in between his workout and when he had to be at work. Normally, he would've just headed in to get an early start, but instead he decided to take his laptop to Baker & Spice and have breakfast and get caught up on his emails.

There was a reminder message from the Shanghai Chapter of Chicago Booth alumnus; they were hosting a cocktail event in a few nights at Bar No. 3, which was near Jack's apartment. He couldn't remember if he saw the first notification or not, but it might make sense if he went, if for no other reason than to try to make some new connections.

There was another email from a college friend who worked at FOX News. A few weeks prior, Jack had written an article about the U.S. government's never-ending discussion with China over trade, stealing IP, and forcing American companies to do joint ventures with local companies. He hadn't planned to write the article, but it was something he spent considerable time thinking about and discussing with others, including some of the people he'd gone to school with—perhaps someone he might see if he went to the alumni event.

Jack read the full email. He knew his friend had liked the article, which focused on a hardline approach to any negotiations—since, as far as Jack could see, China never stuck to any agreement—but apparently this friend had forwarded the article to someone he knew at the *Wall Street Journal*, and they wanted to publish it, immediately.

The validation felt good, especially after everything that had been going on at work. *Maybe you should find another job.*

The thought materialized as if someone else had whispered the idea to him. Jack sat back and looked past his computer screen. Everyone around him seemed completely engrossed on their phones or in whatever conversation they were having. He let the idea unravel a little more—what if he *did* start looking for another opportunity? It wasn't as if he was married to the idea of staying at his current job forever.

He took a sip of coffee, tapped his foot underneath the table, overcome with the desire to act on this new thought. He knew, though, there was no need to rush into anything; he'd pack his stuff up in about twenty minutes and head to work, do his job, and then maybe he'd consider reaching out to some contacts, or even some people at this alumni event in a few days, to see what opportunities might be available.

He was packing his things up when his phone rang. He looked at the display and saw it was his longtime friend, Mike Beckman.

"Mike!" Jack said as he made his way out of the cafe. Mike was a good friend from Los Angeles, someone Jack had known for decades. He and Mike had one of those friendships where they could go months, or even years, without speaking, but then pick right up where they left off, as though resuming a conversation from yesterday.

"Hey, Jack," Mike said. "It's been a little while! How's it going? You find a Chinese wife yet?"

"Ha. No," Jack said. "Though not for lack of trying. Well, sort of."

"What?! It's not like you don't have enough to choose from."

"You're funny," Jack said.

"And right."

"Yes, you're right—there's about seven hundred million women in China."

"So—plenty to choose from."

"Unfortunately, they're not all lining up, waiting for me to pick a lucky winner."

"Then they don't know what they're missing." Mike let out a howl of laughter and Jack found himself unable to stop from laughing, either.

"It's good to hear from you," he said. "But I have a feeling this isn't just a call to shoot the shit."

"Oh, you know me so well," Mike said. "Well, yeah. I'm going to be in your neck of the woods in a few weeks, so you better clear your calendar. I'd like to further diversify my investor base, and I want your help." He cleared his throat. "Let me rephrase that—*need* your help."

Jack smiled. Mike was very successful in real estate, but he had never been able to get any Chinese clients.

"You know I could never say no to my old pal," Jack said. "Actually, I'm going to this Chicago Booth alumni event, so chances are good I'll be able to do a little networking, see what I can come up with."

"Oh yeah? Tell me more."

"Well . . . My feeling is there's a sincere interest in putting Chinese money to work in America."

"Now that's what I'm talking about."

"The thing you need to understand, from what I've seen and heard, is that even many of the larger asset management firms are still unaware that other places exist, aside from the major, well-known cities."

"And that's where we come in and help them realize this is not the case at all."

Jack paused, smiling. According to Mike, everything was so easy. "I'll try to get a better feel for things at the event."

"I don't think I've ever known your senses to lead you astray. All that sounds good. Sign me up. Rather, sign *them* up. Find me some potential investors and I'll be there for a meeting," Mike said. "I'll fly back out there anytime if I have to."

"I'll see what I can do," Jack said. "Tell me something."

"Anything."

"Do you have any larger projects coming up? I'm thinking it might be better to share something concrete. It will also give us a chance to learn more about what they want."

"That sounds good. I knew you'd come through, Jack, you always do. I'll look into what we have and send you something . . . But, is everything okay? You don't sound as chipper as I remember."

"Yeah, I'm good," Jack said. "It's just . . ." He paused.

"Go on," Mike coaxed.

"Nothing, really. It's just work stuff. Just dealing with some unfortunate politics and posturing."

"You still at that bank?"

"I am."

"You gotta get out of there, man. Someone like you has way more potential than the head of some bank. Even if you're president or whatever."

"I'm not."

"Well, you should be! Hell, Jack, maybe it's time to move on. Branch out. Do something different. It sounds to me like you're stuck in a rut.

Don't let these people take advantage of you. How are you going to ramp up your abilities? Your career? You're the sort of person, Jack, you could do anything you put your mind to. Me, I'm good in real estate and . . . well, that's about it. But you—don't waste your talents at some bank that is never going to fully appreciate you anyway."

Jack took a deep breath. He and Mike had come of age together, so whenever Jack heard his friend's voice or was together with him, there was always a bit of nostalgia, and also the sense that Jack was viewing the life he could have had, if he'd stayed in the U.S., the way his father had wanted. He could live in a nice, oceanfront property, go swimming every day, if he felt like it. Mike worked hard but he played hard, too, and Jack knew if asked, Mike would certainly be adamant that he was living his "best life."

"You're not saying anything that hasn't crossed my mind," Jack said. "Especially lately. But, we'll just have to see how it goes."

"The time is now, my friend. You end up hemming and hawing and waiting around and ten years will pass before you even realize it. Don't be passive. The Jack Gold I know would never be passive like that and just 'wait and see.' The Jack Gold I know would quit that shitty job and be out there networking and making connections and raking in the big money. And he'd have a fine lady on each arm."

Jack laughed. "Hey, I think I'd like to meet this guy."

"What about you and I get in on something together? I want more clients in China, you're in China, I mean, hell, let's help each other out, right? What are friends for?"

"Like I said, I'm not closing myself off to any possibilities, including you." If Mike was serious, Jack did find the prospect intriguing; he and Mike had never worked together before but they would likely be pretty successful.

He chatted with Mike for a few more minutes, and then said goodbye, after promising to make sure he had at least a few nights free when his friend arrived into town.

CHAPTER 5

Bar No. 3 was located on a quiet street, a few blocks from Jack's apartment on Xingguo Road. Jack appreciated the bar's low-key ambience and the tall windows and black-tiled walls that greeted him as he walked in. There was just enough space out front for two small, round tables, currently occupied by two couples. Inside, a group of people congregated at the bar, though Jack did not recognize any of them.

He was about to ask the group if they were Chicago Booth alumnus, but then he *did* see a familiar face, a face he hadn't been expecting to see, at least not here, not tonight.

Ari.

He was coming out from behind the bar, carrying what appeared to be an empty duffel bag.

"Ari," Jack said. "I wasn't expecting to see you here!"

"Jack! I was just thinking about you earlier. What are the chances?"

"You didn't mention you also went to Booth," Jack said.

"Oh, you're here for the alumni event? I was making a delivery. You like scotch? Just dropped off a really good bottle of that."

"I enjoy a good scotch every now and then."

Ari smiled and took a step closer, leaning his head toward Jack. "Listen," he said, in a low voice, so Jack had to tilt his head forward to hear. "Something's come up. Something that I'd like to talk with you about." He glanced over his shoulder. "But not now. Are you free Tuesday after work? Want to meet here?"

"Sure," Jack said, his interest piqued. "Six-thirty sound good?"

"I'll be here. Gotta get going, though, have a few more rounds to make." Ari patted him on the shoulder. "Glad I ran into you."

Jack turned to watch as he walked off. *What does he want to talk to me about?*

After a moment, he went over to a table where a woman was sitting, with a sign that said *Chicago Booth Alumnus*. She had name tags laid out in front of her, and she gave him his after he told her his name.

He put the tag on and went to the bar to get a drink. When the bartender came over, he asked, in Chinese, for an Asahi draft beer. It was easy to identify the people here for the alumni event; there weren't many, but they had their name tags on. Jack took his beer and went over and introduced himself to a few people. He spoke in Chinese, which he could tell, by the expressions on people's faces, that they weren't expecting, or at least weren't expecting him to be as fluent as he was.

Jack mingled for about an hour before he stepped outside for a smoke. He walked a few feet past the bar, so the smoke didn't drift toward the people sitting at the two outdoor tables. Another person was there, leaning against the side of the building, also smoking. He saw Jack approach and gave him a quick nod.

"Hey," Jack said. "You here for the Chicago alumni event?" He asked this almost as a joke; the man had one of those youthful faces that could easily be mistaken for very early twenties, though the way he stood and smoked, Jack could tell that he was older.

The man exhaled a cloud of smoke and shook his head. "No. I was wondering what that group was all about. I just had a dinner meeting with a client and after that, I really needed a stiff drink and a smoke. I'm Andrew San." He held out his hand, squinting at Jack's shirt. "And you're Jack, I assume."

"What? Oh, yeah," Jack said, glancing down at his name tag. "Forgot about that thing. So, sounds like a fun client meeting."

Andrew laughed. "Yeah, something like that."

"What do you do?"

"Real estate investment. Here and in the U.S.. I take it that's where you're from?"

"I am. What about you?"

"Well, I like to tell people I was born in Taiwan, grew up in Canada, but I first and foremost consider myself Chinese," he said, with obvious pride. "There is no country in the world as exceptional as China. Wouldn't you agree?"

"It certainly has its good qualities," Jack said, though he certainly wouldn't venture quite so far as to label it *most exceptional ever.*

Andrew laughed. "Oh, come on, *dàgē!*" he exclaimed. Jack couldn't help but smile at the young man's ease and enthusiasm; *dàgē* meant "big brother" and was a friendly way of addressing a good friend who was older than yourself. Though he and Andrew had just met, Jack had a good feeling about him.

"You live here!" Andrew continued. "You must enjoy it. There's a reason you're here."

Jack laughed. "For all the good conversations I have with the interesting people I meet!"

"What do you do?"

"Finance. I work at Global China Banking Group."

Andrew raised his eyebrows. "You must know your stuff, then."

"I'd like to think so. But I'm also exploring other avenues, and I'm involved with a major developer in Los Angeles who'd love some Chinese clients."

Andrew raised his eyebrows, clearly intrigued. "I might know some," he said. "Maybe we could get together to talk some time. I can just tell you're someone I could learn a great deal from."

"That sounds great," Jack said. He was almost finished with his cigarette. "You want to connect via WeChat? Maybe next time we can meet somewhere that's more convenient to smoke." In China, the WeChat app was used by nearly everyone for texting and making payments. He pulled his phone out of his pocket and opened the app. Andrew did the same, and Jack pulled up his personal QR code and then let Andrew scan it, his phone beeping confirmation that the information had been accepted.

"Great," Andrew said. He took a final drag on his cigarette. "Well, glad this evening didn't turn out to be a total waste." He gave Jack another grin. "Really glad to have met you. Let's stay in touch!"

"Absolutely," Jack said. He gave a little wave as Andrew walked off, and Jack turned and went back inside.

There was a large, exposed column at the corner of the bar, and as Jack tried to navigate around that to squeeze into an empty spot at the bar so he could order another drink, he collided with a waitress, carrying a small tray with two drinks balanced on it.

"Whoa!" Jack exclaimed. Somehow, the woman managed to not spill the drinks. "I'm sorry," he said. "I'm not trying to mow you down or anything."

The woman was slim and very attractive. Her dark hair was pulled back and her skin was smooth, flawless. Jack couldn't help but look at her mouth, her full lips, which were not exactly smiling at him, but maybe a little? He hoped, anyway.

"No, that was my fault," she said. "Took that corner a little too fast."

Jack laughed, his mind spinning, trying to think of something to say before she walked away.

"You have great balance," he blurted out, and when she looked at him in confusion, he nodded to the tray of drinks. "I don't think you spilled a single drop."

"That just means I've been working in bars for too long," she said, and then she really did smile and Jack felt the strangest sensation, a giddiness, almost, like he just wanted to set her tray of drinks down, take her hand, and run out of this place together. The feeling was both exciting and surprising and he tried not to let it show on his face—he didn't want to scare her off. "Actually," she said, "I really like working here, and I've enjoyed every other bar I've worked in." She paused. "You get to meet interesting people."

Jack's heart felt like it was about to explode out of his chest; it was so intense he wondered if she could hear it, though of course she couldn't, or at least he hoped that was the case. *What is going on?* he wondered. He wasn't alarmed, but he couldn't ever remember feeling this way, not right away with someone, anyway. As he looked at her, he wondered if the feeling was at all reciprocated, but he couldn't tell.

"So . . . Jack," the woman said. He felt a surge of excitement . . . she knew his name? Oh, but then he remembered his name tag. "I better get these drinks delivered. You have a good night." And she slipped off into the crowd, like a sleek cat disappearing in the night. He was overcome with the desire to go after her, to at least find out her name, but he didn't want to appear totally desperate.

Instead, he ordered another beer and tried to mingle with his fellow alumnus, though he kept glancing over, hoping to see the waitress. He realized that she had an interesting accent. They'd spoken to each other in Mandarin, and her accent was clearly northern Chinese, elegant and well educated. She must be from Beijing.

He talked with two men, both Chinese, one who worked at Booz Allen, the other at Ping An in real estate investing. Jack thought about his earlier conversation with Andrew, and his conversation with Mike a few days ago, as he asked if the man invested in the U.S..

"Only in New York and Los Angeles," the man replied. "Although, my bosses are just learning that Denver and Seattle exist."

Jack smiled. "What size investments do you make?"

"Most have been over two hundred million. But, we're now seeing higher returns on investments that are above twenty million."

"Offices or apartment buildings?"

"Both."

"Under development? Or new?"

"We don't invest in properties under development." The man looked at him curiously. "Are you in real estate?"

"Banking," Jack said, his gaze going across the room, where he spied the waitress delivering another round of drinks. "Though I'm certainly open to new opportunities." He wished he had gotten her name. He was vaguely aware that the man was saying something, he was also vaguely aware that he was nodding along, as if he were paying attention, though the waitress had him riveted.

How is this possible? he wondered. He didn't even know her! But the feeling was undeniable, so strong that he knew he had to at least find out her name before the evening was over. But hopefully more.

His chance came when he went back over to the bar to get another drink. The bartender was chatting with another group, and the waitress was behind the bar, pouring two beers from the tap. Jack leaned toward her.

"Hey," he said. "Could I get one of those?"

She glanced up, and he hoped he wasn't imagining the pleased smile that crossed her face.

"Hey, Jack," she said, and his heart did a somersault, a thrilling, delicious feeling. "I can't give you *this* particular beer, but if you want a glass— hold on one second."

"That would be great," he said, even though he didn't want another beer. But, hell, he'd order an entire keg if it would give him a few minutes with her. "You know what else would be great? If you told me your name. I feel like things are a little one-sided, you knowing my name and all."

"It's Jojo."

He waited until she set the pint glass down before extending his hand. She shook his, her grasp firm, her hand warm, smooth, in his own. He could only imagine the look on his face right now.

"It's so nice to meet you."

"You say that to everyone, don't you?" she asked. She handed him a pint glass. "Here you go. I have to go drop these off. Thirsty customers."

He could've sworn she winked at him, but maybe it was just a blink. Was he imagining the flirtatious tone in her voice? It didn't matter; one thing he was certain of was he *wasn't* imagining this racing of his heart, his sweaty palms . . . *Shit*, he thought, wiping his palms on his pants. Had she felt that when they shook hands? It didn't matter. He knew her name.

And hopefully, in time, maybe he could get to know her much better.

CHAPTER 6

Monday morning started with another call back to the president's office. Considering how his last meeting had gone, Jack did not have high hopes for this one, though he was relieved to see that Priscilla was not there.

"Jack," Mr. Pang said. "Thank you for stopping by. This shouldn't take long, but I wanted to follow up with you about the private banking initiative you promised Priscilla."

"Did Priscilla come talk to you about that?" Jack asked, trying to keep his irritation in check.

Pang offered him a small smile. "You know how Priscilla can be. She just wants to make sure that nothing falls through the cracks, and that things are worked on in an expeditious manner. Not bad qualities."

There was no point in arguing or pointing out the fact that it would have been easier—and more direct—if Priscilla had gone to Jack, instead of taking her complaints to Pang.

"I'm waiting for details from Priscilla," Jack said. "We discussed this. She's supposed to let me know how many high-net-worth customers will justify a banker in a branch. Once she gives me that information, we'll be able to identify the suitable branches and make space. In fact, I just sent her a reminder about this yesterday."

"Really," Pang said. "Are you sure she received it? Because she called me today and said you were dragging your feet in regard to getting things implemented. She said that you are intentionally trying to sabotage her by not getting things done."

Jack stared in disbelief. "Would you like to see my email?" he asked, the calmness of his tone betraying how irate he felt. Why couldn't they all just act like adults? What was so difficult about that?

"Your email?"

"Yes, the email that I sent to Priscilla. Yesterday. So you could see for yourself that I am not trying to 'drag my feet' over this."

"No, Jack, I don't need to see your email. Let's get things taken care of and not let our personal feelings get in the way, okay? That's all."

And, just like that, he was dismissed.

Jack debated his options. He could leave, which was clearly what Pang wanted him to do. Go back to his cubicle and do whatever it was that would make Priscilla happy. Keep his head down and not speak up. Or, he could stay and protest the ridiculousness of the entire situation, but where would that get him?

"Okay, fine," Jack said. "But just so you know, I never drag my feet on anything, and I certainly wouldn't do something like that in an attempt to sabotage a co-worker."

Pang looked up, as if he were surprised that Jack was still there. It didn't matter what Jack said; there would be no getting Pang to see the situation for what it was.

"Thank you for your time," he said before exiting the office.

He made his way back to his cubicle, seething. He never left things unfinished, but if Priscilla was going to continue to be like this, then Jack felt he had no choice: It was time to start looking for new opportunities. He'd been at the bank long enough, and though he'd climbed the ladder, he had a feeling he'd reached the ceiling, and that ceiling was named Priscilla.

CHAPTER 7

Bar No. 3 was not too busy when Jack arrived to meet Ari. He hoped Jojo would be there, but he didn't see her when he stepped through the entrance. He did eventually see Ari, sitting at a table near the back, secluded from the other patrons. Jack went over to the bar and ordered a bottle of Asahi.

"You've made me curious," Jack said when he sat down across from Ari. "What's up?"

Ari did not have the jovial look on his face that Jack had become accustomed to; right now, his expression was rather severe. Was it going to be something bad? Ari glanced around the bar, as if he was making sure no one was eavesdropping, which would be nearly impossible since none of the nearby tables were occupied. Ari leaned forward, motioning for Jack to do the same.

"Something's come up," he said. "Israel's working with America on a project."

"A project?" Jack asked, lowering his voice, too. "What sort of project? How do you know?"

"It's to help the Chinese. It could be significant. Would you be interested?"

Jack frowned. "But how do you know about this?"

"I have connections in the IDF. They've been talking to the American government. That's all I can say right now."

"You're not giving me much to go on," Jack said. His interest was certainly piqued though—what else might Ari know? What exactly was going on? And, if these matters were as serious as Ari was making them out to be, why was he confiding in Jack?

Jack regarded his friend, this time seeing him in a new light, something Jack's father had said the last time they talked drifted into his mind: *If they need something, they'll find you.* While he wasn't thinking Ari was part of the CIA, it seemed he did have connections, ways of finding things out—perhaps this friendship of theirs had not started out as organically as Jack had assumed.

"Let's go for a little walk," Ari said. "We can leave our stuff here." Ari nodded toward the bartender, who was talking with a customer as he wiped down the counter.

"That's okay?" Jack asked.

"Yeah. It'd be better if we left everything here, and it's not like it's so busy someone could slip in and take our stuff without someone noticing." He glanced up, where the wall met the ceiling. "And there's security cameras here. So I'm not too worried about it."

Jack watched as Ari slipped his phone into his bag and then put it behind his chair, near the wall, so it was almost out of sight. Jack did the same with his phone and briefcase, and then followed Ari out of the bar. He turned right at the next intersection and they walked a few blocks to a nearby park. There were some people exercising, a few people sitting on benches, talking. Ari walked to an empty bench underneath a magnolia tree. He sat down and motioned for Jack to sit next to him. Before he started to speak, Ari looked around again.

"Do you have a stalker?" Jack asked.

But Ari didn't smile at the half-attempt at a joke. Instead, he took a deep breath. "So, Israel's now officially pissed off at China's support of Iran." He paused. "And, as you are well aware, I'm sure, Iran's sworn to annihilate Israel."

"Yes," Jack said. "It's not a good situation."

"And you probably also know that President Sutton is livid at China for continuing to steal intellectual property and technology and not living up to their agreements."

Jack nodded. "Yeah. I think everyone in America probably knows that."

"Then you have the Report to Congress on China's lack of compliance with the demands of the WTO where it details everything China promised to do but hasn't. Sutton's convinced the trade negotiations and agreements will yield little long-term benefit or compensation for America for what China's stolen."

Jack felt some sort of sensation—exhilaration, he realized, after a moment. Not because he found what Ari was telling him so riveting—

it wasn't yet anything he didn't already know—but because it was now abundantly clear that he and Ari had similar views in regard to this.

"There's more," Ari continued. "Part of this is conjecture and part is from intercepting internal Chinese communications. The Communist Party leadership has a few priorities, chief of which is preserving its own position. Avoiding chaos in society is related to this. There's evidence that there are two other priorities underlying their actions."

Jack frowned. He hadn't expected Ari to start talking like he was privy to information only available to a select few. "Go on," he said slowly.

"The first priority is they have a plan to keep China less developed, so the average Chinese person doesn't get too prosperous."

"What do you mean?"

"Well, the government, for example, doesn't want people to be able to afford private education. They don't want their citizens becoming more worldly. Realizing that things are done differently in different places. That there is more than one way. In fact, they're spending money on things like the One Belt One Road initiative, instead of education. Why do you think that is?"

Jack paused, waiting for two women to walk past before he responded. "To keep the population in line."

Ari smiled bitterly. "Right. Yet, isn't it ironic that President Zhao's daughter attended Harvard? And at the same time, the government's encouraging people with money to leave China. It views them as a threat and can buy their expertise later, if needed."

Jack nodded, letting Ari's words sink in. "All animals are equal, but some are more equal than others."

Now it was Ari's turn to look confused. "Sorry?"

"You never read *Animal Farm*?" Jack asked. "George Orwell?"

"I think I fell asleep in literature class that day."

"The trouble is that China isn't a developed country. Yes, there are a few cities that seem fully modern, but China's a big country. There are vast areas where things have not changed in decades."

"Tell me about it," Ari said. "There are way too many places where you can't get a cup of coffee or a slice of pizza!"

That was more like the Ari Jack was accustomed to. He laughed. "Not much chance of pizza once you're an hour out of Shanghai. It's like a different world. Like going back in time."

"The point is that Israel and America view China as an existential threat," Ari said, resuming his serious tone. "For Israel, it's because of China's support for Iran; for America, it's China's subjugation of the Chinese people. Oh, and stealing American military secrets."

"That's the first time an American president has classified China as an 'existential threat,'" Jack said. "Do you think he means a threat both internally and externally?"

"Yes, exactly," Ari said. "And given China's close friendship with Russia, the threat's compounded. So, Israel's been working with America to deal with the situation."

Jack took a deep breath and nodded. On one hand, what Ari was telling him was, for the most part, things he already knew. On the other hand, he was also sharing what sounded like highly classified information. Jack looked at his friend, this person he didn't *really* know all that well but had felt an undeniable connection toward since their very first meeting.

Suddenly, the words that had become something of a common theme when he and Ari were together, flashed through his mind: *What can be done?*

Jack cleared his throat. "Wait a second—Are you suggesting *we* should do something? Us?"

Ari gave him a slow, half-smile. "Precisely. And I'm hoping you're interested in learning more and helping out."

"How? And why me?"

Ari cast another look around. "I can't really go into more detail right now. You're just going to have to take my word for it at the moment. But I *can* tell you that I've been talking to people. People who are ready to do something. And I know, after my few conversations with you, that you are a like-minded soul. You are someone that I want to have on my side, because really, Jack, you and I are both on the same team."

"This sounds pretty . . . serious. Your intuition is really that good that you just . . . trust me?"

"Well . . ." Ari gave him a half-smile. "I *do* have great intuition. But . . . you've been looked into."

"I've been looked into?"

"Nothing too invasive. And I've already said more than I should. What you need to know is that *we* need someone else on board. Someone who isn't known for this sort of thing. Someone we can trust." Ari pointed at Jack. "You."

"Me?"

"Why do you sound so surprised? Yes, you."

The wisp of exhilaration Jack had felt earlier bloomed. "Of course I'm interested," he said. "But it's also hard to be completely on board if I don't even know what I'm agreeing to be a part of."

Ari stared straight ahead, and Jack could all but see the wheels turning. "I get it," he finally said. "I'd probably be saying the same thing if I were in your position. But you're going to have to trust me. Which is a big ask, I realize, from someone that you don't know that well. I do, however, think that you are also an excellent judge of character, and I'm going to even go so far as to say that you think the two of us are most certainly operating on the same wave-length."

Jack gave an appreciative nod. "True."

"So, I just need to ask for your trust right now, and I'll get into more details as I can. I *can* tell you that, given the recent events, things will be led by Israel, with close American involvement and support." Ari took a deep breath. "Look, this is serious. I guess I should've started off with that as the caveat. What I'm asking you to get involved in could be dangerous. If things *don't* go according to plan—not that we're going to let that happen—then, it could spell serious trouble for everyone involved. I want to be clear about that, before getting any agreement from you."

"I'm intrigued. But I think I need to know a little more information."

"I know. I presented things kind of backward. I should've given the danger caveat first. I guess I didn't want to scare you off."

"It's going to take a whole lot more than that to scare me off." What, exactly, was it, that Ari had in mind? And if it involved high-level government, the consequences of things not going well would certainly be severe. He had a million thoughts racing through his mind. He wanted more details. He wanted to help. Perhaps, most of all, he wanted to be able to tell his father that he was finally involved in something that could *make a difference.*

"Jack," Ari said, "you know we're off the record here. You don't have to give me an answer now. Or, if you already know you don't want to get involved, just say so. I won't be offended; it won't change our relationship. I think you're great. If you don't want to be a part of it, I respect that, and we don't have to talk about it again."

Jack rubbed his hand over the lower part of his face. "It's surprising, yes," he said. "I mean, I still don't even know *what* exactly, you're talking about. So . . . if I ask you to tell me more about it, I'm in then, huh? Kind of by default?"

"Yeah," Ari said, nodding. "It's a one-way gate, I'm afraid. But take some time and think about it, if you want–"

Jack shook his head. He already knew his answer; there was no point in taking any more time to think about it. "I'm in."

Relief crossed Ari's face, and along with the exhilaration, Jack felt flattered. Like the validation with the *Wall Street Journal* publishing his article, Ari's clear relief that Jack had agreed felt good.

"It's clear that there's a bunch that annoys you about China that also annoys us. And by us, I mean Israel," Ari said. "You're an American, I'm an Israeli, but you're Jewish, too. And hey, I meant what I said about you coming to Shabbat dinner some night at Synagogue Shanghai. You'd enjoy it. And you speak Chinese like a native, unlike most Israelis, who tend to focus on Arabic. You were the missing puzzle piece, Jack. We didn't feel good about moving forward with this until you came into the picture. Now that you've agreed, everything seems to be falling right into place." Ari had a gleam in his eyes. "It's very exciting. But! That's all I can say about it right now."

With that, he stood up, so Jack did, too. As they walked back to the bar, Jack's mind was in overdrive.

What are they planning?

What is the objective?

Who else is going to be involved?

And, perhaps most importantly: *What do they want from me?*

CHAPTER 8

The Synagogue Shanghai community was small, with only about three hundred WeChat members, but it was evolving and growing. When the Jews left Europe, fleeing Hitler, about twenty thousand of them had emigrated to Shanghai. These days, there were far fewer in the city, but that did not stop the Synagogue community from having their own rabbi and holding events for major holidays.

This evening, Jack was meeting Ari and his wife for Shabbat dinner. If nothing else, Jack figured, it would be a good way to make some new connections. According to Ari, the majority of the members were Caucasian, though there were also many interracial marriages, where the mother was Chinese. Traditionally, the children of these unions would not be considered Jewish, but Synagogue Shanghai was more open and accepted all.

When Jack arrived, he saw several large tables where everyone would eventually sit; at the moment, people were standing in small groups, milling about, chatting with each other. Jack saw Ari and a woman he assumed was his wife, standing near a table of drinks, having a conversation with another couple. Ari waved him over.

"Jack!" Ari said. "Glad you made it. And so glad I finally get to introduce you to my better half–this is my wife, Mary. Mary, this is Jack."

Jack smiled and held out his hand. "So nice to finally meet this guy's better half."

Mary returned his smile as she shook his hand. "I can't believe he actually referred to me as 'wife' instead of 'girlfriend.' It's a miracle! Likewise, Jack, it's great to finally meet you–Ari's had a lot to say about you."

Jack winced. "Oh, boy."

"No, no, all good. He even mentioned something about you needing a date. I'm free tomorrow night," she said with a wink. Everyone laughed.

Jack clapped Ari on the shoulder. "Here you are, always looking out for me," he said. "Now that's a true friend."

"Well, when Ari told me that you were looking for a date," Mary said, "I couldn't believe it. Because everything he'd told me about you made you sound like quite the catch, and if you can't find someone in Shanghai, there's something seriously wrong with you."

"It's not that there's an issue meeting someone," Jack said. "It's just meeting the *right* someone. Which can sort of feel like looking for a needle in a haystack."

"Did you see the *Bloomberg* article about China's growing elderly population?" Ari asked.

Jack shook his head. "No. What did it say?"

"That it's dragging down growth and innovation. The median age in China will be fifty-six by 2050. In the U.S., it'll be forty-four. It's the legacy of the one-child policy, and because families have limited incomes, they want fewer children."

"Ironically," Mary said, anger in her voice, "in the past, China forced abortions if a woman got pregnant a second time. Now they're making it more and more difficult to get an abortion. Can you believe that? It's infuriating."

"It is," Jack said. "I mean, I know I'm not a woman and so can't fully understand what it would be like to be in that particular situation, but I can't imagine it would make anyone happy. But, I think China's economic policies will play a bigger role. If they change positively, there'll be more babies and better growth." He looked at Ari. "What's the estimated median age for people in Israel?"

"Thirty-five."

"That's young! You guys must like having babies."

They laughed. People were beginning to take their seats, so Jack followed Ari and Mary over to a table and sat down.

"If China did away with the bride price, that might help more people get married," Ari said.

Jack looked at him in confusion. "What are you talking about?"

"When you marry a woman, there's a bride price. The amount depends on the province."

"What?" Jack said, baffled. "In this day and age, there's still a bride price?" He racked his brain, trying to recall if he had, during all his travels and all the books he had read over the years, come across this information and simply forgot it—no, he was pretty sure he wouldn't forget a fact like that.

"Absolutely," Ari said. "If you want to marry someone from Shandong, the price is twenty thousand U.S. dollars. If you marry someone from Tianjin, it's about ten thousand."

"Really," Jack said. "Interesting. So, how does it work? You hand the father the cash?"

Ari and Mary shared a look. "What we did, we put the money in a special account, and after we married, she gave her dad an ATM card."

"I never talked to my dad about it," Mary said. "It's embarrassing. And such a stupid concept in the first place."

Ari laughed. "Remember how you wanted to try to play it off like it was a loan, and you'd pay me back?"

"Well, it might make me feel a little less like a piece of property."

"Actually . . . now that you're working for Nike, maybe you *should* pay me back."

Mary swatted him on the shoulder.

"It's unbelievable," Jack said. "What's the point?"

"Most people in China still believe that when a daughter gets married, she leaves her family to join her husband's family. The parents feel that their daughter is leaving and they even say, 'I give my daughter to you.' Which is exactly what Mary's mother said to me."

"Again, not a piece of property!" Mary said in a sing-song voice.

"Originally, it was a way to make sure aging parents were taken care of," Ari said. "Then, it became a barometer for whether a man was good enough. No one wants their daughter to be married off to someone who isn't financially solvent. Now, it's evolved into tradition and legacy. If the neighbor gets it, so should you. That sort of thing. The government has tried to stop it, but they haven't succeeded. And with the enormous disparity between the number of men and the number of women here . . . expect bride prices to go up, not down."

"A lot of unintended consequences with that one-child policy," Jack said.

"Yeah," Ari said. "Until recently, if a couple in a village had a girl, they could have another kid to try for a boy. It was common for the mother of the husband to ostracize his wife, as if it were her fault for giving birth to a girl."

"Even though it's the *man's* genetic material that determines gender," Mary said. "And also—younger brother is lucky I'm a girl. Think about all the younger brothers that exist out there, all because their older sibling was the wrong gender. Talk about giving yourself an existential crisis."

"If the first child was a boy," Ari said, "the government wouldn't allow the family to have a second child. Countless girl babies were aborted or abandoned, and now there's close to thirty-four million more men than women here."

"Just one more example of the unintended consequences of misguided governmental policies," Jack said.

Mary elbowed Ari. "Hey, I like this guy."

Shabbat prayers started, and Jack and Mary listened as the others around them said the prayers aloud in Hebrew. Once complete, the Chinese meal was served, and the conversation pivoted from the topic of disastrous government policy to the reasons the people at the table had moved to Shanghai.

The reasons fascinated Jack. To his right sat a corporate attorney who did all his legal work in Chinese, which Jack could not help but find impressive. Less impressive was the man's rather dull personality. Several of the other people at the table had come to Shanghai because they were sent by the companies they worked for or were hired by a local organization because of their specialized knowledge. And a few of the others, like Jack, had ventured to Shanghai to pursue their own dreams.

Ari leaned toward Jack. "There's someone here tonight that I need to introduce you to." He looked past Jack's shoulder. "He's coming over here now. He's the Assistant Consul General for the U.S. Embassy in Shanghai."

Jack turned and saw a tall, dark-haired man, dressed formally in a suit and tie, make his way over to them. He greeted Ari first, enthusiastically. Ari stood and shook his hand.

"Jack Gold, I'd like to introduce you to Sean Smith, who works at your embassy."

Jack set his wine glass down and stood up to shake Sean's hand. "Pleasure to meet you. How's business?"

Sean nodded enthusiastically. "Business is always good in my business. There are more Chinese applying for visas than you could ever imagine."

"About thirty-four million?" Jack asked jokingly.

"It sure as hell feels like that many."

"How long have you been in Shanghai?"

"About six months. Let's just say it's been a steep learning curve."

Sean was about to say something else when a waiter came up and put a Diet Coke down in front of Jack. Jack looked at it, then back to the waiter.

"I think you made a mistake; I didn't order that," Jack said in Chinese.

The waiter took the beverage, as if he'd been expecting that response, and walked off.

"You speak Chinese exceedingly well," Sean said. "*Quite* well. It's impressive. Anyway, gentleman, it looks like the rabbi is about to make an announcement, so I better get back to my seat. But Jack, great to meet you; Ari, as always . . ." They all shook hands and Sean crossed the room to return to the table he had been seated at.

"What was that all about?" Jack whispered, leaning close to Ari, as the rabbi stood at the front of the room behind a makeshift podium.

"The assistant consul general in every embassy is nearly always CIA," Ari whispered back.

The rabbi started to speak, and Ari shifted back into his own seat, eyes glued to the rabbi. Jack, too, straightened and looked at the rabbi, though he wasn't really focusing on what the man was saying. Instead, he was trying to figure out just what was going on here. Ari's response didn't really make sense at all. And what was up with the Diet Coke? It was possible that it had been a genuine mistake, but coupled with meeting Sean, and Ari's response just now, the timing of it seemed . . . a little odd. Or not odd, but significant. Had it been some sort of test? He had replied in Mandarin, after all. Jack tried to replay the exact event back in his mind; he was exceptionally good at recalling events accurately.

The waiter brought the drink over when Sean was right there.

The waiter had not hesitated to remove the drink, or offer any expla-nation or apology—which (though it hadn't happened often), in Jack's experience, was customary—at least some form of apology was always offered. The whole thing did seem a bit . . . staged? No, that wasn't quite the right word, but there had certainly been an air of artificiality to the whole thing; clearly, there was much more going on here than Jack realized.

CHAPTER 9

The next morning was Saturday, thankfully. Jack's irritation over the whole situation with Priscilla had not abated, even after a good night's sleep, which Jack took to mean it really was time to resign. He sat at his kitchen table, drinking his first cup of coffee, composing his resignation letter. He kept it succinct and respectful, thanking the company for the opportunity, but that he felt it was time to move on.

His phone chimed as he was closing his laptop. Text message. It was a WeChat message from Andrew San, wondering if he could give Jack a call.

He poured himself a second cup and then texted Andrew back—*Sure, now is fine for a call.*

"Jack!" Andrew said. "Thanks for indulging me. I'm calling to say hello, of course, but also because you're a man who knows what he's doing, and that's what we need right now."

Jack smiled. "A man who knows what he's doing," he said. "I'd like to think that, at least most of the time."

"Oh, I think it's probably all of the time—that's the feeling I get from you. You make quite the impression, Jack, and take it for the compliment that it is."

"So, what is it that you need help with?"

"I have a big client. One of the biggest I've had. Eager to invest in American real estate—commercial or industrial—but I don't—as much as it pains me to admit this—have the right connections. Which is where you come in. How would you like to work with me on a contractual basis? I'll help you by introducing you to potential clients, and you'll help me by introducing me to some of your American connections. It's perfect!"

This was interesting, Jack had to admit. The timing was—serendipitous? He had not submitted his resignation or given two weeks' notice, yet here was this opportunity. It would be foolish not to take it.

"Well, sure," Jack said. "I'll see what I can do. Why don't you send me some more details on the types of projects you're looking for and I'll start reaching out to some of my connections and see what comes up."

"Hey, that's great," Andrew said. "Thanks, *dàgē*! I knew you were the right person to call. And hey, let's get together soon for that smoke, okay? Actually, do you have plans tomorrow night?"

"Tomorrow?" Jack said. "No, nothing scheduled."

"Great! Well, now you do. We're meeting up at the Roosevelt Club. Some very interesting—and important—people will be there. Why don't you join us? It's going to be a good time."

"Sure," Jack said.

"Excellent!" He could practically hear the grin on Andrew's face, in part, he knew, because it would reflect well on Andrew—bringing an American to a meeting like this, regardless of how little Jack actually knew about real estate. "Why don't you meet me there at seven."

"Looking forward to it. And I'll reach out to some of my contacts and see what I can come up with for you."

"I knew you wouldn't disappoint," Andrew said. "I was sure about you the moment we met."

Jack smiled. "It's that smoker solidarity," he said, though he had a positive attitude about Andrew, too. He liked him, and if this was a start of both a new friendship and business endeavor, well, he was perfectly fine with that.

*   *   *

The meeting was to be held at the Roosevelt Club on the Bund, on the third floor of the House of Roosevelt. It had originally been called the Jardine Matheson Building when it was built in 1922, but China had insisted on the name change because Jardine Matheson was a famous opium trading company back in the day. Jack shook his head, thinking about all the Chinese people who had become addicted to opium. He thought about all the people in America who were now addicted to and dying from fentanyl.

The Shanghai Bund was located along the Huangpu River, famous for the dozens of grand Western-style buildings, with architecture from Dutch gambrel roofs to German Teutonic. During its heyday from 1920 to 1937, the Bund had been synonymous with capitalism and was the epicenter for wealthy people who wanted to party.

Unsurprisingly, China had long ago commandeered the buildings, so while the buildings were still beautiful on the surface, the energy and vibrancy that had previously been there was gone. They lacked the soul they'd once possessed.

Before stepping into the House of Roosevelt, Jack paused and looked up at the tops of the buildings, each adorned with China's red flag, It didn't feel right to Jack, considering the buildings hadn't been built by China. Obviously, the government felt differently.

Andrew met Jack just outside the elevator. "Hey, *dàgē!*" Andrew crowed, and Jack had to smile.

"Hey, Andrew," he replied as they shook hands enthusiastically. "Good to see you. How are things going?"

"It's great," he said. "Come on—lots of important people for you to meet."

Andrew kept up a steady stream of chatter as they entered into the elevator and went to a private room on the third floor. The first of the important people Jack met was Andrew's boss, Stanley Ling.

"Mr. Gold!" Stanley said, giving Jack a warm smile and a firm handshake. "Pleasure to meet you."

"Likewise," Jack said. "Thanks for inviting me to join you tonight."

"The more the merrier! That's how the saying goes, isn't it? Well, no matter, because you know what I mean! Come in, come in, get comfortable. Here, have a cigar. Have two. Whiskey? Scotch? Red wine? Something else?"

Jack couldn't help but laugh as he looked at the two cigars Stanley had just given him. This guy was like someone out of a movie or something, with his blue, white-collared shirt, big Rolex, gold rings on both ring fingers.

"I haven't had a cigar in a while," Jack said. "Though when I have one, I always enjoy a good whiskey with it."

"Ah, smart man. I like you. Want to meet someone else I like? We call him Mr. Big. He's the smartest person I know!"

Stanley guffawed, and Jack wondered how many drinks he'd had already.

Perhaps unsurprisingly, Mr. Big was short. He was older, too, and from a generation that did not have nutritious food to eat. His face remained impassive as Jack was introduced, and when Jack said, "Hi, it's nice to meet you," Mr. Big just grunted.

Stanley, though, did not seem to think anything was amiss with this reaction, and so Jack figured Mr. Big was maybe a little rude, or maybe just took a while to warm up to people he didn't know.

Jack was seated next to Andrew, and across from Mr. Big, who continued to glower at him like he was nothing more than some piece of trash that had somehow found its way inside. Jack picked up one of the cigars that Stanley had given him—a Partagas D4, an old friend—and lit it. Andrew handed him a whiskey.

"You're a good friend," he said.

"I'm so glad you were able to join us tonight. I told Stanley that you had—"

"Why have you given THAAD to South Korea?"

Mr. Big's voice cut through the conversation like a blade; everyone stopped talking and looked to him, then Jack, because Mr. Big was still staring intently at him. It sounded more like an accusation than a question.

For a moment, Jack thought about simply ignoring him, but his frustrations from work came bubbling back as he looked Mr. Big right in the eye. The man stared back, his eyes dark, hooded, his skin sallow and pock marked.

"Excuse me?" Jack said in Chinese, despite having heard him perfectly fine the first time.

Mr. Big repeated the question.

"I'm sorry," Jack said, "but you're mistaken in your assumption that I represent the United States government. I didn't give THAAD to Korea; America did. *Why* did America do that? To protect South Korea from North Korean missiles. Friends help friends."

Mr. Big frowned.

"Plus," Jack continued, "you should remember that in World War Two, it was *America* who defeated Japan. If it wasn't for America, Japan would have conquered China and you, sir, would be speaking Japanese right now."

A strained silence descended.

Mr. Big was seething underneath that detached exterior, Jack could tell, but he was also doing everything in his power to keep his emotions in check. The only real evidence of this was the crimson color his ears were turning.

Jack picked up his glass, downed the rest of his drink, and then turned to Andrew. "Is there anymore whiskey?"

Andrew shot out of his seat and grabbed the bottle, poured Jack a generous measure.

"To good friends!" Stanley said, holding his glass to Jack, then to Mr. Big. "And good business!"

Everyone stood up and touched glasses, the tense exchange hopefully over. As the evening continued, though, Jack couldn't help but be aware of Mr. Big's presence, the hostility that seemed to emanate from him. Jack had met people like him before, and he knew they could be dangerous, completely consumed by the mentality of the Chinese government. He also knew there was zero use in trying to reason with people like that, at least in his own experience.

After everyone sat back down, Andrew turned to Jack, excitement in his eyes. "So," he said. "Stanley and I have looked over your LinkedIn profile. Your education and professional experiences are quite impressive. We'd like you formally involved on our real estate team. If you can source some good projects for our investors to invest in, then we'll give you part of the acquisition and general partnership fee."

"Ah," Jack said. To receive an offer so quickly was surprising, though he knew they weren't taking much of an initial risk; if he was unable to find them good investment opportunities, they would have lost nothing. "I knew you had an ulterior motive for inviting me here tonight; it wasn't just the pleasure of my company." He smiled. "What's the fee sharing you're proposing?"

"Point-three percent commission on investment below one hundred million, and point-two-percent above that. The general partnership fee we can share—twenty-five percent each."

Jack mulled this over. He knew standard industry practice, and what Andrew had just proposed were not unfair terms. The key was that they could go around him after he introduced the sources of investment opportunities.

"Take time to think about it, if you need to," Andrew said.

"What you've said so far sounds good. I'd like to continue receiving commission from introduced clients for five years after introductions are first made."

Andrew's eyebrows shot up, his smile wavering. "*Five* years? That's a long time. I'll have to discuss that with Stanley."

"Of course. It's a reasonable request. It's nice to hear about companies wanting to get their money out of China." Jack let his gaze rest on Mr. Big as he said this.

"Tesla is doing great in Shanghai now," Andrew said. "Lots of foreign companies will now start to come in. It's very exciting."

"Tesla's the favored stepchild. The free trade zones aren't too free, except for the world's leading maker of electronic automobiles. They do not allow for the free flow of currency. If they can't be successful—which they aren't—what will happen to China's economy?" Again, Jack couldn't help but eye Mr. Big as he spoke, who sat stone-faced, arms folded across his chest.

Since 2013, China had established areas to attract foreign investment, but the promise of free-flowing currency within those areas was untenable.

Mr. Big uncrossed his arms and leaned forward. "China is a big country with lots of people. It can do everything on its own. It certainly does not need America."

"We live in a global marketplace," Jack said. "There's no country that can do everything on its own. An open market and free-flowing currency would only benefit the people of China. Are you familiar with Milton Friedman? He's a Nobel prize-winning economist. Read what he wrote in *Free to Choose*."_

"Why are you so concerned about benefiting the people of China? You're an American. Why not go back there and enjoy your incredible country?"

He had a choice—he could continue this pointless argument, with a man whose opinion would never be swayed, no matter how compelling the argument or evidence presented, or he could let it go and enjoy the rest of his evening. Jack was pretty sure that no one else here wanted to hear this back and forth anyway, so he picked up his glass and held it in Mr. Big's direction.

"I'll consider it," he said, and though he had to force it, he gave the man a grin. Jack finished off his whiskey and then turned his attention to Andrew, resolving to just have a good time for the remainder of the night.

CHAPTER 10

Jack met Ari upstairs at Taste Buds, an overpriced cocktail bar that somehow managed to exude both a warm and an exclusive atmosphere. The décor was a little over the top, with the hanging lights ensconced in what looked like old-fashioned birdcages without the bottom, and decadent, Victorian-style oversized sofas. It was a regular haunt of Jack's, and over the years, he'd come to know the owner, Daniel An, quite well.

"How's it going Daniel?" Jack asked. "How's everything with the new bar coming along?"

"Things are great," Daniel said. "New place opens in two weeks. Lots to still finish, but I hope you'll drop by."

"Absolutely," Jack said, glancing around. No Ari yet.

He turned his attention back to Daniel, who handed him a business card. "There's the address," he said. "Really hope you can make it by."

"I will," Jack said, pocketing the card. He took a seat at the bar as Daniel moved off to talk with other patrons. Whenever Jack came here, he liked to sit right at the bar so he could watch the drinks getting mixed. Daniel was an award-winning bartender, and the people he hired really knew their stuff.

The current bartender nodded at Jack. "What would you like?"

Jack thought for a moment. "A Grey Goose martini," he said. "Straight up, with frozen grapes, please."

The bartender gave a little smile at the mention of frozen grapes, which had been Jack's idea, one of the first times he'd come into the bar, years ago. He'd asked if they had any, which they didn't, though Daniel had furrowed his brow for a second and then smiled, declaring it a great idea that should be included in the menu immediately.

Jack watched as the bartender worked. Some bars served small drinks, to save money, but that was not the case at Taste Buds. Their drinks were large, and Jack was happy to see the three ripe grapes at the bottom of his glass. He took a big sip, enjoying the smooth flavor. Grey Goose wasn't easy to find in Shanghai; he hadn't properly appreciated the huge bottles he used to get at Costco until he came here.

He turned on the bar stool as he took another sip of his drink, right as Ari walked through the door. Jack held up his glass, a gesture meant to get Ari's attention but probably looked more like a toast. Jack watched as Ari started to make his way over, paused to speak with Daniel for a few moments, and then continued on his way.

"Sorry I'm late," Ari said. He looked at Jack's drink, then at the bartender as he held up two fingers. "That looks good. What is that at the bottom? Those aren't olives."

"No, they're frozen grapes."

Ari smiled. "Genius."

When they had their drinks, Ari suggested they go up on the balcony. That sounded good to Jack, because it meant he could have a smoke if he wanted to. The balcony was sparsely decorated, with some benches and a single table, and a few tall trees that acted as a canopy, the big leaves fluttering lightly in the breeze. Aside from the two people smoking cigarettes, Jack and Ari had the place to themselves.

They sipped their martinis. Ari gave Jack a serious look. "Mary and I are likely to leave Shanghai next year."

"Really?" Jack said, unable to keep the surprise out of his voice. "How come?"

"Oh, lots of reasons. We want kids, eventually, and the smog bothers us. Also, just a change of venue—and food."

"I hear you," Jack said. "It took me a little while to get used to food being on the sweeter side here. You getting tired of the Shanghainese?"

Ari gave Jack a pointed look. "That's one way of putting it."

"Yeah," Jack said. "I'm actually exploring a different avenue right now, too, though I'm not planning to leave Shanghai any time soon."

"Oh yeah?"

"I've moved on from the bank. I should still be finishing out my time there, but they gave me the boot right after I turned down the president's offer to head up their bank in Thailand." After commenting on his surprise to be receiving Jack's resignation letter, Pang had tried to offer him a different position in Thailand, but it was too little, too late at that point. Jack had been set to finish out his two weeks, but after he'd returned to his desk, a security guard arrived shortly after to escort him out. And that was that.

Ari raised his eyebrows. "Sounds like a big offer to pass on."

"Yes and no. I also wasn't sure if I wanted to go to Thailand, but it was really the fact that they didn't give a damn about trying to straighten out any of the interpersonal stuff that was going on. I'm not the sort of guy that tries to screw people over just so I can get to the top, and unfortunately, that's not how all of my co-workers seemed to operate."

"I wouldn't say that's the typical American attitude," Ari said. "But I'm glad to hear screwing people over isn't a top priority of yours."

"It's not. Actually, an old friend of mine will be out here soon and going out on the town is definitely always part of his travel itinerary. You should meet us for drinks or something. He's in real estate; he's actually been talking to me about getting involved. Which . . . honestly, isn't the worst idea. Chinese investors would do very well in America."

"That they would, if only they were aware that America consisted of more than New York and Los Angeles. But hey, that sounds great—I could see you being very successful in real estate."

"What I'd really like to do—"

"Hey!" one of the guys across the balcony shouted before Jack could finish. "Are you Americans?" he asked in broken English. He ground his cigarette out in the ashtray on the table, his friend doing the same, as they staggered toward Jack and Ari, clearly intoxicated. Jack didn't like the guy's tone; he might be drunk and mouthy, but Jack could also tell he was aggressive and looking to take it out on someone.

"Yes, I'm from America," Jack said.

The guy took another several steps closer. "And you think you can come to China and take our women and do whatever you please? You think that's okay? That we're supposed to be fine with that?"

Jack glanced at Ari. Many Chinese men felt this way, and some even went so far as to beat up any foreign man they came across, just because he wasn't Chinese.

"I respect people," Jack said. "I wouldn't take another man's woman, because I wouldn't *take* a woman in the first place—she's not a possession. Maybe that's your problem—you need to treat women with more respect."

"*Cào nɪ mā!*" the second guy yelled. "Fuck your mother!"

Jack's anger flared, even though he knew he should just suggest to Ari they leave. Then again, there was a part of him that wanted to give these two a fight, if that's what they wanted. But he wasn't going to be the one to throw the first punch—in China, the person who hit first was at fault.

Jack stood up. "I think you're just upset over the fact that all Chinese women find foreigners more attractive than the two of you." Jack paused. "Including your mother."

It happened fast, as all fights do—one of the guy's threw a punch, which Jack easily sidestepped, right as the second guy tried to land one. It grazed Jack's shoulder as he unleashed a front kick into the stomach of the first guy, who immediately keeled over, groaning. Jack pivoted to his left, catching the second guy square in the jaw with a right hook. Now, they were both sprawled on the ground, no longer looking like the tough guys that they had just been trying to be.

Jack stood there, adrenaline coursing through him. He glanced at Ari, who was looking intently at the two men as they struggled to get to their feet. Jack could tell by the way they were moving that their egos might be bruised but there was no real damage.

"Listen, guys," Jack said, as his adrenaline started to ebb. What was the point of all of this? "Let's just stop this. Why don't we sit down and have a drink together. They're on me."

For a moment, he thought they were going to accept his attempt at extending an olive branch, but then the guy he hit in the jaw tried to come at him again, swinging wildly. Jack kicked him in the shin and hit him once in the side of the head. He ducked an incoming punch from the first guy and countered with two hard hits to the ribs. The guy was hunched over, and Jack grabbed him by the back of the shirt and threw him over the balcony. They were on the second floor, but the building wasn't particularly tall, and there were bushes to break the fall, so Jack knew there was little chance of the man being mortally wounded. The second guy, undeterred by what had just happened to his friend, rushed forward as if he were going to use sheer momentum to send Jack over the balcony. Instead, Jack waited until the guy was almost upon him, then he reached out and, almost like they were doing some sort of dance, grabbed the guy's shoulders and sent him flying over the railing to join his friend below. He could hear both of them, cursing and yelling as they tried to extricate themselves from the shrubbery.

"Who knew taking out the trash could be so satisfying," Ari said. He had his phone in his hand, but then he slipped it into his pocket.

"Yeah, thanks for the help," Jack said.

Ari smiled. "I was enjoying the show, and, I wanted you to have fun. I mean, where the hell did you learn moves like that?"

"I've practiced karate most of my life."

Ari shook his head in amazement. "Is there anything you can't do? I think we need to go in for a refill."

Jack followed Ari back inside. He hoped those two fools wouldn't try to come inside looking for round two. He didn't see any sign of them, so he slid into an empty seat next to Ari at the bar and ordered another round of drinks. "What a night," Jack said. "This wasn't exactly how I thought things were going to turn out."

"Me neither, but at least things went in our favor."

No sooner had the words left Ari's mouth when Jack saw two police officers walk in. Next to them was one of the guys Jack had tossed over the balcony.

"Shit," he muttered. He signaled the bartender. "Can we get our bill, please?"

The bartender came to scan Jack's phone right as the police officers made their way over.

"Would both of you come with us?" one of the officers asked.

"Sure," Jack said. Instead of feeling anxious, he felt calm, and he knew that was what he was projecting.

They followed the policeman outside, only to find there were five more officers waiting. Jack glanced at Ari, who did not look particularly pleased at this new development, but also seemed to be exuding an air of calm, which was certainly not the vibe Jack was getting from the two guys, both of whom were seething.

One of the police officers looked at Jack. "Did you hit these two men?"

Jack looked at the two guys. *This could be a problem*, he thought, and that calmness began to give way to a little bit of anxiety.

"I did," he said. "That's true. But I only did so because I was protecting myself. They attacked me, not the other way around."

The two guys immediately started yelling in Chinese, disputing what Jack said, gesticulating wildly, mimicking being thrown over a balcony.

"Here," Ari said suddenly, almost having to shout to be heard over the yelling. He had his phone out. "I recorded the whole incident; you can see for yourselves."

The officers gathered around and Ari pressed play. From his vantage point over his shoulder, Jack watched the video unfold. Was Ari about to implicate him in this whole thing? Defending himself, yes, but how was he going to explain throwing them over the balcony?

But before it arrived to that part of the action, the video ended.

"So now you see," Ari said. "They started it."

"Play it again," one of the officers said. They all watched it a second time. The officer looked at the two guys, then at Jack.

"Did you throw them over the balcony?"

Jack knew, in this instance, that lying was the only way. If he admitted to throwing them over the balcony, who knew what would happen, and at this point, it was their word against his. He widened his eyes as he shook his head vehemently.

"Absolutely not," he said. "Why would I do that? I was just trying to protect myself. My friend and I are just sitting up on the balcony, enjoying the evening, and these two start insulting us and then trying to get physical. I tried to both defend myself *and* defuse the situation—which I thought I had. My friend and I then went back into the bar to get a drink, and now this."

For several long seconds, no one said anything. The police officers looked at each other, the two guys looked at the officers, and Jack glanced over at Ari, who just raised his eyebrows and shrugged.

"Okay," one of the officers finally said. He handed Ari his phone back. "You're free to go. Goodnight."

The two men began yelling in protest, but Jack wasn't interested in sticking around to hear any of that. "Come on," he said to Ari. "Let's get out of here."

"Don't have to ask me twice," Ari said.

"Celebratory drink at Bar No. 3?" Jack asked.

"Sure, why not. What are we celebrating? Not being detained and thrown in prison?"

"Nah—your awesome assist there."

Ari grinned. "Don't let my size fool you—I don't have an ounce of the physical prowess you displayed back there."

"I was actually talking about the fact that you recorded it; I didn't realize you'd done that."

"Let's go get that drink."

Bar No. 3 was crowded when they arrived, the air full of chatter and laughing, the sounds of people enjoying themselves. Jack hoped there wouldn't be any further issues tonight; he just wanted to have a good time. His spirits lifted even further when he saw that Jojo was working.

She smiled when she saw them and came over to their table to take their order. "Hi, Jojo," Jack said in Mandarin. "Nice to see you again."

"Nice to see you, too," she said. "What can I get you guys?"

"I'll let you decide," Ari said.

"How about two Grey Goose martinis? With olives. Pretty sure Bar No. 3 doesn't carry frozen grapes."

Jojo looked at him curiously. "Frozen grapes?"

"Yeah. They're good in martinis."

"Huh. I never thought of that before, but now that you mention it, yeah, it does sound pretty good!"

She laughed, and Jack couldn't recall seeing a more beautiful woman in his entire life. He laughed along with her, feeling as if they were the only two in the whole crowded place. What *was* this feeling?

"I'll be right back with those drinks," she said, and Jack felt a deep longing as she walked away.

He turned to Ari, certain that his friend was going to give him a hard time about the obvious puppy dog crush he had on this woman, but perhaps he wasn't exhibiting it outwardly as much as he thought he was, because Ari only leaned toward him and said, "The more I think about what happened earlier, the more it seems straight out of a movie. I admit—that's not how I thought things were going to end." He leaned a little closer, dropped his voice lower. "Why'd you throw them both over the balcony? You didn't have to do that."

He could tell from Ari's tone, though, that he did not disapprove. "They deserved it," Jack said. "I wouldn't have done it if I thought they could get seriously hurt. Hopefully that taught them a lesson, and maybe next time they won't be so quick to mouth off. Remember—I offered to buy everyone drinks. They could've agreed, but instead they acted like spineless snakes. So, I just put them where snakes should go—in the garden."

They both laughed and were still laughing when Jojo returned with their drinks.

"I'd love to stay and find out what's so funny, but as you can see, we're really slammed right now!" she said. "Enjoy."

She was off before Jack could say anything, so he smiled and took a sip of his drink. "I'd be more than happy if I never had to have an encounter with guys like that again," he said. "I'm certainly not the type of person who goes out looking for that sort of thing."

"Fighting has never been a strength of mine," Ari said. "I used to get picked on at school. I really didn't think I'd enjoy my time in the IDF, but I did. But still . . . never developed a taste for fighting. Physical fighting, anyway." He gave Jack a half-smile. "There are other ways to win battles." He leaned back and pulled something out of his pocket, which he handed to Jack. Jack looked at the folded-up papers in his hand.

"What's this?" he asked as he unfolded the two sheets.

"An article from the *Telegraph*. Dozens of U.S. spies were killed after Iran and China uncovered a CIA messaging service using Google."

Jack squinted against the bar's low ambient lighting as he skimmed the article. *Things are getting worse*, he thought. *But it's hard to get the full picture. No one's looking at the situation as a whole.*

He folded the article back up and slid it into his own pocket. Ari was looking at him closely. "I'll give this a more thorough read-through tomorrow," he said.

"It's getting bad, Jack."

"I know."

Ari nodded. "I know you do. Maybe it's my heritage, but I just don't want to be one of those people who stands around and does nothing. Thinks that someone else will handle it."

"I agree."

It seemed, for a moment, that Ari was about to say something else, perhaps delve into the details that Jack *really* wanted to hear about, but then he stopped.

"We can talk more about this another time."

"Okay." Jack nodded, trying to keep a calm exterior, yet wanting to know more details, lots of details—what exactly was going on? What was the objective, the end goal? Who was behind all of this?

CHAPTER 11

For his first night out when his friend Mike Beckman arrived into town, Jack suggested a bar called Boom Boom, with an outside sitting area along the street. They had the perfect vantage point to people watch—people on foot, on bikes, in cars, parents playing with their kids and walking their dogs in the park across the street. As Jack sipped his beer, he watched Mike's eyes follow any attractive woman who walked by.

"This place is great," Mike said.

Jack smiled. "I thought you'd like it. Look at the walk-by traffic."

"Yeah, no shit! The traffic's astonishing." Mike turned his head, looking into the bar. "But the bar isn't even full yet."

"Give it time. In two hours it'll be packed. There'll even be a guy selling Greek food right over there," Jack said, pointing. "It's still early for most people." He glanced at his watch. "Though I do expect Ari to be coming through any time. You'll like him."

"How'd the two of you meet?"

"At a nearby bar. I was on a date—"

"A date! Good for you!"

"It didn't end up going anywhere. But, Ari was at the bar, and I wound up sitting next to him. After my date left, we started talking and . . . we just hit it off." Jack paused. "He's a very interesting person."

"So, it sounds like the date was successful after all, just maybe not in the way that you originally imagined." Mike slapped the table and took a big swig of beer.

"I guess I hadn't thought of it like that," Jack said. "But . . . you're right."

"What is it that Ari does again?"

"He imports and distributes liquor to various restaurants and bars."

"A man after my own heart."

"He does other things, too, of which I'm not entirely clear on, but . . ." Jack shrugged.

"A man of intrigue. Where is he? Sounds like he should be my new best friend."

"We'll see about that. He should be here any minute. Never mind, there he is."

Jack waved when he saw Ari stroll up. Introductions were made and more beer was ordered.

"Ah," Ari said, sitting down. "I've been looking forward to this."

"So," Mike said. "Jack tells me you're involved in importing and distributing liquor. Which is the exact thing I'd be into, if I wasn't in real estate, that is. How's business?"

"It depends where you're talking about," Ari said. "Hong Kong is solid and growing. Taiwan's also growing, but not near the rate of Hong Kong. And China? China's pretty dead."

"Then why are you here?" Mike asked. "If this place is dead—which, it doesn't really seem that way to *me*—I'd pack my stuff up and get out."

"There are some compelling reasons to stay," Ari said, his gaze resting on Jack for a moment. "My girlfr—I mean, wife—and I are talking about moving. But . . . she also recently started working for Nike, and it's not the sort of opportunity you just want to walk away from."

"It's funny," Jack said, "I never thought of it before, but liquor sales are probably a pretty good barometer of economic growth."

"Don't people drink when they're depressed and unemployed, though?" Mike asked. "I know that's all I'd be doing. But . . ." he said with a grin, "I sure as hell don't feel like that now, so, who wants to indulge in a cigar or two?" He reached down where his leather satchel lay at his feet and pulled out three Cuban cigars.

They each took one and lit up. Jack held the smoke in his mouth for a second before exhaling . . . Ah, that was good. He took a sip of his beer. Even better.

"So, if you're planning on bailing," Mike said to Ari as he exhaled a cloud of smoke, "then you should definitely help me talk Jack into getting out of here too." He set the cigar down in the ashtray at the center of the table and fixed Jack with a long look. "I mean, hell, you should come back to America and do real estate with me, Jack. You'd make so much money your head would explode. And think how proud your dad would be!"

"I was enjoying the evening—let's not bring up my dad," Jack said.

"You don't have a good relationship with your father?" Ari asked.

"It's not that. We actually do have a decent enough relationship, and I think both of us would be happy if it were better, it's just . . . I don't know. We have different ways of seeing things, I guess. My father thinks that I could be doing more with my life, helping more people, making more of an impact, than with what I'm doing now." Jack shrugged. "At this juncture, I can't say that he's wrong, but . . . I'm still not ready to leave China just yet."

"I'm glad to hear that," Ari said. He looked at Mike. "Sorry, I don't think I'm going to be much help in your campaign to get Jack to go back to America with you."

Mike waved him off. "Yeah, yeah, I figured. Well, I guess that means Jack will have to work for us out here. I'll have to come out and drink and smoke with you guys more often."

After Jack was done with his cigar, he excused himself to go the bathroom. He made his way through the crowded bar and felt that it was a bit of a respite stepping into the restroom, which he had all to himself.

Jack was coming out of the bathroom when he sensed a commotion, noticing the shift of energy before he heard the cacophonic sounds near the entrance. The indistinct chatter gave way to quiet as he saw what seemed to be a horde of police pouring through the door.

He could see out the window a large bus and several police cars. Ari and Mike, along with the other patrons who had been outside, were herded in, and then the officers stood there, blocking the two exits. Jack caught Mike's eye and tried to give his friend a reassuring look, as he could tell from the way Mike's eyes were darting around that he had no idea what was going on.

Though probably a shock to anyone from America, the Chinese citizens were quite used to this sort of thing, and the police had the process down to a science.

Ari and Mike managed to make their way over to Jack, and the three of them stood there while the police tried to get everyone else to put their drinks down and line up.

"What is going on?" Mike whispered.

"I hope it's been a while since you last smoked pot," Ari said under his breath.

Mike gave him a confused look. "I stopped three months ago."

The officers were going around handing people little plastic cups, and then directing two lines, one into the men's room, the other into the women's room. Jack looked at the cup. He knew right where this was headed.

"Wait a second," Mike said, his eyes going from the cup to Jack, then back again. "Is this . . .?"

"Yes," Jack said, though before he could add "It's to pee in" they were nudged along toward the bathroom, where two officers were supervising.

It was ridiculous, but Jack knew better than to try to say something about it, unlike some of the other people around him, tourists, he assumed, likely from Europe, saying something about knowing their rights.

All that goes out the window, Jack thought, *when you're on another country's turf.*

He knew Mike was probably having similar thoughts of disbelief that this was actually happening–there was so much that was done in China that would shock the average Westerner. People from the U.S. and Europe often took their civil liberties for granted, not realizing that things were not at all like this in other parts of the world.

Jack's turn. He stepped up to the urinal, and, ignoring the officer the best he could, peed what little he could into the cup. He made sure the lid was on securely before handing it over. The officer took it, and then the second officer stepped forward and pulled off several hairs by the roots of Jack's hair. Jack inwardly recoiled but said nothing. He hoped Mike would have the sense to do the same.

Jack stood amongst the others who had already peed in cups and gotten their hair sample taken, and he watched as two medical personnel conducted the tests.

"Would someone like to tell me what the hell is going on?" Mike asked, walking up behind Jack. "Cause I'm pretty sure that guy back there just took a hair sample."

"I heard they've been assigned an aggressive arrest quota," Ari said. "And that quota for foreigners is much higher."

Mike smiled nervously. "Okay . . . So what happens if they catch you? I mean, they're testing that shit right here, right now? What is this?"

"Let's say you smoked pot in California last week. That was the last time you'd done it. Your test would still come up positive, and no one would care that you hadn't actually done it here. You'd get ten days in jail and then deported, unless you gave them the names of five others who have been smoking pot."

A police officer approached, a severe expression on his face, and Jack found himself hoping that Mike was not incorrect about the last time he smoked pot. That was not how Jack wanted this evening—or any evening—to end.

"You three," the officer said. "You can go."

"We can?" Mike asked.

"Yes," Ari said, wasting no time in making for the door. "The tests were clean." He looked at Mike. "Guess you were right about that three months."

Once outside, they hurried away from the bar.

"What the hell was that about?" Mike asked. "Why did that happen? Jesus Christ, that was insane. Have my rights been violated?"

"This is becoming increasingly common," Ari said, a grim expression on his face. "Notice that it's really only the bars owned by foreigners. They're not doing this to any of the Chinese-owned bars." The frown on Ari's face deepened. "A buddy of mine told me last week that they were planning to raid another bar, this one Canadian-owned. Except one of the owners was friendly with one of the police officers, who tipped him off. The owner then told him that the majority of the patrons were either Canadian or Australian, and conducting such a raid had the potential to cause significant diplomatic conflict. So, they decided not to. Particularly because the place was not frequented by that many 'blacks.'" Ari shook his head. "Their words, not mine."

"Blacks?" Mike said. "Like, African-Americans?"

"Well," Jack said, "not necessarily African-*Americans*."

"People from Nigeria and South Africa," Ari said. "Those involved in the drug trade. They don't want them here."

Mike's eyes widened. "Wait, really?" he said. "I mean, come on. China and all the shitty fentanyl it dumps on the U.S.? Why don't they worry about that first? I don't know what sorts of drugs Nigerians and South Africans are pushing, but I doubt it could be anything worse than fentanyl."

"The whole thing is not good," Ari said, and something in his voice told Jack he wasn't just talking about the bar getting raided. He could feel Ari's gaze on him. "Something needs to be done."

"Well, what needs to be done this very moment is, we need to go to another bar and get a drink because I am not having the last thing I do tonight be pee in a cup," Mike said. "So . . . Where are you guys taking me?"

"How about Bar No. 3?" Ari suggested.

"Never been, but sounds great," Mike said. They both looked at Jack, and he nodded, feeling hopeful that maybe Jojo would be working, but also a little skeptical since he'd be there with Mike; he was afraid Mike would say something dumb, and ruin Jack's chances before things even really started.

"Maybe just one more drink," Jack said. "I'm not trying to be on an all-night bender, here."

"What are you talking about?" Mike said. "How could you *not* want that, after what we were just subjected to? Holy shit, I still can't believe that happened."

Jack half-listened to the conversation as they made their way to Bar No. 3. The closer they got, the more heightened his nerves became at the prospect of seeing Jojo. His palms were actually starting to sweat, and he wiped them on his pants and tried to remind himself to breathe.

And when they stepped into the bar, there she was. She was dropping off a round of drinks to a table of four, and she was slightly turned away from them so she didn't see Jack until she turned to head back to the bar.

"Hi, Jojo," he said.

She didn't recognize him right away, he could tell by the smile that crossed her face, it was the sort of smile you'd give a customer, someone you didn't know, which, Jack realized, was really all he was to her.

"Oh, hey Jack," she said, and he didn't think that it was his imagination that her smile deepened a little when she recognized him. "I have to get some drinks delivered, but I'll come get your order right after that."

They took a seat at an empty table near the front. "You know her?" Mike asked. "She's hot. Hell, there's hot women all around. Seriously, Ari, can you help our friend here find a date?"

Ari laughed. "I don't think Jack needs any help in that department."

Jojo was making her way over to them, and Jack positioned himself so he could give Mike a swift kick to the shins if necessary.

"So," she said, once she reached their table. "What can I get you guys?"

"Something strong—you wouldn't believe the experience I just had!" Mike exclaimed. He looked at Jojo attentively. "What do you recommend?"

"Hmm," she said. "I have it on good authority that a Grey Goose martini with frozen grapes is the way to go. If you're looking for something both strong and refined."

"Strong and refined!" Mike said. "That's me to a T. I'll take that."

Jojo caught Jack's eye and gave him a little wink. Or was it just his imagination?

"You have frozen grapes?" he asked.

"Yes," she said. "We got a tip from a customer with good taste that frozen grapes were the way to go when it came to martinis, so we started freezing grapes and it's been very popular." She looked at Ari and then back to Jack. "So, will that be three Grey Goose martinis with frozen grapes?"

"That sounds like perfection," Jack said, and he felt as though he and Jojo were sharing in some sort of private moment, even though there were two others involved in the conversation.

"Frozen grapes, no kidding," Mike said after Jojo had left. "I wonder what genius thought that up. I mean, I haven't even had it yet, but I can tell it's going to be good."

The drinks were, indeed, quite good when Jojo brought them over. It was the best-tasting martini Jack had ever had, as if Jojo had somehow imbued it with some sort of magic. That's how he felt anyway; he was having a hard time staying focused on whatever it was Mike and Ari were talking about as he was hyperaware of Jojo. He tried to push the idea out of his mind that he was bordering on stalker. No, that wasn't it at all. If Jojo told him she wasn't interested, didn't want him to show his face around here again, well, he would oblige her.

It was getting late as they finished their drinks, and Jack could tell that Ari was getting ready to call it a night. Mike could probably go for another five or six hours, but Jack wasn't feeling up to some wild night out drinking.

"Let me take care of this," Mike said when Jack tried to pay the bill. "Our waitress was great; I'm gonna leave her a hell of a tip."

"No, you're not," Jack said. "People don't leave tips in China," he added, when Mike gave him a confused, almost hurt, look. "It has nothing to do with the quality of service; it's not a custom here. And let me take care of this—my treat."

He did not make a big show out of saying goodbye to Jojo; he simply paid the tab, and, catching her eye on the way out, he nodded his goodbye, even though what he really wanted was to ask her, right then and there, for her contact info. The idea had been in the back of his mind ever since he first stepped in and saw that Jojo was working, but he knew that tonight would not end without him at least asking to get her details.

He just didn't want to do it with an audience.

So, he followed his two friends outside. "Wow," Mike was saying. "Tonight was something else. Always an adventure when I go out with Jack!" He clapped him on the shoulder. "And damn, that martini was good."

"Glad you had a good time," Jack said.

"I'll be in touch about getting together in a day or two to talk about all your ideas on how I can further diversify my investor base," Mike said, giving Jack a half-hug, another slap on the back, did the same with Ari, and made them both promise that they'd all go out again before he left.

"Oh, and one more thing," Ari said, "If you get a chance to acquire a new real estate client in Washington DC, I suggest you take advantage of the opportunity. They'll invite you to Washington, where you can learn more. They should contact you within the next few weeks."

Jack glanced at Mike, who was looking at his phone, and didn't seem to hear what Ari had said.

"Okay." He nodded, wanting to hear more details but knowing that Ari likely wouldn't offer them.

Jack gave his friends one more wave and then walked off, as if he were heading back to his apartment. Really, though, he turned the corner and walked around the block, circling back to the bar. There were only a few people left, and Jojo was going around, wiping down tables, clearing away empty glasses.

She looked up as he approached, and if she was surprised that he had returned, she didn't let it show.

"Oh, hey," she said. "Did you forget something?"

Jack smiled, hoping his nervousness wasn't showing. He couldn't remember the last time he'd felt like this, that a person had made him feel this way. Nerves were generally something he was pretty good at keeping in control of.

"Well . . . yes, actually," he said. "It's been something that I've been meaning to do . . . since I met you, I guess you could say. I was hoping

I could get your WeChat ID." He cringed inwardly, wondering if he sounded as awkward as he felt.

A hint of a smile touched the corners of her mouth, and right when Jack thought for sure she was going to burst out laughing and tell him to get lost, in that beautiful accent of hers, she looked him right in the eye and said, "I was wondering when you'd finally get around to asking."

Relief and happiness flooded Jack, as Jojo pulled her phone from her back pocket. Jack took his out too and he opened the WeChat app so he could scan her code.

"Great," he said. "Thanks."

"Sure. Is there is anything else? We're not closed just yet."

He thought about ordering another drink but decided not to. If he stopped now, there was good chance he'd avoid a hangover tomorrow, and also the possibility of making a fool of himself tonight. Instead, he was already thinking what his first message to Jojo might be.

CHAPTER 12

The next day was beautiful, with bright sun, relatively low humidity, little smog. Jack showered and dressed, gathered his stuff and left the apartment. He walked up Wukang Road to Anhui Road, where the large-leaved Wutong trees shaded him as he passed by houses and apartments in different styles of architecture—Mediterranean, French Renaissance, English, Art Deco. Just one of the many things that made the former French Concession so distinct from other places in China.

It was still early, so Baker & Spice hadn't yet filled up with the break-fast crowd. He went over to the counter and order bacon and eggs and an Americano, and then took a seat in the middle of the café, where there was a long common table with benches. He preferred sitting here, as opposed to one of the smaller tables by himself, because of the likeli-hood of meeting someone interesting to talk to, which had happened on many occasions when he'd come here to do a little work.

After Jack settled in and pulled out his laptop, he checked his phone and saw that he had a WeChat alert—Jojo had accepted his invitation to connect. His heart rate picked up a little. He didn't message her back just yet; he wanted to think about it, make sure he got it right.

Then again, maybe he was overthinking it. From what he'd seen of Jojo so far, she played it cool—Jack couldn't even say for certain if she *liked* him, though he had to believe she did, otherwise why would she connect with him via WeChat?

He shook his head, trying to clear the thoughts, grateful when his Americano arrived.

Good morning, Jojo, he typed. *It's your martini coffee drinking customer. I hope you're not still working.*

He wrote the message in English, even though they'd only spoken Chinese to each other. Often, the Chinese wrote English quite well but had a harder time speaking it, though Jack knew he shouldn't assume anything.

He sent the message right as one of the waitresses brought his food out. "Here you are," she said as she slid the plate down in front of him. "Enjoy."

His appetite, which had been considerable on the way over, seemed somewhat diminished now as he waited for Jojo's reply. Not that he was expecting it to be instantaneous or anything. It occurred to him, suddenly, that perhaps it was too early to send a message. It was seven forty-five, so it wasn't like he was texting her at four in the morning, but, still. Maybe she was a night owl. Maybe she had gone out with friends after her shift was over and had only been asleep for a few hours when the alert of his message woke her up because she had forgot to put her phone on silent before she went to sleep . . .

He forced the thought out of his mind and picked up his silverware, despite the fact that he was not a bit hungry now.

Give me a break, he thought. *What is this, amateur hour? She'll get back when she does. And if she doesn't—oh well.*

He broke the yolk on one of the eggs, sopped up a bit of the yolk with a piece of toast, took a bite. Chewed. Took a bite of bacon, a sip of coffee, checked his phone, casually. No new alerts.

He took a few more bites and then pushed his plate to the side so he could take out his laptop. He purposefully did not look at his phone, instead checking his emails, then a news site, where he skimmed a few articles. Checked the weather—Sunday was going to be the better day of the weekend. He had another bite, some more coffee. The place was starting to fill up, and the aroma of freshly brewed coffee was strong.

His phone beeped. Incoming message. Jack took one more bite of his toast before picking up his phone, knowing before he looked that he'd be disappointed if it was a message from anyone other than Jojo.

It was from Jojo.

Ha, it read. *I'm working, but not at the bar.*

Are you still drinking?

Jack smiled. He wondered what work she was doing, if she wasn't at the bar.

I'm finally eating, he replied. *What do you do besides hang out at the bar?*

Only after sending it did he realize that it could be interpreted as brusque, which was not how he intended it at all.

Maybe I'll tell you someday.

The smile deepened; okay, she could play this game, too.

But what he didn't want to do was get caught up in a messaging loop, where they traded flirtatious texts back and forth but never actually met for that first date. Then again, he also didn't want to come across as impatient.

The weather this Sunday looks like it's going to be great, he wrote. *Would you like to join me for an early evening picnic at Jiao Tong University?*

A minute went by after he sent the message, no reply.

Another minute.

Jack tried to keep his thoughts in check and not let his imagination get too carried away, but he hoped she wasn't going to make him wait all day, or even several hours, before she replied.

Then again, maybe she wasn't replying because she wasn't interested.

He reached for his coffee. There were other people who had come in and taken seats at the large table with him, most had laptops or phones in front of them. Jack wondered who else among them here were waiting for a response about a potential first date.

The people seated closest to him, two Americans, probably in their mid-twenties, were talking about Tony Ma, one of the best-known figures in China. He was the founder of one of the largest e-commerce platforms and a charismatic leader.

"It's crazy," one of the Americans was saying, "how the government kicked him out of his company and took it away."

The second guy shook his head. "Not if you think about it."

"I *am* thinking about it, and that's why I think it's insane. They forced him to step down when he was fifty-five. Fifty-five! Can you imagine Steve Jobs doing that?"

"No, but Steve Jobs wasn't in China. The point you're missing is that Tony Ma not only had crazy wealth, but he could also speak English exceptionally well. So if he can speak English and Chinese, he can basically communicate to the entire world."

"And what's wrong with that?"

"If you're the Chinese government—a great deal. Just think about . . ."

Jack probably would've continued eavesdropping on their conversation, but then his phone beeped.

Sounds like a great idea! When and where would you like to meet?

The excited relief that flooded through him was palpable, and he knew there was a foolish grin on his face as he typed back his reply.

How about 5:30 p.m. at the northern entrance to the university on Huashan Road?

No sooner had he sent the message off than he received an alert of a new message, this time from Ari.

Been meaning to send this to you, thought you'd like to see the full, unedited version. NSFW? Haha.

Jack waited for the file to download, curious. While he waited, Jojo's reply came through, confirming their date for Sunday. Once the file had downloaded, Jack opened it and began to watch the video.

It was from the other night at Taste Buds, and it was strange to be watching himself as he fought with the two guys. Unlike in the version Ari had shared with the police, though, this version included the grand finale, and it was almost like he was watching someone else throw these two jokers from the balcony.

Jesus, he thought. Jokers or not, it was painfully obvious now how much trouble he could have gotten into, as clearly, he took it way too far. He sent a quick reply to Ari, thanking him for commemorating the night, and also for his good editing job, which surely had prevented Jack from getting detained by the police.

He finished eating and then began to read his new emails. The first was from a man named Gary O'Reilly, from a DC-based real estate company, a developer of large retail and condominium projects. He'd heard of them; they were ranked number three on the East Coast.

One of our mutual friends suggested we contact you. They felt you might be of assistance in raising funds from Chinese investors. We have a number of projects in the DC area that will become available soon. Might you be free for a chat this Thursday, nine in the morning Shanghai time?

Jack went to their website and saw that their chairman and CEO had gone to Stanford, and most of their top management had served in the military. Ari's words floated back to him: *If you get a chance to acquire a new real estate investment client in Washington DC, I suggest you take advantage of the opportunity. They'll invite you to Washington, where you can learn more . . .*

He sent a reply back, saying Thursday morning would be fine. He couldn't know for absolute certainty that this was what Ari had been talking about, but it seemed likely. What, exactly, was their conversation going to entail?

*   *   *

He met up with Mike and Andrew San the next morning on the executive floor of the Ritz-Portman. Both Mike and Andrew were eager to meet each other to begin to feel out ways that they could structure a mutually beneficial business relationship.

"I'm surprised to see you up at this early hour," Jack said as he slid into the chair across from Mike.

Mike grinned. "Who says I've been to sleep? Actually, I have—I'm feeling good about the possibilities here, Jack, I really am."

They went over to the buffet station to get some coffee while they waited for Andrew to arrive.

"So," Mike said when they had sat back down. "Do you think it's going to be a problem that an investment package hasn't been put together yet? For the Moore Park Business Center?"

Jack took a sip of his coffee and shook his head. "Not a problem at all. In fact, it might even work in your favor. The Chinese, in particular, like to hear about things early; they might have a unique angle that makes the investment even more attractive to them. Oh, here's Andrew."

Jack gave a little wave as Andrew made his way over, an eager smile on his face as he shook first Jack's hand, then Mike's.

"So great to meet you, Mike. I had a really good feeling about Jack when we first met, and now here we all are, I hope to discuss some good opportunities."

Jack sat back and let Mike give Andrew all the details about the development. "We purchased Moore Park Business Center in 2013, and since then, the area has expanded faster than anyone ever expected. It's a twenty-four-acre property with several low-rise commercial buildings. Given the surrounding area demand, our architect has put together a one billion dollar project, which includes thirteen buildings, 1.2 million square feet of office space, eighty thousand square feet of ground-floor commercial space, eight hundred forty-two rental apartment, one hundred sixty-eight condominiums, and a two-hundred twenty-eight key hotel."

Andrew raised his eyebrows. "Wow. Substantial project."

"All the parking will be underground," Mike continued. "Building will occur in five phases over fifteen years. We're currently waiting for final city approval of the plans."

"Stanley was just talking to me about this area," Andrew said. "He knows it well. I bet there are several Chinese insurance companies who would love to be involved. Is there an investment package put together yet?"

Mike shot Jack a look. "Um, not yet."

"What if we went out there and put one together?" Andrew asked. "Some of the insurance companies might offer a premium price for the entire development if they can put their name on it."

"We have to wait for the city permits," Mike said. "Then we'll have a package ready. In the meantime, we're converting all the existing leases to month-to-month as they roll over. So let's hold off for now, but I'll keep you guys updated every step of the way if you think this is something you're interested in."

"Oh, absolutely," Andrew said. "I'll be seeing Stanley later today and I'll relay all this information to him."

"That's great," Mike said. He picked up his coffee cup. "I'm going to grab a refill and maybe something to eat. Excuse me for a moment, gentlemen."

Jack reached for his own cup, which was about halfway full. "Hey, Jack?" Andrew said. "Could I speak to you for a minute?"

"Sure."

Andrew glanced at Mike, who had reached the buffet station at the other side of the room. "This sounds like a big development. Is there any way you can convince Mike to let us put an investment package together? We'll make it worth your while. There must be some leverage you have that can help us get in on this deal early."

Jack smiled. "Mike is an old friend; I know him well. He's not going to change his mind. He has good reason for not entertaining offers now—without city approvals, investors always want a discount. He's not willing to do that."

"Are you sure there's no leverage you have?"

"Sorry," Jack said. He appreciated Andrew's eagerness, but now was not the time to pull strings or call in special favors. "There really isn't anything I can do to speed things up. But trust me—Mike is as interested in working with you and Stanley as you guys are with him. And if he said he's going to keep you updated along the way, he will."

Disappointment crossed Andrew's face, but only for a moment. "Okay," he said brightly. "I trust you, Jack. And I hope you know that you can trust us, too."

"Of course I do," Jack said. "Don't worry, Andrew—many good things ahead, I just know it."

*　*　*

On Thursday, at precisely nine o'clock, the Skype call came in from Washington DC. Jack was at his desk, wireless earbuds in. He answered, and two faces appeared on his laptop screen. He recognized Gary from his photo on the website. "Good evening, Gary," Jack said.

Gary smiled. "Good morning, Jack. Nice to meet you. I'd like to introduce you to Rick Smith, our head of acquisitions."

"Hello, Jack," Rick said.

"Hi Rick. Nice to meet you."

"We thought it would be good to have a call to learn more about you and what you do," Gary said. "And then we could discuss potential projects we have coming up that we might be able to work on together."

"Sounds good," Jack said. "Would you like me to share some background?"

"That would be a good place to start."

Jack gave the two men a brief history of what brought him to Shanghai, and what he'd been doing there, including his most recent involvement with Andrew and arrangement with Mike.

"So you have a good understanding of what investors want," Gary said. "What types of opportunities they're looking for."

"I'd like to think so," Jack said. "Chinese investors still focus on well-known markets, like Los Angeles, San Francisco, New York, Seattle. But my gut tells me there'd be strong interest in DC."

"Is there a preference regarding the type of development they like to invest in?"

"Typically, they like newer developments, deals with a value-added component."

"Pete Peterson has a few condo development deals in construction," Rick said. "One is right near Johns Hopkins University. Would there be any interest in that?"

"Quite possibly," Jack said. "I'll talk with my colleague Andrew and some others."

"How do you suggest we structure working together?" Rick asked.

"I'd like a portion of the acquisition fee and a small cut of the general partnership fee, if there is one." Jack figured he'd have his bases covered in case Andrew's side did not receive the fees.

Gary and Rick looked at each other, smiling, and then looked at Jack. "That's very helpful," Gary said. "You're making this easy for us. Do you ever get to the East Coast?"

"Unfortunately, I haven't been out that way in a while."

"What if we fly you out here so we can meet in person and discuss collaborating? We'll pay for everything."

Jack considered this. Taking an eighteen-hour flight was no one's idea of a good time, but they were offering to pay, and it had been a while since he'd last been back to the States. But—it did sound like they had some interesting projects, and Ari's words were still in the back of Jack's mind, though he still couldn't quite put the pieces together to see the full puzzle.

"Sure," he said. He could renew his visa, too—he'd been working in the country on a visitor's visa, which he didn't like doing, but China made it very difficult to do business there without having a local partner. Such partners often cost more than the benefit they added, though Jack knew that Chinese companies going to America had no such difficulties.

"Great," Gary said. "So it's settled then. Why don't you look at your calendar and email me what dates work for you. The sooner the better, of course, but I don't know what your schedule is looking like."

"I'll get back to you about that right away," Jack said. "Nice talking with you two, and looks like we'll be seeing more of each other person."

They both smiled. "Yes," Gary said. "Thanks for your time."

The call ended. Jack sat there for a moment, then opened his calendar. He could go any time, but there was his date with Jojo that he certainly wasn't going to miss. A week from today, the following Thursday, seemed good. He typed a quick email to Gary, suggesting a week from today, and also cc'd Rick with the terms he had proposed.

Then he leaned back in his chair and stretched. A week from now, he'd be in DC.

CHAPTER 13

Finally—Sunday.

As the weather report had predicted, it was warm and sunny, with a light breeze and record low pollution levels. Jack took this as a good sign that things would go well this evening, not that he was the sort of person who usually looked for signs. A nervous, excited energy had been coursing through him ever since he and Jojo had set up the date, and now that the day had arrived, his energy levels felt at an all-time high.

To keep himself from counting down the minutes until it was time to head to Jiao Tong University, Jack spent the morning at the gym, in one of the unused yoga studios, running through his martial arts warm-up routine, then practicing different combinations of counter moves. Jack had started practicing martial arts in middle school, initially hoping to find an activity that might impress his father. He soon realized, though, just how much he himself enjoyed it, and had continued to practice it to this day, having earned his third-degree black belt five years ago. He visualized the two guys from Taste Buds as he practiced. He followed this by going through about twenty-five karate forms, finishing with a series of rapid kicks and punches.

A few people stood at the door of the studio, watching him. He gave them a wave as he wiped the sweat from his face; he was accustomed to people watching him, though their numbers had certainly dwindled from when he had first shown up at the gym. The communist government had banned martial arts when they took control in 1949, seeing it as a potential threat. Though the ban had been lifted around 2010, many people were still not used to seeing martial arts in action. Jack had never been someone who needed to be the center of attention, but for some reason, he never minded when he had an audience at the gym.

* * *

Jack waited by the entrance to Jiao Tong University. He wore a black button up shirt and jeans, along with his gray fedora and Italian loafers. He hoped he looked nice, but not too formal.

The school had been established in 1896 by an imperial edict from the emperor, with the idea that it would be renowned as the "MIT of the East." The goal had not been achieved, though, and the university ranked over one hundred out of all the universities in the world.

Still, it made a nice place for a first date, with all its trees and open spaces. Jojo arrived in a Didi a few minutes before five-thirty, and Jack couldn't help but smile as he saw her step out of the car. She wore a blue and white pencil skirt and a light green blouse, both garments contrasting nicely with her dark hair and her eyes, though Jack was fairly certain she could have shown up wearing a trash bag and he would've thought she looked great.

"Hello," she said, returning his smile as he walked over. She closed the door and the car drove off. "I like that hat."

"You look wonderful," he said. "I think we go together quite well, actually."

"I never would have thought of coming here for a picnic, but it's actually a great idea."

"I was thinking we could set up near the track, since you'll get the best view of the sunset there."

Jojo nodded, looking up at the sky. "I bet it'll be a good one."

They started to walk along a quiet street, flanked by large Phoenix trees and old buildings. They were about as close to each other as one could be without physically touching; Jack was overcome with the desire to hold her hand, but he restrained himself. Yes, it would've felt like the exact right thing to do at the moment, but this was also their first date, and he didn't want to come across too strongly.

"Did you have a good day today?" he asked.

"I did. Though I have to be honest—I was a little nervous." She laughed. "I don't go on many dates."

"I find that incredibly hard to believe."

"Well, you shouldn't. So this isn't really something that I'm used to."

"You're doing a great job so far." He cleared his throat. "If we're being honest, dating isn't really my forte, either."

She gave him a coy look. "Okay, now it's *my* turn to be completely disbelieving. You wouldn't own a hat like that if you didn't enjoy dating."

"True . . . I guess it just has to be with the right person. I had a recent date that most certainly was *not* the right person."

"We could spend the whole evening talking about dates with the wrong person," Jojo said. "More like, almost an entire *decade* with the wrong person."

Jack winced. "Yikes. That doesn't sound good."

"It was good in the beginning, and then not so good in the middle, and then a total shit show by the end of it. Luckily, it's done and over with."

"Poor guy. He must've had it for you bad."

He meant it as a joke, though he could tell the moment he said it that Jojo did not find it particularly funny. "That's one way of putting it," she said.

They walked in silence for several moments, Jack mentally kicking himself for his last comment. *Why the hell would we even start talking about exes on our first date?* He had been enjoying the easy flow the conversation had, and he wanted to get it back to that.

As they approached the field, Jack could see there were many people out taking advantage of the nice weather—walking, jogging, riding bikes, kicking a soccer ball around.

"How about over there?" Jack pointed to an area that was far enough from the soccer game that a ball wouldn't likely get kicked over.

"Looks good," Jojo said, as they navigated their way over. "I'm surprised no one else is here having a picnic. It's such a perfect evening for it." Jack set his bag down and pulled out the picnic blanket. He spread it out, then took off his shoes as Jojo did the same. They sat down on the blanket, and Jack began to unload the rest of the bag.

"What do you have in there?"

He pulled out the first item—the portable Bose speaker. "Because no first date could be considered a success without some music."

She laughed. "Oh, is that what I've been doing wrong all this time?"

He turned the speaker on and then pulled his phone out and found the right playlist. "Be Alright" by Dean Lewis began to play.

"Now that we have the music taken care of . . . let's see what we have in here to drink."

He rummaged through the bag and pulled out a bottle of wine. "I hope white wine is okay?"

"Most certainly," she said. "White wine's great. I was actually wondering what else you drank, besides coffee and vodka. Oh yeah, I have this." She reached into her purse and pulled out a small paper bag, which she handed to Jack. He peered inside.

"Brownies?"

"Yeah. I made them earlier today, when I was trying to figure out what I could do to keep my mind off of this evening."

"Are these pot brownies?" he asked jokingly.

"No, I only make pot cookies," she deadpanned. "Chocolate chip."

They looked at each other for a moment and then burst out laughing.

"These are perfect," he said. "Thanks for making them."

He set about taking the rest of the things out of the bag: tuna sandwiches, chicken, carrots, and celery, three soufflé dishes with different sauces—Caesar dressing, ranch, and Sriracha.

"This looks delicious," Jojo said.

"Well, I can't take all the credit—I didn't make the chicken, but it's from one of my favorite places. Oh, and I almost forgot—grapes." He took the grapes out, as well as the glasses and the chopsticks.

He poured Jojo a glass of wine, then poured one for himself, as "Little French Song" began to play. Jojo took a sip of her wine and then turned to him and said something he didn't quite catch, in Mandarin.

"Sorry," he said. "What did you say?"

"Is this Carla Bruni?" Jojo asked, switching to English. "The French President's wife?"

Jack nodded, trying to hide his surprise—this was the first time he'd heard her speak English, and she had done so exceptionally well—with a French accent!

"I have to say," he said, "I find you to be a very intriguing person. I knew when I first heard your accent that you were from somewhere north. But now I hear you speaking English—quite well, might I add—and is that a French accent I hear? You must have quite the interesting history."

Jojo laughed. "That's one way of putting it. You're right—I grew up in Beijing. I went to school at Tshinghua, then I spent five years in France studying sculpture and art."

"So, how long have you been in Shanghai?"

"About three years. I'm a sculptor. But I also enjoy working odd jobs. It's inspiring and is sometimes the only social interaction I get. Sculpting is not really a group effort. At least the kind of sculpting I do."

"I'd love to see your work some time," Jack said, trying to push the image of the pottery wheel scene from the movie *Ghost* out of his mind.

"Maybe," Jojo said. "What about you? Tell me your history."

"It's not as exciting as yours, I'm afraid . . . Let's see. I grew up in Southern California. Went to college. After graduating, I decided I'd come to China, much to my father's chagrin. I thought there might be some good opportunities."

I wasn't wrong, he thought as he watched Jojo take another sip of her wine. A song by Andrea Bocelli came on and Jojo's face lit up.

"I like your taste in music," she said. She reached out and picked up a pair of chopsticks, deftly selected a grape, and put it in her mouth.

I could watch you do that all day, Jack thought. Instead, he took a big sip of wine.

"Are these chopsticks from Haidilao?" She paused, waiting for his answer, the grape delicately nestled between the two chopsticks, just a few inches from her mouth. Jack had to force himself to look away.

"Yes," he said, clearing his throat. "How did you know?"

She put the grape in her mouth and held one of the chopsticks out to him, pointing at the imprint of the restaurant's name.

"I like long chopsticks," he said, "and these are pretty good quality. So, I asked them a while back if I could buy a few pairs." He smiled at the memory. "And you know what they did? They gave me five pairs. I use them when I'm cooking."

He took his own chopsticks, using the reverse ends to pick up a sandwich for Jojo, which he put on a plate and handed to her.

"I have to warn you, I make a mean tuna sandwich," he said. "Prepare yourself."

She looked down at the plate, then up at him with a smile. "I see you show no mercy to crusts."

"My mother used to cut the crusts off my sandwich, even as I was older, and I always enjoyed that. It irked the hell out of my father; he felt like she was babying me." Jack shook his head. "My father couldn't stand the idea of my mother trying to make things easier for me or my brother. He always wanted us to make our own way, suffer through our own struggles, come out the other side as stronger men. That's basically him in a nutshell."

"Your mom sounds sweet."

"She was. She was an artist, too. She died a while back. So, whenever I make myself a sandwich and cut the crusts off, I think of her."

"I'm sorry," Jojo said. "It's hard to lose a parent no matter how old you are."

"What about you?" Jack asked. "Do you get along with your parents pretty well?"

She took a bite of her sandwich and chewed a while before responding. "Let's not talk about parents," she said. "I'm pretty sure that's a no-no on any first date. Look at the sky."

Jack followed her gaze, past the copse of trees, where the sun had started its westward descent. The sky was a brilliant palette of crimson and rose, and as he took in the immense beauty in the sky, along with the incredible beauty sitting next to him, Jack felt a full and complete sense of happiness and contentment settle over him. Had he ever been happier? He didn't know. It certainly wouldn't have surprised him if the answer was *no*, that this was the happiest he'd ever been, because there seemed to be some sort of unspoken magic in the air, something that might not be tangible or able to be seen with the eyes, but there nonetheless. It was a most curious feeling, and something Jack couldn't remember experiencing to this magnitude before, not even all those years ago with his beloved college sweetheart.

But did she feel the same way? It was hard to tell. Their conversation certainly flowed, there had been—at least in Jack's estimation—no uncomfortable silences or awkward moments.

"That is quite the view," Jack said. "The best views are the ones that change, like this one. Seeing the same thing in a new light."

"I love that you said that, because I am constantly trying to do that," Jojo said, giving him a look of genuine appreciation. "Nothing can be more stagnating for an artist to get stuck in the rut of seeing the things around you the same way that you always have."

"I'm probably as far from an artist as you could get," Jack said, "but I do have great admiration for what people like you do."

"What do you mean?" Jojo asked. "You're not as far from an artist as you could get—it sounds like you have it in your DNA."

"Yes, well, I can draw a mean stick figure."

She laughed, which Jack decided was surely the most wonderful sound in the world.

"If the whole art thing doesn't pan out, you have real potential as a gourmet sandwich chef."

Now it was Jack's turn to laugh. "It's hard to find bread in Shanghai."

"Tell me about it. The bread in Paris was to die for."

"Want to see a picture of me in Paris?" Jack asked. "With a sculpture, as a matter of fact."

"I would love to."

He scrolled through the photo app on his phone until he came to the collection of photos from a Paris trip, years ago, now. The first photo he showed her was one of him, standing next to a Rodin sculpture, imitating the pose.

"I know, I'm so original," he said, as he swiped to the next photo, which featured him next to another sculpture, again copying the pose.

"Let me see these," Jojo said, and she took the phone from him, zooming in on the photo.

"I like Rodin, as you can see," Jack said. "In fact, when I go to Paris, I don't bother going to the Louvre; instead, I go directly to the Rodin sculpture garden behind it." He smiled. "I'm sure you're vastly more knowledgeable than me, but 'The Thinker' statue looks like someone sitting on the toilet."

Jojo handed him his phone back. "It may look like that, but it mattered enough to have been originally put in front of the Gates of Hell statue that was commissioned in 1880."

Jack nodded slowly, as if he was considering her point, though he already knew what she was telling him. She narrowed her eyes, a smile appearing at the corner of her mouth.

"You knew that, though, didn't you?" she said. "Were you testing me?" She paused, raised one eyebrow, almost imperceptibly. "Or were you teasing me?"

Jack raised his eyebrows and gave her a playful look.

"You were doing both!" she exclaimed, and they laughed. "You're naughty," she said, still laughing. "The pictures you took with the statues are interesting, though. I never thought of emulating them in that way."

"No? It just seemed like the thing to do. Maybe because I know I'd never be able to actually sculpt something like that with my own two hands."

"The emotional component and then reflecting that in your posture is tricky. How long did it take for you to get the right shot?"

Jack tried to keep a straight face. "Oh, I was there for a good three hours. I really wanted to get the correct shot, and I'm so glad you noticed my effort."

She stared at him, his expression wavering until he wasn't able to hold it back any longer, and he started laughing. "The truth?" he said. "It took under five minutes. And here, look." He scrolled through until he arrived at the last photograph, a selfie Jack took with the Japanese tourist who had taken the other pictures for him.

He put his phone away and they ate some more food while watching the sunset. It had almost disappeared, bathing everything in a warm, orange glow. Jack was about to say something to Jojo about it when she let out a shriek.

A small dog had appeared, seemingly out of nowhere, and made a beeline for the piece of chicken Jojo had on her chopsticks. "You scared me!" she gently scolded the dog as it yipped and jumped and—so it seemed to Jack—did its best attempt to look as adorable as possible, its eyes never once moving from the food it wanted so badly.

"He's rather cute," Jack said. The dog sat down, held perfectly still, except for its thumping tail. A young Chinese man came running up, holding a leash that the dog was presumably supposed to be on the end of.

"I'm so sorry," the young man said. "I don't know how he does it, but he's always escaping. He's always trying to go home with whoever he thinks has the best food!"

"He's very cute," Jack said. "No harm done."

The man clipped the leash back onto the dog's collar and then had to tug several times to get the dog to finally follow along. Jack could hear him admonishing the dog as they walked off.

"He *was* cute," Jojo said.

"I hope you're referring to the dog," Jack said with a smile.

"Ha. Yes. His owner was probably still a teenager." She sighed. "I miss having a dog. I had one when I was young, and I really loved him."

"Maybe you should get one."

"It hasn't been practical for so long that I've just kind of pushed the idea from my mind. But maybe it's something I should look into."

"We had a couple good dogs when I was a kid," Jack said. "A Golden Retriever and a German Shepherd. The German Shepherd was sort of like my dad's other son. His favorite one, of course."

"Sure; dogs can't talk back."

Jack laughed. "You know, I never thought about it like that, but you're exactly right. Which is not to make my father out to be some sort of tyrant or anything—he's actually a very respectable guy." He paused. "Oh yeah, I forgot we weren't supposed to talk about our parents. Does this mean our first date was not a success?"

"I actually quite enjoy hearing about you," Jojo said. "You're an interesting person. So, let's amend that—*you* can talk about your parents all you want; I just don't want to have to talk about mine."

"Fair enough," Jack said, though he couldn't help but wonder why she seemed so against even mentioning her parents. Perhaps they didn't get along so well, or there was some bad history. He hoped, over time, that he might have the chance to talk with her about it.

Now that the sun had set, dusk was rapidly turning to darkness.

"I've had such a good time," Jack said. "I hate to have to end things now."

"I did too." Jojo handed him a few of the containers as he began putting the things back in the duffle bag. She held up the pair of chopsticks she had used. "Mind if I keep these? I collect chopsticks."

"Sure," Jack said. "But let me give you a clean pair." He reached into the bag and found the container that he had put the chopsticks in and extracted a clean pair for her, which he wrapped in a napkin.

"Thanks," she said, putting them in her purse. "Did you know that chopsticks were originally used for cooking—not eating—about five thousand years ago?"

"I did not," he said. "That's interesting."

She gave him a coy look. "I guess I can be interesting, too."

Now that it was dark, there were only a handful of people left on the field, a few walkers and one woman running around the track. A pleasant silence descended.

They were nearing the entrance, and then they would have to part ways. He would be easygoing about however it was that Jojo wanted to leave it, but he really hoped that she would be interested in seeing him again.

"Thank you again for going out with me," Jack said. "That was the best picnic I've had in a long time."

"I really enjoyed myself. It's kind of like you said—I've been here before, but tonight it was like I was seeing it in a different light. So, thank *you.*

And . . . I was also wondering if you might want to see my work some time."

She said this last part quickly, addressing the ground, and he realized that she was nervous. So far, she hadn't given him many signals indicating how she felt toward him, but he took this as a good sign, both that she wanted him to see her work and that she wanted to see *him* again.

"I would like nothing more," he said. "How can we make that happen?"

"What's Wednesday looking like for you? Say, early evening? You can come to my studio, and this time it'll be my turn to impress you with my culinary skills."

"That's perfect."

"Great. I'll send you the address. This is me," she said when the Didi she had requested pulled up.

Jack opened the door so she could get in. He wanted nothing more than to give her a hug and a long, lingering kiss, but he also wanted to take things slowly. Develop a solid foundation for their relationship—if there was to be one.

Jack shut the door and took a step back. The window went down and Jojo leaned her head out. "Just a thought," she said. "But for Wednesday, can you bring *two* bottles of wine?"

The car pulled away before he could respond, and Jack stood there, marveling at what an incredible evening it had been.

CHAPTER 14

On Tuesday, Jack awoke to find another day almost as stunning as Sunday had been, a rarity for Shanghai, a city that was usually choked with smog. First thought upon awakening: *I get to see Jojo tomorrow.*

He showered and dressed and then packed up his laptop and set out along Wukang Road, then turned onto Julu Road. Julu Road was one of Shanghai's coolest and up-and-coming streets. It wasn't full of shops or flashy restaurants; instead, it was mostly residents living in older, renovated homes. There was a new development called "Lost Heaven," within which was a French bakery which connected to a series of small restaurants, all who shared a common seating area. There was even a restaurant that made its own Western-style hotdogs.

Jack bought a coffee and an almond croissant from the bakery and then found a place to sit in the general seating area. He checked his email while he sipped coffee, saw that he had two emails from Mike about new real estate investment deals, which he forwarded to Andrew and his contacts at two different investment firms. Really, this job was all about knowing the right people—though some might argue the fact, it wasn't difficult. Or, at least, Jack did not find it so. After he heard back from his contacts, he'd need to set up a conference call to get a better understanding of the deals, though when it came down to it, it was also pretty simple: Either they were interested in investing, or not.

With the business part of things taken care of, Jack read an article in the *South China Morning Post.*

Lately the Chinese government is making it more difficult to send money outside of China. Previously, individuals and companies could use the services of a third-party who would get the funds out of China for a two-percentage fee. But the government is now cracking down on these types of transactions, making it nearly impossible to get funds out of the country.

Jack frowned. How could China continue to grow? There was too much money in China as it was, with nowhere to go, and real estate prices were unattainably high. It would take the average Chinese individual one hundred years to pay off a mortgage. Those who were married fared a little better, Jack supposed, and sometimes, getting help from their parents was also a possibility, but for many, the possibility of owning a home was well out of reach.

There was also the fact that there were simply too many people in the country given the low economic growth. Not that people didn't leave China all the time—many to become students in America, never to return to their country of origin—but something would have to change. Something big, something that would really wake people up, make them take notice. Though Jack had no idea what this big change might be, he knew it needed to happen if China was not going to be crippled by national debt.

He read a few more articles. The government had recently announced they'd be putting party members in private Chinese companies. Under President Zhao, China was definitely moving to a more Maoist mentality. The previous president, Deng Xiaoping, had been more open, but now Zhao had changed China's constitution, and could potentially end up ruling for his entire life.

Jack closed his laptop and finished the rest of his coffee and the croissant. While he'd been hoping to find distractions today, he wasn't in the mood right now to be reading about the ways the government was trying to keep their stronghold on its citizens. He packed up his things and walked around the corner to the local market, where the air was pungent with the smell of fish, which were sitting in big buckets on ice, their mouths gaping, as if in surprise. He walked past the fish and picked up a basket. He was running low on soap, and though he'd taken a shower this morning, he might take a second before he went over to Jojo's. He found his preferred soap and then walked a few aisles over and put a few bottles of wine in his basket. He bought some tin foil, and then, because he passed right by them on his way to stand in line— and because they were beautiful—he picked a small bouquet of flowers, shrouded in cellophane, out of a large bucket near one of the registers.

As he stood in line, he watched an old woman slowly make her way to the front of the line, bypassing Jack and all the other people who were waiting. Jack heard her say she would like to pay for her items, and could she be helped? The cashier shooed her away, but the woman, unde- terred, made a limping trek to the other cash register, where a second cashier was helping another employee pay for their things.

"This register is closed," the second cashier said rudely. "Go get in line."

Jack had heard enough. "You help an employee," he said in Chinese, "but not an elderly woman? That's shameful."

The two cashiers stopped what they were doing and looked at him. He felt the eyes of those standing in line with him on him, too, but that didn't bother Jack at all. While it was true that most did not want to be cut in line, it was also true that most people would be willing to make an exception when it was warranted, as it clearly was here. The people Jack stood in line with were probably either his age or younger, and he could tell as he glanced over his shoulder that they did not disagree with him speaking up.

But why was he the only one to speak up? It seemed as if they were waiting for someone *else* to say something, and he had, and they could give their sympathetic looks to the woman, or their looks of agreement to him, and feel as if they had done something, too, when the fact was, they hadn't—they'd just stood there and waited for someone else to take action.

"Surely I'm not the only person who speaks Chinese here," he said. No one said anything, and those who had been nodding their approval of what he had just done stopped looking so friendly and instead looked back down at their phones.

It was his turn at the register, and as the cashier scanned his items, he couldn't help himself. "What type of society will we have if we don't help the elderly? Or those who need it?"

The cashier's eyes darted to him and then quickly back down as she mumbled the total that he owed. Jack was glad to get out of there, though his irritation lingered as he stepped outside and waited on the corner for the light to turn green. There were people standing on the other side of the street, also waiting to cross. Every single person Jack saw was staring at their phone, most likely playing games or on WeChat. Their phones gave them no access to real news or opinions—only what the government wanted them to know. And most people seemed fine with that.

The light changed, and Jack stepped off the curb. He didn't know if it was still lingering irritation over what had happened back at the store, or the fact that literally every person he passed was staring at their phone, but he was overcome with the desire to grab the next person and shake them by their shoulders and yell *Wake up!*

Someone fell in step next to him, their arms brushing. This was not strange; it had happened to Jack plenty of times when he'd been walking in a crowd. But instead of the person moving off, he stayed right there by Jack's side.

"What are you doing?"

The man said this in a low voice, so low that Jack almost missed it. Jack glanced at him, wondering if perhaps he was talking to someone on Bluetooth, but the man was looking right at Jack. He wore jeans and a paint-flecked white t-shirt over which was a faded green fatigue jacket, adorned with safety pins and various patches.

"You better watch yourself," he said. "Leave Wang Min alone."

Jack rolled his eyes. "Fuck off," he said. "You must have me confused with someone else, because I have no idea who you're talking about." He gave the guy a hard look, one that said, in no uncertain terms, how he was not in the mood to deal with this shit.

The guy tried to give him what was supposed to be a menacing look, but really just came across as cartoonish. He had the thinnest of scars along his left cheek, maybe three inches long, almost as if it had been done with a surgical instrument.

"You want to add another scar to the other side of your face?" Jack said.

The guy narrowed his eyes and slowed his pace as Jack continued on. Jack shook his head. Undiagnosed mental illness was rampant in China, so random, unwanted interactions like this were not too uncommon, but it wasn't what Jack felt like dealing with right now.

He took a deep breath when he arrived at the next intersection. As he exhaled, he tried to envision letting go of all his stress and frustration—he'd be seeing Jojo tomorrow, and just the thought put a smile on his face.

CHAPTER 15

Jojo's place was located amongst a mix of residential dwellings and shops. Jack was reminded, though, that just thirty minutes from the center of Shanghai, things were quite different. Gone was the impressive architecture, the elevated expressways, the vast number of restaurants and shops; away from Shanghai's center, it was like taking a trip back in time. There were no coffee shops, no internet cafes, the buildings were unpainted and in disrepair. It was almost like being transported to a different place entirely, despite technically being a part of the same city.

Jack double-checked the address before he got out of his Didi, then thanked the driver. Jojo's building was a two-story structure, painted white with a dark blue front door. He knocked and then stepped back and waited. He took a deep breath and hoped he didn't look too foolish, standing there with the little bouquet of flowers. What if she hated flowers? No, he'd never met a woman who hated flowers. But were flowers, at this point in time, appropriate? Would she think he was taking it too far, too fast? Maybe the flowers were a bad idea. Maybe he should—

Before his thoughts could spiral too out of control, he heard the muted sound of approaching footsteps. Too late to do anything with the flowers now, so he took another deep breath and hoped for the best.

The door opened. There she was.

The smile that crossed his face when he saw her was automatic; just the sight of her put him in a good mood. He could not recall anyone ever having this effect on him.

"Hi," she said. "You made it."

She returned his smile as she stepped back and invited him in. Her long, dark hair was twisted up into a bun, and she wore a man's white dress shirt with the sleeves rolled up, and a pair of black leggings. Wisps of hair had escaped and framed her face and Jack had to resist the urge to touch them, to brush them back.

"I made it," he said as she shut the door behind him. "These are for you," he added, handing her the flowers.

"Why thank you," she said. "They're beautiful. Come on in."

Jack took a few steps inside and looked around. The floor was made of polished concrete, the walls white. There were maybe a dozen square display pedestals, atop which sat a different sculpture. There were several perfect copies of Rodin sculptures, both in larger and smaller versions than the originals.

"Wow," Jack said, walking over to one of the sculptures. "You did this?"

Jojo nodded.

"It's stunning. Truly. You're really talented. What are they made out of?"

"I use clay. It's easy to handle and work with. But, it can easily dry out, so you have to get it fired, then treat it. If a statue is commissioned, I sometimes cast the clay composition into plaster. This takes more time, though, and I don't have assistants like Rodin did."

"What about this one?" Jack said, nodding to a sculpture that had been covered with a sheet. "Work in progress?"

"It was, but I just finished it yesterday. Would you like to see?"

"I'd love to."

It took his brain a minute to catch up with his eyes after Jojo removed the sheet. He was looking at himself. And Ari. The two of them were laughing.

"Oh my god," he said. "This is incredible. It's Ari and me. How . . . how did you do that so quickly?"

"Clay is wonderful to work with if you know what you want to create. And I think it was the first or second time I saw the two of you at the bar, there was just this good energy you guys were giving off, and I knew I wanted to sculpt you. This was *before* you came back and asked me out on a date," she added.

"I see. So this sculpture was meant to be anyway, not something to try to impress me," Jack said jokingly. Really, though, he couldn't get over just how exquisite it was to see this sculpture, not just because it captured his likeness perfectly, but also because it meant that Jojo had been thinking about him. A pleasant shiver shot down his spine.

"No," Jojo said, laughing. "If I wanted to impress you, I'd probably head for that thing." She nodded to a full-sized Steinway in the corner that Jack hadn't noticed until now.

But even a beautiful grand piano couldn't hold his attention—he was captivated by the sculpture. He took a step closer and drew in a breath. She must have a photographic memory, there was no other way she would've been able to get the details of their faces so accurately.

"You have immense talent," he said, thoroughly dumbstruck.

"Thank you."

He could've stood there for the rest of the evening, admiring the sculpture, but that was probably not what Jojo had in mind when she invited him over. He forced himself to look away and handed her the bag with the wine.

She looked inside. "Ooh, you brought *three* bottles. Good man."

"It's not possible to have too much wine."

"Let's get one of these open, shall we? And get these flowers in some water."

He followed her toward the back of the loft. They passed a spiral staircase that led to the second-story loft, where Jack assumed there must be a bed, though he tried to push any thoughts of Jojo's bed out of his mind—at least for now. There was a small kitchen and a round table large enough for two. She put the wine down and retrieved a wine opener from one of the kitchen drawers. Normally, he would've asked if there was something he could do to help, but it was clear she had the situation under control and plus, he loved to watch her. She moved effortlessly, easily, like she herself was some sort of art, something to be looked at and admired. He accepted the wine glass she handed to him, and they clinked glasses before taking the first sip.

"I like your hair up like that," Jack said, as he put his wine glass down.

She looked confused for a moment, and then her hand went up to her hair, felt the bun. "Oh, I totally forgot. I always keep it up when I work." She pulled the chopstick out of her hair and it cascaded over her shoulders in dark, luxurious waves.

"I like your hair down, too," Jack said. "So that's what you wanted the chopsticks for?"

She laughed. "No. Though, I *did* use one of the chopsticks to make your sculpture. It seemed appropriate." She nodded to his wine glass. "Want to take this outside?"

She took him through a door at the back of the loft, to a quiet outdoor area where there was a large table and chairs. Several trees provided a canopy of shade and, along with the various plants and flowers, made the area really feel like a sanctuary.

"It's delightful out here," Jack said.

Jojo smiled. "It is. It's one of the reasons I rented the space to begin with. It's hard to find nice, outside private areas in Shanghai."

"Is that a watermelon plant?" Jack pointed to a delicate-looking vine with lobed, light green leaves.

"Yes," Jojo said. "I plant a few each spring. My dad and I used to grow them in Beijing, in a greenhouse. We'd even cook the rind and eat it. I cook the seeds and save them for Chinese New Year."

"Wow," Jack said. "How long do they take to grow?"

"About three months, if the weather's good. I don't really have enough space here, but they're pretty easy, so it's always worth it to at least try. You just trim them periodically and make sure to remove the smaller, abnormal fruit. My dad used to tell me that a watermelon, although it doesn't look it, is a berry."

"Huh," Jack said. "Interesting. I didn't realize that."

"And I just realized—I broke my rule," Jojo said. "Talking about parents," she added, when Jack gave her a confused look.

"Oh," he said. "Well . . . does that even need to be a rule at this point? Just hearing you talking about it—I can picture you and your dad, I can see him telling you that a watermelon was a berry. It's charming, really."

"I promised you food." Jojo stood up. "I'm going to go get that started—unless you want watermelon for dinner."

Jack also stood, wondering why it was that Jojo was in such a hurry to pivot the conversation away from her father—even though she had brought him up first. It was almost as if she'd forgotten the self-imposed rule, which Jack still wasn't clear about. But if she didn't want to continue the conversation about her father, he would leave it at that.

He followed her inside and poured them each more wine while she rummaged around in the fridge, pulling things out and placing them on the counter.

"You want to put some music on?" she asked. "There's a Bluetooth speaker in the gallery."

Jack went out in the gallery where he found the speaker on a small table. He synced it with his phone, selected a song, and turned up the volume. The song had a Charleston-like beat, but the lyrics were in

Chinese, and Jack began to tap his foot to the beat as he took a seat back in the kitchen.

Jojo began to nod her head to the beat, too, as she filled a pot with water and put it on the stove.

"This is a cute song," she said.

"It is, but I like the next one even better."

The next song was "Give Me a Kiss" and it had a jazzier feel to it.

"I like this one, too," she said. "You have good taste in music, Jack."

He got up and poured them each another glass of wine as the water on the stove began to boil. While she put the pasta in the pot, he took his glass and wandered back out into the gallery, again looking at the sculptures, marveling at the exquisite detail in each one. It was almost impossible for him to wrap his mind around the fact that she had created such things with her own two hands. It was incredible, and though he tried to refrain, his mind kept wondering what *else* she could do with those hands . . .

He stopped at a small bookshelf and perused the titles. Many art history books. A few novels. Nestled at the very end was a worn copy of *Le Petit Prince*. Jack slid it out and looked at it. It had been one of his favorite stories as a child, though he hadn't thought about it in a long time. This was a well-loved copy, he could tell, as he thumbed through it, the words and sentences familiar as the pages passed by.

Something fluttered out, a bookmark, he thought, but when he bent down to retrieve it, he saw that it was a photograph. It showed a man, young, maybe in his mid-twenties, with a head of thick, dark hair. He was holding a little girl who was probably four or five, her hair cut just above her shoulders, short bangs cut straight across her forehead. Neither were looking directly at the camera; instead their gazes were something skyward, the man's left arm was extended, the little girl's eyes wide as she looked whatever he was pointing at. Jack imagined he was telling Jojo something about a bird that had just flown by, or a flower on a tree branch that was way out of reach. He glanced toward the kitchen and saw that Jojo's back was to him as she rummaged through the fridge for something. He looked down at the photograph again, its edges discoloring with age.

Though decades had passed since the photograph must have been taken, Jack knew this was Jojo, and, very likely, her father. He wanted to ask her about it, but he also didn't want to push her to talk about something she didn't want to. There was no need to push things—he wanted to take his time.

So he gently tucked the photograph back into the book, then slid the book back onto the shelf. Back in the kitchen, Jojo had almost finished her wine and was giving the pasta another stir.

"Almost there," she said. "You hungry?"

"I am," Jack said. "What are you doing over there? Can I do anything?"

"You could pour me a little more wine. We're having linguini with lemon and mushrooms, in a cream sauce. And a Caesar salad."

Jack poured Jojo another glass, and then topped off his own. She drained the pasta and mixed it with the sauce and then made up their plates.

"Wow," Jack said, as they sat down at the table. "This looks incredible. Thank you so much."

It had been a long time since a woman had cooked for him, and he realized, as the savory aroma wafted toward him, how much he missed that—not that he needed to be cooked for, but there was something wonderfully intimate and caring about having a meal prepared and then getting to indulge it together.

He took a bite of salad and tasted the pungent spiciness of the garlic and the saltiness of the anchovies, the tang of lemon juice, the slightly nutty flavor of the grated Parmesan. The Romaine lettuce was crisp, and as Jack chewed, he sighed contentedly.

Mozart began to play in the background. "Where were those two songs from?" Jojo asked. "That were playing earlier? The jazzy one and then the one before it?"

"They're from that movie *Crazy Rich Asians*. The book was great, but I didn't enjoy the movie—I walked out, actually."

"You didn't like the movie but you're listening to the soundtrack?"

"Yeah. That, I would say, was one of its few redeeming qualities. The music had good energy." Jack set his fork down and took a sip of wine. "I can send you a screenshot of the songs, if you'd like."

"That'd be great. Thanks."

Jack took his time twirling linguini around his fork. The lemon cream sauce went perfectly with the Caesar salad. The mushrooms added depth with their meaty texture, and he honestly could never recall if he'd had a better meal.

His whole body thrummed with happiness. "This is so delicious," he said. "You should adopt me."

Jojo laughed. "I should adopt you," she repeated. "Jack, you're hilarious."

"Anything to make you laugh."

And the thing was—he meant it. Just seeing that she was happy made *him* happy.

"So," he said. "Tell me what brought you to Shanghai."

She finished the mouthful she was chewing and then took a sip of wine. "Well," she said. "I'll go ahead and break my rule and tell you that I wanted to be closer to my dad, who's in Beijing. But not too close. He can be . . . a little protective. And Beijing is spread out and the traffic and pollution are awful. It's just not as beautiful as it is here." She smiled. "Should I go on? I can probably come up with a couple more things."

Jack considered mentioning the photograph, since she had brought the subject of her father up, but before he could, Jojo waved her hand dismissively. "What about you? Do you like it here in Shanghai?"

"I do," he said, though in his head he was thinking, *I do much more now.* "I don't know if this is where I'll end up forever, but if I do . . . it's certainly not the worst place to be."

"No, it's really not. I do like to travel, though."

"Speaking of traveling, I'm heading to DC tomorrow. Well, technically tomorrow, the flight leaves fifteen minutes after midnight."

She raised her eyebrows. "For how long?"

"Less than a week. It's a short trip, considering the length of the flight. For business."

"Well, we better be sure not to make it a late night, then. We don't want you to miss your flight. Pudong Airport is an hour from here—and that's only if there's no traffic."

"Are you trying to get rid of me?"

"Of course I'm not. But I don't want to be responsible for you missing an important business trip."

"I've already packed and sent my bag to the airport. So, I'm good." *Besides*, he thought, *missing this flight because of you would be more than worth it.*

When they were finished eating, Jack helped Jojo clean up. Once the dishes were in the drying rack, he poured them each another half glass of wine. Their fingertips brushed when he passed her the glass. He lifted his own toward her. "To an incredible chef and an even more incredible artist. Thank you for a wonderful evening."

She grinned and touched her glass to his. "Thanks so much for coming by. I enjoyed the evening, too."

Jack set his wine glass down. "The evening doesn't have to end just yet," he said. "Hey Siri, play mixed music."

The classical music switched to an upbeat, jazzy big band song called "Swingers." He held out his hand. Jojo hesitated, but only for a second, before reaching out to take his, and he pulled her to him and they both started dancing.

And despite never dancing together before, it felt completely natural to be this close, and moving in sync with Jojo. It felt as if they were moving as one, and Jack wished the song would never end.

But it did, and they were both laughing as they stepped back from each other.

"You're a good dancer," Jojo said. "That was fun."

"It was. We'll have to do it again. Soon."

"Maybe when you get back from your trip."

"*Definitely* when I get back from my trip. I suppose it'll be my turn to do the cooking."

Jojo raised her eyebrows. "Ooh, you cook, too? What do you like to cook?"

"All sorts of things. Mexican food, I can do a decent Burmese dish. White people food," he said with a laugh. "Unfortunately, I don't have a nice gallery and incredible sculptures to impress you with."

She gave him what was most certainly a coy smile. "I'm sure you could come up with other ways to impress me."

They smiled. The air seemed to tingle around them, and Jack wanted nothing more than to once again close the distance, take Jojo in his arms, and give her a kiss. But he had to get going, and he didn't want their first kiss to happen right as he was about to leave the country for a week.

"I guess I better get a Didi," he said. "Not that I want this night to end."

He was hopeful that the closest Didi would be at least a few minutes away, but of course there was one less than a minute away. Jack sighed. Didi never went at the speed you wanted it to.

"I'll be in touch," Jack said as they walked toward the door. He glanced at the sculptures once more, again struck by her immense talent. *What a remarkable person.* "Thank you again, Jojo."

"Safe travels, Jack. I look forward to your return."

He stepped outside. Oh, how he wanted to kiss her. His Didi pulled up and he glanced over his shoulder one last time, took in her smiling face. Yes, he wanted to kiss her more than anything, but he would wait. It would just make returning back home even better.

CHAPTER 16

Ronald Reagan airport was cool and rainy, exactly the sort of weather Jack expected. He took a taxi to the W Hotel right next to the White House, where his room had a magnificent view of the Washington Monument. His meeting with Gary and Rick was scheduled for the following morning, so for the rest of his evening, Jack planned to relax and unwind, first with a shower, then some room service.

Throughout it all, Jojo was constantly on his mind. What was she doing, was she thinking about him at all? He wanted to message her but didn't want to come across as needy. Also—she hadn't messaged *him* yet, and maybe it would be better if he let her make the first move. Still, the idea of the entire week passing by with no contact seemed untenable.

* * *

The next morning, Jack was up early, feeling surprisingly refreshed. He put on a dark blue suit with a yellow tie, then fastened his Luminox military watch to his wrist. Finally, he put on his Officine Creative shoes. They fit perfectly, which, at six hundred dollars a pair, they should. If taken care of properly, the shoes would last forever, offsetting their steep price tag.

Gary and Rick were waiting for him in the hotel restaurant, at a private table, away from the other guests. They both stood up and everyone greeted each other, shook hands.

"How was the flight in?" Rick asked.

"It was great," Jack said. "Nothing compares with Chinese airlines."

"Are you serious?" Rick said skeptically. "Better than American?"

Jack nodded. "Absolutely. Asian airlines don't have lifetime employment, so their staff are typically younger and more motivated. The food is usually better. And they actually clean their toilets during the flight. United and American are the worst."

Rick shot a look at Gary. "Guess we should stick to private jets."

Everyone laughed, and then Gary suggested they sit down and check out the menu and order something. Jack decided on poached eggs, corned beef hash, an English muffin, and a double espresso.

"And I'll have a glass of watermelon juice," he told the waitress as he handed the menu back to her.

The waitress smiled and looked at Gary, who ordered a coffee, and then Rick, who also ordered a coffee.

"I'm the only one eating?" Jack said.

"I already ate," Rick said.

"And I can't eat anything until I have at least three coffees," Gary said. "But I thought we could have a casual chat here and then go by our office. There are more details and mock-ups about our developments there."

"Sounds good," Jack said as their waitress returned with their coffees and the watermelon juice.

Rick eyed his glass. "Watermelon juice," he said. "Now that sounds exotic."

Jack smiled as he took a sip, thinking of sitting out back with Jojo, her watermelon plants. "It's quite good," he said. "You should try it some time."

Gary poured some sugar into his coffee and gave it a stir. "So," he said, "it would be helpful, Jack, if you could give us your perspective on China."

Jack nodded. "Sure. But there are many different things I have a perspective on, so before I start waxing on about something you have no interest in, did you have something a little more specific that you were interested in hearing about?"

"I'd specifically like to hear about what it's like to live in Shanghai. I'd like your perspective on that."

Jack took a small sip of his espresso. "Shanghai's a beautiful city. All different types of architecture and neighborhoods. The foreigners are diverse and interesting. And the business environment is more open than elsewhere in the country." Gary and Rick nodded, as if this was exactly what they wanted to hear. "There's a great deal of real estate development, which I suppose shouldn't be surprising, considering it's the most populous city in the world. But if you go just outside the city center, it feels like you've gone back thirty years in time."

"Interesting," Rick said. "How many people live there?"

"Twenty-six million."

He let out a low whistle. "Incredible."

Jack's food arrived a few minutes later, and Gary shared a little more information with Jack about some of the projects they were doing while Jack devoured his breakfast. Ah, he had missed this sort of food. It was the little things.

When he was finished eating, they left the hotel and walked a few blocks to Gary and Rick's office. The building had been gutted and was now a large, open space with a modern, industrial feel. The big windows showcased a remarkable view of the White House and Washington Monument.

Jack followed the two men into a room with floor-to-ceiling windows. In the middle of the room was a miniature three-dimensional rendition of their developments. As Jack looked at them, Gary described how much they would be investing and the expected returns. Jack nodded as he listened, couldn't help but feel impressed at the figures Gary was rattling off.

"It'd be great to get potential investors to visit your office," Jack said. "This is the sort of thing that would impress them. Let's aim to get a few project documents out whenever you feel it's appropriate, then I'll circulate them to my contacts and arrange some calls. Typically, they won't invest in the first project but will use it as a way to get to know you. I'm just giving you the head's up about that."

"It's good to know," Rick said. "Would you like to go and see one of the projects?"

"No, that's okay," Jack said. "I'm a numbers and strategy guy. When it comes to doing due diligence, you'll have plenty of other people visiting."

"Sure," Gary said. "Oh, but before we forget, we have a friend. We mentioned you to him and he'd love you to drop by and say hello. He's in the same building." He reached into his jacket pocket and pulled out a business card. "His name's Harold Task. He's an attorney and may have other real estate-related contacts for you. He hoped you'd have a few minutes to drop by his office when we're done."

Jack looked down at the card. "Well, if we're all done here, I guess I'll head over now."

* * *

Jack was curious about Harold and what he might want to talk about. The elevator let him out on the eleventh floor, where he found himself in what was clearly a corporate attorney's office, with its high ceilings and dark, gleaming wood.

He walked over to the reception area. "Hello," he said, when the woman looked up at him. "I'm here to see Harold."

"Do you have an appointment?"

"I do not, but I believe he's expecting me. My name's Jack Gold."

The receptionist gave him a brief smile and picked up her phone. She said something in a low voice that Jack couldn't quite make out, but then she put the phone down and looked up.

"You're all set. Just go to the conference room down the hall that way," she said, pointing. "The room will be the first door on your right."

Jack thanked her and walked down the hallway, into the conference room. It was like every other conference room Jack had been in, with a gleaming wood table that sat eight people, though presently, he was the only one in the room. He took a seat in one of the black leather executive chairs and leaned his head back. Immediately, his thoughts flowed to Jojo, and he felt a tingle of excitement thinking about getting back to see her. It was like being a teenager again, this way that he felt, and it was a most pleasant surprise.

Jack lifted his head and sat up straight when a man, who he assumed was Harold, strode into the room. He looked to be around sixty, and he wore a dark blue suit with a light blue tie. Jack stood up and introduced himself, shook Harold's hand, then sat back down. Harold shut the door and took the seat at the head of the table.

"Do you have your passport on you?" Harold asked.

The question surprised Jack, but he didn't let it show. Was this what Ari had been referring to? "I do," he said, without missing a beat. He reached into the inside pocket of his jacket and pulled it out. "Here you go."

He sat back and watched as Harold flipped it to the third page and looked at Jack's photo and his name. He looked at Jack, then back down at the passport once more, before he closed it and handed it back. "Thank you."

Jack tucked the passport back into his jacket.

"So," Harold said. "We understand you're willing to assist the U.S. government with a problem in China. I'm not here to fully brief you, but rather to formalize your interest. Is what I just said accurate?"

"Yes."

"The current situation in China presents an existential threat to itself and others. Because of this, America and Israel are considering covert action to alter the current situation's trajectory." Harold leaned forward, looking closely at Jack. "The intent of such action is not to kill people, but it will be dangerous and may result in loss of life." He paused. "Do you understand what I have just said?"

Jack took a moment to let Harold's words sink in. He still wasn't any clearer on the specifics of the plan, but he knew he wouldn't learn any further details unless he agreed. Did he want to lose his life? No, of course not, but he could not sit on the sidelines and let someone else take on the dangerous, the important work. This was something that could make a difference, not just in a single individual's life, but an entire nation.

He thought of his father, what his father might say if he were to find out what Jack was involved in. He would be proud, no doubt–he would say that Jack was finally starting to live up to his potential.

"Yes," Jack said, looking at Harold. "I understand everything you've said."

"Are you interested in assisting America in this matter, given the issues I've outlined?" It sounded as if Harold had had conversations like this many times before.

"Yes." Jack nodded. "I will need verifications that the endeavors have been officially sanctioned."

"Certainly. We've arranged a tour of the White House for you tomorrow morning. You'll meet someone who can go into more detail and provide you the assurance you require. As a matter of fact, I have the ticket right here." Harold reached into his own inside jacket pocket and handed the ticket to Jack. "As is typically the case with such endeavors, it will be essential that America has deniability if something goes wrong." He slid a piece of paper in front of Jack.

Jack knew a non-disclosure agreement when he saw one, and there was nothing out of the ordinary with this one. He pulled his pen out of his jacket pocket and signed, slid the paper back to Harold.

"Have a good tour tomorrow," Harold said. They stood and shook hands. "And remember to take your passport with you."

Jack said he would and then he made his exit, replaying what had just happened as he stepped into the elevator. *Dangerous and may result in loss of life.* Not necessarily the words anyone wanted to hear before agreeing to be a part of something, but also, this seemed like the exact type of situation Jack had been waiting for. This was going to be his chance to be a part of something that mattered. To make a difference in people's lives. The elevator doors opened at the first floor. He stepped out into the lobby.

I miss Jojo, he thought.

CHAPTER 17

Excitement coursed through Jack as he made his way to the White House the next morning. He'd never been there before, and as he walked toward the East Wing entrance, he thought about his favorite president, Harry S. Truman. Truman had been a senator from Missouri, didn't have a college education, and had not been successful in saving China from communism. But he *had* been successful in dealing with Japan, and he didn't hesitate when it came to bombing Hiroshima and Nagasaki. Most people didn't know that Winston Churchill had once said to Truman, "I misjudged you badly. Since that time, you, more than any other man, have saved Western civilization."

What a thing, Jack had thought, more than once, to be a person, a single individual, in the position to save or protect an entire society–and most of the people who would benefit from it were not even aware.

A line of people had formed at the East Wing, and Jack took his spot at the end. A young man, dressed in a dark suit, walked from the front of the line to the back, telling everyone to form a line and have their invitations and IDs ready to show. Jack double checked his pants pocket to make sure that he had both.

The line moved slowly, and Jack shuffled along, thinking of Jojo. He'd send her a message via WeChat later today, he decided, whether or not she messaged him first. It would be a simple message, just to say hi and let her know he was thinking about her.

He made it to the front of the line, and as he handed the guard his passport and his invitation, he made a conscious effort to push Jojo out of his mind. Right now, he wanted to focus on being here at the–

"Sir," the guard said, "there's an issue with your ID. Could you come with me, please?"

The people standing closest to him looked his way curiously, and Jack frowned. What was the problem? The guard probably didn't know, so there was no point in asking. Jack nodded. "Sure."

The guard said nothing as he led Jack into the East Wing and then up a stairway. It seemed like a long way to go just to get his ID verified. Something, he felt in his gut, was about to happen; he just wasn't sure what.

They made their way down a long hallway, the dark hardwood floor laid out in a herringbone pattern, large windows with columns to his left, several sets of closed double doors to his right. The guard opened one of the doors, and Jack found himself in an office with three chairs and a table.

"Please wait here, Mr. Gold," the guard said. "Someone will be with you shortly."

He motioned for Jack to sit down, and only once Jack had, did he return his passport.

"Thanks," Jack said. Before the guard was able to make his exit, though, another man walked into the room. He was slightly overweight and wore a white shirt with a tie, but no jacket.

"Thank you, sergeant," he said to the guard, before turning his attention to Jack. "Hello, Mr. Gold. I'm Officer Cooper, and I'll be your point person."

Jack stood and they shook hands. "Nice to meet you. I guess I'll have to take that tour another day."

"Yes, indeed. Let's get down to business, since time is limited." Jack sat back down, and Cooper took the seat next to him. "I'll get right to the point. The ultimate intent of our plan is to share factual information with the Chinese people and let them have free access to information. The rest is up to them."

Jack nodded. "Okay."

"But to do this, we need to remove China's leadership for a few days, thereby distracting everyone. Then we'll be able to take control of their broadcasting and internet capabilities. We have a guy by the name of Tony Woo who will be explaining the reasons for our actions to the general population. And we have documents that will be shared." Cooper paused and then leaned a little closer to Jack. "We have support for this. There's a good percentage of the Chinese government that's aligned with us on this project. Likewise, there is military support. Everyone is reluctant to act alone, since they fear President Zhao's power. But if we can all come together toward this common goal . . ."

"How are you going to remove the leadership?" Jack was intrigued but skeptical. That seemed like the biggest hurdle of all, and if that wasn't done correctly, the whole plan would be–

"That's where you come in," Cooper said with a hint of a smile.

Jack raised an eyebrow. "Come again?"

"You will be positioned so you can shake hands with certain people in leadership. You'll have a neurotoxin on your hand that you'll pass to them. They, in turn, will pass it on to others. The neurotoxin takes twelve hours to kick in and it'll take them three to five days to build up a resistance, by which time we'll be done."

"Okay," Jack said slowly. "But how sure are you that the neurotoxin won't spread? And won't I become infected, if I have it on my hand?"

"Good questions; let me try to put your mind at ease. The viral factor declines steeply, so we don't infect too many people. We've run a number of scenarios, and the maximum infection number is ten thousand, with a point-five potential mortality rate."

"Ten thousand," Jack repeated. Not a huge number, compared to over a billion, but still. He didn't like the idea of possibly harming innocent people. And despite the fact that the mortality rate was almost non-existent, there was still the chance. Sometimes, though, such sacrifices needed to be made if things were going to be accomplished.

"And that's the maximum," Cooper said, as if he could hear Jack's thoughts. "It will likely be much lower. As for you, we'd like to give you an immunization today, and then one more before you leave DC."

There was a knock at the door. "Ah, perfect timing," Cooper said. "Come in!"

The door opened, and an attractive young woman in a beige pantsuit came in. "The nurse is here to give you the first injection," Cooper explained as the nurse gave Jack the thinnest of smiles. "And while she's doing that, may I please have your phone?"

Jack pulled his iPhone out of his pocket and handed it to Cooper. "Thanks. We'll return it to your hotel front desk later today. We just want to modify it slightly. Is that okay?"

"Yes."

"We'll go step-by-step. Your friend Ari will introduce you to a gentleman named Joshua Adler, who sells jet fuel from Israel to China. You'll befriend Joshua, and he'll introduce you to some of China's leadership. Afterward, we'd like you to be around and help us gain access to the CCTV's Headquarters Building. We'll need to broadcast from there. I'm sure you've seen the building?"

Jack frowned. "I'm not sure."

"It's the big building in Beijing that looks like a huge chair. Or a toilet." To Jack's surprise, Cooper smiled.

"Oh, okay!" Jack said. "I know where you mean."

The nurse cleared her throat, and when Jack looked at her, she asked him to please roll up his sleeve.

He did, the sharp smell of antiseptic filling the room as she dabbed his upper arm with a cotton ball. The injection was quick and stung only for a second.

"Here you go," she said to Jack after he rolled his sleeve back down. She gave him a vial of what appeared to be eye drops.

"That's the neurotoxin," Cooper said. "All you need is four or five drops on your right hand. Keep it in your briefcase; don't check it through luggage when flying. The cold temperature will ruin it."

"Got it," Jack said.

The nurse left without saying anything, and Jack turned his attention back to Cooper, expecting to be given more information. Instead, though, the door opened again, and, much to Jack's surprise, there stood the President of the United States.

"Hello, Jack."

Jack stood immediately. "President Sutton."

"It's a pleasure," Sutton said as they shook hands. "I want to emphasize the importance—and the risk—of what we're asking you to do. As I'm sure you know, this is an Israeli operation with full U.S. support. And they wanted you involved. I want you to know that we have the support of Britain, France, Japan, and South Korea. China is messing with its own population, stealing American national security secrets, and colluding with Russia and Iran. We can never trust what their administration says. We have to do this in order to give the people of China a chance." He smiled. "I just wanted to stop in and wish you good luck. And thank you for being willing to step up."

"Yes, of course," Jack said, once more shaking Sutton's hand.

The president turned to leave, but then stopped and turned, looking at Jack once more. "That was a great video of you throwing those two guys off the balcony." He shook his head, laughing just a little, and then left before Jack could respond.

"He wanted to come by and speak to you in person," Cooper said.

Jack blinked. Everything felt so surreal. Not only did he meet the president, but the man had somehow seen the video of him throwing those two guys off the balcony—and he *liked* it.

Cooper slid an all-black phone across the table to Jack. "For texting us only," he said. "And for life and death situations, of which there will hopefully be none. We pre-programmed in a number for you, and we've added a few of your contacts as well. The one you won't recognize—Sam—is us. Otherwise, use your ordinary phone as normal. We will be monitoring you via both phones." He leaned forward and slid a folded-up piece of paper out of his back pocket, which he opened and gave to Jack. "Here's the phone contract. Please sign it—we've already set up direct payment for it from your bank account." Cooper held up his hands. "Sorry, but that's a necessity in case anyone looks into it. On the plus side—here's the cash to cover it." Jack took the envelope from him and then signed the phone contract. "And there's one more thing for you to sign."

"How many papers do you have in that pocket?" Jack asked.

Cooper gave him a tight-lipped smile. "Last one, I promise. Signing for the cash."

Jack lifted the pen once more and signed his name.

"So you're sure you're up for this?" Cooper asked as he folded the papers back up.

Jack raised his eyebrows. "Hell of a time to ask," he said, "after I've already signed on. But, yes. I am. Do you need me to repeat anything?"

"No. I think we're set. We'll keep you updated periodically via text, so please keep both phones with you. Make sure you delete each text once you've received it. It'll then be completely removed from your phone."

"Understood," Jack said. Everything seemed very still, almost as if he could sense each individual molecule in the room, in the air, all around him. He was in it now—no going back. Any anxiety about possible danger or the consequences if things did not go as planned had to be pushed aside. He looked Cooper right in the eye and gave him a brisk nod. "I want to help out however I can."

"Excellent," Cooper said. "And now I'll let the sergeant return you to your tour group."

The guard was standing there when Cooper opened the door. He shook Jack's hand. "You'll be hearing from us. And hey, that was pretty good the way you threw those guys off the balcony. It could've been straight out of Hollywood!"

"Uh, thanks," Jack said. Cooper laughed and shook his head, then turned and started to walk down the hallway. Jack followed the guard in the opposite direction, wondering if everyone in the administration had seen Ari's little video.

*   *   *

Jack sat in the busy terminal, waiting to board his flight back to China. His mind was spinning, as it had been since his visit to the White House. He wanted nothing more than to call his dad and tell him about it, but he knew such a thing would be prohibited, and, possibly, quite dangerous. But this was the exact sort of thing his father would be over the moon proud about—Jack, finally living up to his potential.

The final days of his DC trip had been relatively uneventful—his phone had been returned, which he'd picked up from the hotel front desk, and the nurse had stopped by to give him his final shot. He'd had another moment where it felt as though he had stepped onto the scene of a movie—the nurse was dressed in jeans and a sweater, and she looked like just another regular hotel guest. It felt strange knowing his movements were being tracked. That he could be found at any time.

He wanted to clear his thoughts, so he started to count babies. There were four, and more would likely show up. There were newborn babies on almost every return flight from America to China; couples would arrange to visit America before they were about to give birth, so their baby would automatically get U.S. citizenship. Only the wealthy couples could afford the visitor's visa and the airfare and travel accommodations. But it was for no other reason than to give their children a better chance, which was any parent's wish, wasn't it? Jack couldn't fault the couples who made such a journey, though he did find it surprising that the Chinese government didn't see it as a huge no-confidence vote, a quiet revolution with a whole new generation of children being born elsewhere.

CHAPTER 18

Jack was famished when he woke up the next morning, so he headed to Baker and Spice. After coffee and a few bites of breakfast, he was feeling more like himself. He picked up his phone and sent Jojo a message. *Back from the colonial power headquarters. How are you?*

He sipped his coffee and typed the URL address for Hong Kong's main newspaper into his browser. The headline read: *China cracking down on illegal underground forex trading in bid to control capital flight.*

The article described how China was cracking down on unregulated banks that were assisting people in getting money out of the country. Selling renminbi meant there was less demand for it, weakening it. China preferred a relatively strong renminbi because Chinese exporters were paid in American dollars, which they would then convert into renminbi.

But the government just didn't get it—everything was economically interlinked. It seemed so obvious to Jack, yet much of China's leadership did not seem able or willing to understand this. Trying to manage one variable would inevitably impact another—it was impossible for central planning to manage every scenario effectively.

He took a sip of coffee and glanced over right as his phone alerted him to a new message. From Jojo. *Welcome home. All is good. On a delivery run.*

Before he could write a response, though, a text came through from Ari.

Heading to Beijing next week. I have a few people there I'd like to introduce you to.

I can do that, Jack replied. Cooper's words echoed in his mind: *Your friend Ari will introduce you to a gentleman named Joshua Adler . . . You'll befriend Joshua, and he'll introduce you to some of China's leadership . . . We'd like you to be around and help us gain access to the CCTV's headquarters building . . .*

He finished writing to Ari, telling him to let him know the dates he planned to go up there, and then he turned his attention back to Jojo's message.

Just seeing the words made him smile, and he wished that there was some way he could've gone along on the delivery run with her—just being around her was all he wanted.

He typed back a reply, asking if she wanted to get together for dinner that weekend.

I'll cook, he added.

Her response came a few minutes later, and Jack smiled when he saw she'd accepted his invitation. They settled on Sunday evening, at his place.

CHAPTER 19

For their third date, Jack decided to cook lamb ribs with eggplant, string beans, and Italian squash in a Burmese curry-like dish, served atop rice. It was relatively simple to make yet the flavors were exuberant, and Jack had a feeling Jojo would enjoy it. He spent the first part of the day making sure the apartment looked presentable—it did—and then he began prep work on the food.

She texted him when her Didi got close, and he quickly slipped his shoes on and made his way outside to meet her. This was common practice when someone was visiting for the first time, as so many of the buildings were interlocked that it could be difficult for people to navigate, if they did not know exactly where they were going.

When her car pulled up, he stepped forward and opened the door. She got out, and his breath caught in his throat at the sight of her. She looked completely different than the last time he'd seen her—she wore black square glasses, tight jeans, and a black button-up shirt. Her hair was down, and he did not think a woman could look more gorgeous.

"Hi," was all he could manage to say at first, with his big, happy smile. She held out a bottle of wine.

"Hello."

They stood there and smiled at each other for a moment, Jack overcome with the desire to hug her, to smell her hair, to feel her arms around him. But he refrained, because this was only their third date, after all. He'd see how tonight went, and if it seemed the right thing to do, he would probably try to kiss her.

It was a bit of a reversal from their last date—now Jack showed Jojo around his apartment, and she looked around, commenting on the architecture.

"The ceilings are higher than in traditional apartments," she said, gazing up. "But I like it. Certainly makes everything feel bigger."

"I love the architecture in this building," Jack said. "Clearly, I'm not much of an interior decorator, but I feel like that's less noticeable in a place like this."

Jojo smiled. "As far as bachelor pads go, yours isn't so bad at all."

Jack put the bottle of wine she had brought in the fridge to chill and pulled out a bottle of French Chablis. He poured them each a glass.

"What are you making?" Jojo asked. "It smells good."

"Lamb ribs and a spicy Burmese dish, with rice. I have the vegetables simmering and I just put the rice on and the last thing to do is get the lamb in the oven. I hope the menu is okay with you."

She raised her eyebrows as she took a sip of wine. "I'll have to get back to you on that."

Jack returned her playful look as he started to cook. "So, how did your trip go?" Jojo asked as she slid onto one of the tall counter stools and watched as he set the lamb onto a rack in a shallow baking pan.

"Pretty tiring," Jack said. "Thirty-six hours of flying. I didn't even get to go on the tour of the White House."

"How come?"

"My passport information didn't match what was listed on the ticket, apparently. But it's okay. I walked around instead, and that was nice." After the lamb was in the oven, he set the timer, trying to ignore the prickly discomfort he felt at deceiving Jojo. "What about you?" he asked. "How's business going? You mentioned the other day that you were out on a delivery."

"Yeah, I was delivering a statue to one of my long-time clients. It was of his wife, for their upcoming anniversary." She traced her index finger along the stem of the wine glass. "I can't say I'd want a sculpture in my image for an anniversary gift, but . . . Who am I to say? And I appreciate the business. I actually have a waiting list."

"That's great," Jack said. "Did you ever think about increasing your prices, seeing as you have people waiting?"

"I charge what it's worth. I know I'm very fortunate to get to do my art and make money from it. Art in this country is seriously undeveloped. It's hard for most artists to exist because they can't make a living, and most of the people who are interested in art want to see foreign art, not domestic art."

Jack nodded. "I've thought about that before," he said. "How China has such a huge population but produced so few artists. Present company excluded, of course. Though really, Jojo, how could someone with your talent not find success? Your work is incredible." *So are you*, he wanted to add.

He took a sip of wine and then grabbed his phone and put some music on before stirring the Burmese dish. Another song came on, "Wonderful Tonight" by Eric Clapton. He reached over and turned up the volume. It was the most romantic song he knew.

He went over to Jojo and held his hand out, and when she slipped her palm into his, he gently pulled her to her feet. "Dance with me," he said. "It's one of my favorite romantic songs."

Jack wasn't sure if it was just that Jojo was a good dancer, or maybe the wine, or maybe some combination of the two, but slow dancing with her felt like the most natural thing ever. And it didn't matter the song, it didn't matter the place—If Jojo was there, Jack would be more than content to dance with her.

"I don't know what it is about you," Jojo said as Jack twirled her. "But I'm at ease with you."

"It's funny," Jack replied, "because I feel the exact same way about you."

She stepped closer to him, so close that the length of their bodies were touching, and Jack could feel the energy between then, something tingling and tangible that he could reach out and grab.

After the song was over, Jack went back into the kitchen to check on the rice and the vegetables, which were done. He took plates out of the cupboard and refilled their wine glasses, then took the lamb out of the oven and set it under foil to rest for ten minutes.

"Oh my god, that smells incredible," Jojo said.

Jack emptied the pot of rice into a serving bowl and did the same with the vegetables. The steam curled up, and he had to admit, every-thing both smelled and looked delicious. He made the plates, starting with the rice first, then the vegetables in their sauce, then the lamb, with a little more sauce drizzled over the top.

They sat down at the table. "May I?" Jack asked, gesturing to Jojo's plate.

"Please," she said. "I'm not even sure where to start with this."

He spooned up some of the rice and vegetables and then cut a piece of lamb, which he also put on the spoon. He wanted to feed it to her but wasn't sure if she'd be interested in that. He started to hand her the spoon, but then she opened her mouth and looked at him expectantly. He gave her the bite.

"This is how they eat it in Burma," he said. "The flavors blend."

She chewed slowly, a look of mild concentration on her face. "It's *really* good," she said. "I wasn't sure how I'd feel about it, but it's a great combination of flavors."

Jack slowly began to eat, enjoying the taste of the food, the pleasure of the company. DC, the neurotoxin, Cooper, Ari . . . all of that seemed a distant memory, like it was a movie he'd seen long ago, or a story someone else had told him. The only thing that mattered in this moment was Jojo.

"Do you feel like dessert?" Jack asked when they were finished eating. "Do you like chocolate?"

Jojo grinned. "Is that a trick question? Of course."

He had the perfect thing. He wasn't much of a fan of desserts, but he had a frozen soufflé he could quickly heat up in the oven and serve with a scoop of ice cream.

"You're not having one?" Jojo asked when he set the soufflé dish and ice cream in front of her. "This also looks delicious, by the way." She picked up the spoon and took a bite. "Jack, is there anything you can't do? This is better than what you'd get in a restaurant."

It was not so much the compliment but the fact that she was clearly enjoying herself so thoroughly that made the smile stretch across Jack's face. "One of the first people I met when I came to Shanghai was a guy who was a chef at this French restaurant on the Bund, and he gave me his recipe."

"I've had some good soufflés before, I mean it—this is right up there with the best ones I had in France."

"It took me quite a while to get the hang of it."

"It was well worth the effort." She took another bite. "Though I do find it interesting that someone who doesn't like desserts would spend the time to learn how to make it. That's one of the things I like about you though—you're not someone who only does things just because it personally benefits you. Most people are not like that."

"Now you're making me blush," Jack said, and he was glad he made the joke because he did in fact feel like his face was flushed. Probably just the wine. Yes, that was it.

"You shouldn't blush; you should take a bow. You put together an incredible meal and you made it seem effortless. I can't help but be impressed."

"I'm just so happy you were able to come over," Jack said. "It's great getting to see you. I have to confess; I did think about you quite a bit when I was away."

Jojo took her final bite of soufflé. "Did you," she said as she set the spoon into the empty bowl. "That's interesting, because I found myself thinking about *you* quite a bit."

There was a moment of silence, which stretched to another, then another, but it didn't feel awkward, and Jack did not feel the need to fill the space with words.

"Would you like to see the rest of the apartment?" he asked.

"I'd love to."

He realized, too late, that this probably seemed like a ploy to get her into the bedroom, as there wasn't much that she hadn't seen yet—kitchen opened into the living room, there was a short hallway with the bathroom, and then his bedroom. But the room had two windows side-by-side that looked out on the street and the tall, leafy trees. It was a view Jack had always enjoyed, and he went to the window now to look out, thinking he'd show Jojo, but she had moved to the other side of the room to look at his bookshelf.

Jack looked out the window to the street below. A few people walked by, someone rode past on a bicycle. He was about to turn away when he saw someone standing on the other side of the street, just standing there on the sidewalk, looking up at Jack's building. The person wore a sweatshirt with the hood pulled up, and because it was dark and the glow of the streetlight did not extend far enough, it was impossible for Jack to make out any distinguishing features. Other than it seemed odd that someone would be standing out there like this, looking up at his building.

It could be nothing; or, it could be something, but have nothing to do with him. He stood there a moment longer, watching. He doubted that anyone in China would know the role he had been recruited to play, yet he also didn't want to be willfully ignorant. Cooper had told him that there was danger involved—perhaps this was someone trying to send him a message.

He turned away from the window, pulling the curtain across, nearly bumping into Jojo, who had come up behind him.

"You have a nice bedroom," she said. She took a step closer to him, close enough that he could easily reach out and encircle her waist with his arms, which he did. He kept his eyes on hers as he slowly leaned closer; when their lips met he closed his eyes and let himself get lost in the sensation—her arms going around his neck, the feel of her lips moving against his, the tips of their tongues touching, lightly at first and then with more force.

Finally, they pulled apart, both breathless and smiling. "I'm glad you think I have a nice bedroom," Jack said, his arms still around her waist. "I have a nice bed, too, that I'd be more than happy to show you. Only if that's okay with you, of course."

He would understand if she didn't want to, if she felt things were progressing too quickly. But he hoped otherwise.

"It's more than okay," she said. He smiled as they slowly made their way over to his bed.

Several hours later, they lay next to each other in the dark, the muted light from the full moon trying to muscle its way through the closed curtain. Jack stood up and pushed the fabric back, letting the milky light spill into the room.

"I love moonlight," Jojo said when he climbed back into bed next to her.

"There's an app that controls the timing, size, and location of the moon," he said. "The *Moon App*. I used that tonight for us."

"Could you be more of a gentleman? I guess there is an app for everything."

They both laughed. Jojo rolled to her side and rested her head on Jack's shoulder, draped an arm over his chest.

"So," she said. "I was wondering . . . Would you mind if I spent the night?"

"There's nothing I'd like more."

"Then I guess you probably won't mind if I just stay curled up against you all night."

"I would love that. And I hope you're not just teasing me."

"I wouldn't joke about something like that. Although . . . maybe we won't stay curled up *all* night . . ." She tilted her head back to look up at him and he leaned closer and they started to kiss again.

Morning arrived too soon, but Jack couldn't think of a better way to wake up than his limbs entwined with Jojo's. She was still fast asleep, and he just lay there for a few moments and watched her. He could see her as a child, the little girl in the photo that had fallen out of the book that night he'd been to her place, and he again found himself marveling at the fact of her existence, at the fact that they had found each other. Because that was how he felt about it—he'd been looking for her all this time yet hadn't realized it.

She sighed but didn't wake, and rolled over, her long hair dark against her pale shoulder. Jack slipped out of bed and quietly went into the bathroom. When he was done in there, he checked his two phones, then his email. No urgent messages from Ari or America. That was good.

When he returned to the room, Jojo was beginning to stir. She stretched and yawned, and Jack went over and sat at the edge of the bed.

"Good morning," he said. "How do you like your coffee?"

"Black. With cream and sugar," she deadpanned.

He cracked a smile and then she did too. "You stay right there," he said. "You deserve coffee in bed."

"I will not argue with that. Although after last night, you probably deserve coffee in bed." She gave him a coy look. "Three times in one night is quite impressive."

He returned her smile but felt himself blushing, so he hurried out to the kitchen to get started on the coffee. Last night had been spectacular, yes, beyond what he had ever imagined. Had it been four times? He'd lost track, because everything just sort of blurred together in this almost transcendental experience of the best sensations Jack had ever felt.

While the water was heating for coffee, Jack cleaned up last night's dishes. He had a few blueberry muffins he'd picked up at the nearby bakery a day ago; they wouldn't be as fresh, but they'd still be good, and he didn't have much else to offer in the way of breakfast.

He returned to the bedroom and put Jojo's cup on the bedside table next to her. She sat up and reached for it, and he placed the plate of muffins in front of her.

"This is all I can offer you," he said. "If I had known you were going to stay over—"

"You would've had the ingredients for a five-course brunch?" she asked, taking a sip. She closed her eyes. "Oh, but this coffee is good. Mmm." She held her face over the cup and inhaled.

"It's Peet's. From California. They do make good coffee." He reached for his phone. "Care for a little music to go along with your coffee?"

"That would be excellent."

He scrolled through until he found what he was looking for. George Winston playing Pachelbel's "Variations on the Kanon." He wondered if Jojo would recognize this version.

A few seconds in, she frowned. "I know the song," she said, "but I don't think I've heard this version before."

"George Winston," Jack said.

She listened for a few more moment. "It's . . . interesting," she said. "Do you know Ping Ping?"

"I do," he said. Ping Ping was a famous Chinese pianist whose work Jack was familiar with. "He's great."

He sat on the bed with her and took a sip of his own coffee. "So. What do you have on your agenda for today?"

"I have to meet up with a client about a possible sculpture he wants to commission. And after that, I'm going to do some work at my studio and then I'll be at the bar tonight. I'm free tomorrow, though . . . If tomorrow isn't too soon for you to see me."

"What are you talking about? I'd see you every day if I could. Maybe I'll stop by the bar tonight. But yes, I'd love to see you tomorrow."

"Great. It's a plan then."

After they finished their coffee, Jojo went and took a shower. Jack cleaned up their coffee cups and the muffin plate, and then went back into the bedroom and made up the bed. He stopped and looked out the window, the sunlight dappling the sidewalk as it shown through the canopy of leaves.

And then he saw the person.

It was the same person from last night, Jack was certain of it. He squinted, trying to make out anything that might clue him to who this was, but he was too far away. He was now leaning against the trunk of one of the trees, looking rather casual and not too out of place, but there was something about his stance that made Jack certain it was the same guy.

He could hear Jojo singing something in the shower, though he couldn't quite make out what it was. And then the water turned off, and she appeared a few moments later, her hair damp, her face bright. She had the smoothest skin.

"I don't think I've ever felt this relaxed," she said. "But unfortunately, I have to run to meet with that client on time."

She ordered a car and Jack walked her outside, on alert for the person. And there he was, still leaning against the tree. But when he saw Jack he abruptly turned and hurried around the block, so when Jojo stepped out, a few steps behind Jack, he was gone.

Jack stood there, adrenaline coursing through him. It *might be nothing*, he thought, but he knew that wasn't true. It was something; he just wasn't sure what.

But he pushed the concern from his mind as he took a step back toward Jojo. He smiled at her as her car pulled to stop in front of them.

"I had such a great time with you," he said. "Thank you."

"I did, too. Have a great day, and I'll be in touch later about tomorrow."

She stepped into the car and Jack closed the door behind her. He had wanted to take her in his arms, give her a Hollywood-worthy kiss, but he knew she needed to get on her way, she didn't want to be late.

And he had all his nice memories of last night to buoy him through the day, until he was able to see her tomorrow.

CHAPTER 20

Jack arrived in Beijing with one thing on his mind: Jojo.

He knew he was supposed to be focused on whatever it was he needed to do to see that things went smoothly, but the past several days had been more magical than anything Jack could ever recall. It was only natural, then, that he would not be able to stop thinking about her—not just being intimate, but walking down the street together, sitting close at the little dumpling restaurant near her place, trying out a new recipe at Jack's that he had found online.

But now he was here in the executive lounge of the JW Marriott Beijing, at a table with Ari while they waited for Joshua.

"He'll be with this guy, David," Ari said. "An American. He's involved in the music industry, but he came to China because . . . Well, guess why."

Jack took a sip of his beer. "Um . . . he's into karaoke?"

"Ha. Close. He wants to recreate the 'We Are the World' song with singers across the world."

"Ambitious."

"He's a hoot; he'll be good comic relief."

A few minutes later, they arrived. Joshua was young, maybe in his early thirties, Jack guessed. He had short, light brown hair and hazel eyes and one of those open, friendly faces that made him seem like someone you had met before.

"I don't know you from somewhere, do I?" Jack asked, half-joking.

Joshua smiled. "Doubtful. Though you're not the first person to ask me that."

"I have some good news," David said. He was tall and lanky, with a headful of unruly, steel-colored hair. "We've selected a date for the performance."

"That's great," Ari said.

"Yes, well, the venue and scheduling was easy; the hard part will be securing sizable sponsors to fund the venture. But come on—who could resist something like this?"

"You have a partner?" Jack asked.

"I do. And they want the money to go through them, instead of straight to me, but we're going to figure out the details later."

Jack made a mental note to talk to David in private later, and maybe give him a few tips, if he was interested. David's partner was likely a government related entity and if David gave the group control of the money, he wouldn't be able to access it unless he first paid a hefty fee. If he was receptive to Jack's advice, he'd tell him to never allow his business to be controlled like that.

"We should go celebrate," David said. "Who feels like some duck?"

It had been a while since Jack last had duck, and at the mention of it, his mouth immediately started watering. "I'm in," he said.

The place they walked to was called Da Tong, one of the best duck restaurants in the world. It was located in a modern building with an open floor plan, and nearly every table was occupied. Toward the back of the restaurant, Jack could see the uncooked ducks hanging from a rack, waiting for their turn to be placed into the wooden oven.

"This place is always hoppin'," David said. "Just a minute, please."

Jack watched him approach one of the staff members, but he was too far away, and the chatter in the restaurant was too loud for him to be able to hear what he was saying.

"David knows everybody," Ari said.

"It sure seems like he does," Jack replied, watching as another staff member came over to hear what David was saying. Then, the conversation appeared to end and David turned and walked back toward them.

"I bet he's going to tell us he received—"

"Follow me if you will, gentlemen, down to our private room," David said, grinning. "Boy, doesn't that duck smell good."

The room was down a corridor away from the bustle of the main restaurant. There was a large round table in the center of the room, and the walls were covered in wallpaper featuring delicate pink cherry blossoms against a marbled, cream-colored background.

David looked over to Jack. "I understand you speak Chinese. Why don't you order for the table."

"Sure." Jack took the menu and spent several minutes asking questions and ordering from the menu as the waiter leaned over his shoulder.

After the waiter left, Joshua looked at Jack. "Your Chinese is impressive," he said. "It's like you're from Beijing."

Jack smiled, despite always feeling a bit of embarrassment whenever someone said something like that. "I was fortunate to have some great teachers in school and when I first arrived here," he said. "Most were from Beijing."

"Wish I had a similar experience," Joshua said, and he did sound regretful, which Jack found oddly touching. "It would make doing business easier."

"Doing business in China is hard."

"No kidding. If you only knew what I went through."

"Tell me."

"Well, China needs high-quality jet fuel. It doesn't have the capacity to produce what it needs. At the same time, Israel has excess capacity and is willing to sell. Sounds like a win-win, right? But getting approval in China is a nightmare."

"I bet," Jack said. "What made you decide to get into jet fuel business anyhow?"

"My dad suggested it; he's in the Air Force. But it's not like this is plutonium," Joshua said, sighing. He looked truly perplexed about the whole thing. "It's pretty basic to test it to check the quality. Anyway, the transfer mechanisms for the fuel, funds processing, verification, and approvals took a huge amount of time and investment. Approval from China's military took nine months alone. They had to do background checks on everyone!"

David leaned over and clapped Joshua on the back. "Don't let this face fool you," he said. "It was his homegrown charm and his boyish good looks that eventually won them over."

Joshua's face reddened and he looked down, clearly uncomfortable with the compliment. "I don't think it was that."

"Did you do national service in Israel?" Jack asked, hoping to steer the conversation back to more comfortable territory.

"I did, for five years. It was the most physically challenging experience of my life. I learned so much and I did some things I'll never forget. Also made some great, lifelong friends."

"I can only imagine." Jack found it reassuring that Joshua had served for so long and had what sounded like very solid experience.

"Let's connect via WeChat," Joshua said.

Right after Jack gave Joshua his WeChat ID, two ducks arrived, and Jack's hunger kicked into high gear just at the sight of them. He grabbed his chopsticks as the others around him did the same. He took a thin pancake and set it on his plate, then grabbed some duck, dipping it first in plum sauce. He placed the duck on the pancake and then added some sliced cucumber and onion. He took the first delectable bite and couldn't help but sight at the rich, savory flavor of the tender duck meat, the spice of the onion, the mellow coolness of the cucumber. It was so good he immediately thought of Jojo and wished that he was sharing the meal with her.

When everyone had eaten their fill, David insisted on taking care of the bill, with little fanfare. They all thanked him as they stepped outside.

"That was delicious," Jack said. He felt beyond satiated; and, the only thing he wanted to do now was go back to his hotel room and send Jojo a message.

"One of my favorite places," David said. "And it's even better when I get to share the meal with good company! You ordered perfectly."

Jack fell in step next to David; Ari and Joshua were a few paces behind them. They stopped as they neared an intersection, and Jack observed the wide sidewalks with trees, the bike and scooter lanes, the way Beijing was clearly engaging in a concerted effort to make the city green.

They started to cross the street. Jack looked before he stepped off the curb, but it seemed a car suddenly appeared out of nowhere, careening toward them. Jack put his arm out, stopping David mid-step.

"Jesus Christ!" David exclaimed. "He totally just brushed me!"

The car had to stop a few feet past them anyway, as there was traffic, and it seemed the driver waited until the very last moment to slam on the brakes and come to a screeching halt. Jack had become so accustomed to how dangerous many of the drivers in China were. Not because they were malicious or trying to hurt anyone, but because things were generally quite chaotic. Bicycles and motorcycles zipping along on the sidewalk, cars trying to beat the light before it turned red, flying through intersections, the cacophony of horns blasting nearly all the time. It was dangerous to be a pedestrian.

Before Jack realized what was happening, David had gone over to the car and reached in the open window. Though it was darker inside the car, it appeared to Jack that David had just slapped the driver in the face. A light slap, but a slap nonetheless. The driver's side door flew open and a middle-aged man in wire rimmed glasses, got out, sputtering in anger. Jack hurried over, Ari and Joshua right behind him.

"Don't hit him," Jack said to David. "Unless you want to end up in jail. Let me take care of this."

He positioned himself between David and the driver, whose eyes darted back and forth angrily, first on David, then Jack, then back to David again. "Do you see that camera?" Jack said to the man in Chinese. He pointed to the camera affixed near the stop lights. The man looked where Jack was pointing. "Do you think the police might be interested in reviewing the video and seeing that you hit my friend?"

"I did not hit your friend!" the man snapped. "Your friend hit *me*."

"After you hit him with your car."

"That did not happen. Your friend isn't hurt."

"See, the video is going to show otherwise. Just because you didn't mow him down doesn't mean you didn't make contact with him. Should we get the police down here to sort things out? Or do you want to get back into your car and be on your way? If you choose that option, we'll do the same."

For several moments, the man didn't say anything. He looked at Jack, then David, then he appeared to notice that Ari and Joshua were right there, too. He was outnumbered, and Jack could see that he was not completely sure if he had hit David or not. Finally, he turned and got back in his car, muttering something under his breath. Jack exhaled and looked at David, who grinned and started to clap.

"That could not have been handled any better," he said. "I mean, I could've handled myself better, but when is that not the case?"

"I'm just glad that didn't escalate," Ari said.

"Yeah, are you okay?" Joshua asked. He shook his head. "It doesn't matter how long I live in China, I don't think I will ever get used to the way people around here drive."

"That's the point," Ari said. "They want to keep you on your toes. Being a pedestrian in China—the next big extreme sport. Like mixed martial arts, except instead of an octagon, it's the roads and sidewalks."

"Hey, I think you're onto something," David said. "That sounds like it would be wildly popular!"

Ari grinned. "Something to work on after your musical project is wrapped up."

"I love it. Keep the ideas coming. So long as we have Jack around to de-escalate any situation, I think we'll be good." David looked at him. "Sound good, Jack? You're available, right?"

"Yeah, but only if it's called something like *Pedestrian Death Match*."

David laughed and clapped him on the back. "I'll start getting the merchandise made up tomorrow."

* * *

Jack was tired when he finally arrived back to his hotel room, and glad for the respite of quiet after his evening out with Ari, Joshua, and David. Not that he hadn't a good time—both Joshua and David were interesting and intriguing people.

He sent Jojo a message, stopping short of saying he missed her, but that he had tomorrow night free and was wondering if she had any recommendations on what he should do. He figured she'd be able to give him a few good suggestions. What he wasn't expecting, though, was her response: *How about having dinner with me?*

I wish, he wrote back. *Still in Beijing. Be back in a few days, though.*

I know. I was thinking I might come up there tomorrow. We could do dinner. Maybe I could even spend the night. Then see my dad the next day.

Jack felt his spirits lift immediately, a smile spread across his face, as he wrote back and told her that would be perfect.

CHAPTER 21

At five-thirty, Jack went down to the hotel lobby to wait for Jojo. He sat in the lounge, near the large front window so he could see her arrive. When she stepped out of the car, wearing slim black pants and a white button-down shirt, Jack felt a fluttering in his solar plexus, a pleasant feeling spread across him just at the anticipation of being near her. He hurried outside. She was wearing the glasses he liked.

"Hey," he said, and she turned toward him, brushing her hair back as she did so.

"Jack! Hello." Her smile matched his as she took a step closer but stopped short of hugging him. That was okay; Jack didn't mind that she didn't want to display affection in public. Some people just didn't. Being here next to her was enough, and besides, he hoped to display all of the affection he wanted to later, in the privacy of his hotel room.

"You look great," he said.

"I never feel that great after traveling, no matter how short the trip. But, thank you. You're looking quite handsome yourself."

"Why thank you," he said. "Let me take your suitcase."

Jack picked up her small black suitcase and they made their way into the hotel. When they arrived to his room, he unlocked the door and they stepped inside. He put Jojo's suitcase down and they both stood there for a moment, neither saying anything. He looked at her, and her eyes seemed to be communicating something, seemed to be saying to him that the only thing she wanted was for him to wrap his arms around her.

"You're a tease," she finally said.

His eyebrows shot up. "Me?"

She walked right up to him, stopped when less than an inch separated the length of their bodies. She reached her hand up and gently placed it on the back of his head, pulling his face toward hers. His eyes closed as their lips met–bliss. He kissed her back, but then she pulled away, and he opened his eyes. She took a step back, serious expression on her face.

"What?" he asked. "Is everything okay?"

The serious look remained on her face for another second, but then the façade broke and she grinned as she jumped onto him, wrapping her legs around his waist, her arms around his neck.

"Now it is," she whispered, her breath warm on his ear.

*　*　*

The next morning, they ordered room service and had breakfast in bed. Jack would've been more than content not to move from the bed for the rest of his time here with Jojo, but he also wanted to go out and do things with her.

"I told my dad I'd visit with him today," Jojo said as she rifled through her suitcase. Jack was dressed and finishing up his second cup of coffee, fully enjoying the sight of Jojo in her underwear, looking for whatever outfit she planned to wear. "I'm not sure about the exact timing yet, though. And I also need to meet up with a few art world people."

"Sounds like you have a packed schedule. Thank you for fitting me in." He downed the last of his coffee. "What do you have to do with the art world people?"

She pulled a rose-colored long-sleeve shirt over her head. "I need to meet with Zhang Wang, the ex-chairman of the Department of Sculpture. At the Central Academy of Fine Arts. They've commissioned me to do a statue for the 798 Art District." She smiled, clearly proud of this development. As she should be, Jack thought.

"Zhang Wang was largely responsible for bringing contemporary art to China. His Mao series is historic."

"You're absolutely right. He draws on the powerful image of the Mao suit, not as an element of revolutionary attire but as a symbol of restriction and limitation. He's perhaps the most important and influential artist in China. Are you familiar with 798?"

"A little," Jack said. "But tell me more about it. Where will your statue be? What is the statue going to be? What materials are you going to use?"

Jojo laughed. "You have a lot of questions."

"How could I not? I can't help but be impressed by how accomplished my girlfriend is." The word slipped out before he was able to censor himself—but if he were to be honest, that was how he felt. Things felt right when Jojo was around, and he hoped that they would be able to spend more time together. "Err . . ." He looked at her. "Did I just say that?"

"Girlfriend," she repeated, a smile on her face. "Is that what I am to you? I could get used to that."

"Well . . . We haven't had that conversation yet. And to be honest, I've been *thinking* of you like my girlfriend for . . . a while now. So, I guess it would be nice to make it official. Only if you want to, though," he added.

She dropped whatever article of clothing she had been holding and came over to him, in her shirt and underwear, and sat in his lap. He put his arm around her lower back, his hand resting atop her smooth thigh.

"Hmm," she said. "Do I want to . . . I suppose I could be convinced."

She leaned down and kissed him.

"Okay," she said, brushing his hair back from his forehead. "I'm convinced."

"You've just made me a very happy man."

"Do you know the history of 798?" Jojo asked, sliding off his lap. She began rummaging through her suitcase again.

"I don't, not really."

"Well, it produced military and civilian equipment in 1951, but as a state-run facility. It underwent a gradual decline and eventually became obsolete. That's when artists moved in to take advantage of the low rents, and so did the galleries. They liked the large factories and the fact that the windows faced north because the light in that direction casts fewer shadows."

"Interesting," Jack said. "I didn't know that. But I'd heard it was very successful."

"It's become a victim of its own success. Now you have lofts, publishing firms, design companies, high-end tailor shops, cafés, fancy restaurants. All that stuff. And nearby there are all sorts of developments. The rents have skyrocketed and artists can't afford to rent space there now. And, to be honest, I want my statue to take this into account. Also, I'd like to meet up with some of my classmates from Tsinghua University."

"What was that like, going to school there?"

"Oh, it was incredible. I loved it. And the campus is beautiful."

"What school were you in?"

"The Academy of Arts and Design. It's great for connections. But the enrollment system isn't fair. They decide how many people will be admitted from each province, so some people get in with low test scores." She shook her head. "I even had one classmate whose dad paid a bribe to a police commissioner in another province to take the Gaokao test there."

"I can't say things are much different in America," Jack said. "I mean, they are, obviously, but there's also plenty of bribery and scandals when it comes to getting into college there. Not to mention the scandal in plain sight, which would be how insanely expensive tuition has gotten. I'm glad I'm not graduating now; some kids are graduating close to one hundred thousand dollars in debt. I was fortunate to go to a good school and not to have to take out any loans, but that's certainly not the case for most people."

"I agree," Jojo said. "A decent education should not just be the right of those who can afford it. I know I was really lucky, too, and I try to never take it for granted. I've had many opportunities that other people have not. But . . . sometimes it does seem like a great deal of what happens—in life, not just with education—seems to come down to good luck."

"Some," Jack said. "But it's not the only thing. You have to help luck along."

Jojo gave him a skeptical look. "Help it along? How do you do that?"

"Well, I think some people would say something like that person's dad paying the commissioner is helping luck along."

"Really? I'd just call it bribery."

"That too. It's fairly common everywhere, though. Everyone just wants to have an advantage. It's like all the babies I see going back to China from the United States. Their parents just want to give them an advantage. Your own parents might not go so far as to bribe someone to get you into a certain program, but I bet they want what's best for you. And I think sometimes, that desire of wanting what's best, can fog an otherwise rational person's mind."

Jojo nodded, a frown on her face. "I hear what you're saying. But that still doesn't excuse it, right? I mean, just because you're well-intentioned does not mean that it's now okay to be out there doing something illegal."

"So if your father paid a bribe to get you into a school you otherwise probably wouldn't get into, you would refuse to go?"

"I'm not saying that. I don't know, to be honest. What I *do* know, though, is that my father would never do something like that. He's not that sort of person."

"Oh, I'm not saying that he is—I've never even met him." Jack paused, let the sentiment hang in the air a moment. He wasn't expecting to tag along with Jojo and meet her dad, but he'd be lying if he said he wasn't curious about the man. "What's your dad's name, by the way?" he asked.

But Jojo didn't seem to hear him. She stepped into a pair of form-fitting black pants, and Jack took a moment to just appreciate the view. She turned to face him, a thoughtful expression on her face.

"You're right," she said. "As much as I'd like to think I'm my father's daughter and would always act with honor and integrity, if that was the only way I'd get into a good school, I probably would do it." She shrugged. "I guess I'm lucky that my dad would never do something like that in the first place, so I won't be faced with that situation."

"It is hard to know exactly what you'd do, until you're in the situation," Jack said. "I know we'd all like to *think* we'd do the right thing, but it can be an entirely different matter when you're right in the thick of it."

When Jojo was done getting dressed, they headed out into Beijing. There was a bookstore Jojo needed to go to pick up a gift for Zhang Wang before she went to see him, and Jack thought it would be nice if they spent a little time together walking around the city.

Jack had lived in Beijing when he first came to China, and he enjoyed the city, though the pollution was worse here than in Shanghai, as it was surrounded by mountains.

They went to Sanlitun, a district in Beijing known for its upscale stores and eclectic restaurants and cafes. Jack was familiar with the bookstore that Jojo wanted to go to, though he was not familiar with the book that she was picking up.

"I had to special order it," she said, "but they called me yesterday to say that it had arrived."

It was a large book, like the sort of thing someone might display on their coffee table.

"Here it is," she said. He happened to catch sight of the price, and he blinked, certain that he had seen it wrong.

Two thousand dollars?

No, that had to be a mistake—

But he stood beside Jojo as she paid for it, and it certainly was two thousand dollars. A price tag she did not even bat an eyelash over. He fidgeted, vacillating between not wanting to say anything because it wasn't any of his business how much Jojo paid for a book, but also being unable to fathom how someone could do such a thing.

"That's . . . that's quite the expensive gift you have there," he said as they were leaving the store. "I didn't even realize a book could be that expensive."

"They can be more expensive than this," Jojo said. "But I know Zhang Wang will appreciate this."

I would hope so, Jack thought, though he had the sense not to say it out loud. It wasn't, after all, up to him to decide how much Jojo could spend on a gift for a friend; the amount seemed completely over the top to him, but he knew that many people of means in China gave extravagant gifts—when he had first come to China, one of his co-workers at the bank he was employed at told him about his sister, who had an entire cabinet full of expensive electronic gadgets—iPhones, tablets, Airpods—that she would give as gifts.

"I'm sure he will," Jack finally said. "Though I bet he'll be even more happy just to see you."

They were approaching a Starbucks, and Jack asked Jojo if she wanted to get a coffee. They took their drinks and sat at one of the empty tables outside and people watched.

"I was thinking of maybe trying out a class there," Jojo said. Jack looked in the direction she had just pointed, saw several storefronts, then his eyes alighted on an orange sign that read, in white sans serif font: SpaceCycle.

"SpaceCycle?" he said. "What's that?"

"It's a nice boutique yoga and spinning studio. I've heard good things about it."

As if on cue, the SpaceCycle door opened and a crowd of flushed, smiling people in workout attire came out.

No better marketing than that, Jack thought. He'd never done a spin class, but he knew they were intense, and he imagined the high you experienced after completing a class was probably pretty good.

"Unfortunately," he said, "I didn't pack my cycling kit."

Jojo grinned. "No worries; I wasn't going to take a class here; they also have a studio in Shanghai."

"Oh boy," Jack said, groaning. But he'd do most anything with Jojo; he was just happy to be around her.

Several of the people who had just exited SpaceCycle headed toward Starbucks, and Jack had to admit, they all looked the picture of health. One of the girls in the group, who wore cropped pink leggings and a gray hoodie, veered over to their table, a big smile on her face.

"Jojo!" she exclaimed.

Jack could tell that for a second, Jojo didn't recognize who this was, but then she did and she stood up and he watched as the two hugged.

"It's so funny I'm seeing you right now," the girl said, "I was just visiting with my parents the other night and my dad said he went out to dinner with your dad the other night. Which made me wonder how you were doing—and now here you are! What are the chances?"

"It was meant to be," Jojo said. She turned to Jack. "This is my boyfriend, Jack." He smiled at the introduction, liking how it sounded. "Jack, this is Amy, who I went to school with."

"*Oui, il y a une vie*," Amy said, grinning.

Jojo laughed. "Yes, it does feel like a lifetime ago."

Amy held out her hand, and Jack stood up and shook it.

"So nice to meet you."

"You too." She shot a conspiratorial look at Jojo. "This must be a new relationship, because apparently our fathers were talking about the fact that both of us are still single!"

"Yes, every father's worst nightmare—that his daughter is going to become a spinster." Jojo rolled her eyes. "You're right, though, Amy, this is a new relationship, and I haven't told my father yet. Soon, though."

"I won't say a word."

"Thanks. You want to hang out for a little bit?"

"I would love to, but I actually have to get home and shower because..." She paused, her grin widening, "I have a date! We're just getting lunch, but... I'm pretty positive about this one!"

"That was a blast from the past," Jojo said, after Amy had left. "I can't remember the last time we saw each other. We went to school together at Tsinghua and then we lived together in France for a while. Our parents have known each other forever, so Amy and I pretty much started hanging out when we were babies. And our fathers have remained good friends all these years. I'll have to tell my dad I ran into Amy."

Jack thought of asking whether or not Jojo was also going to tell her father that she had a boyfriend, but he didn't want to pressure her if she wasn't, and it didn't matter to him either way.

After their coffee, they walked around a little more, and then it was time for Jojo to go meet up with Zhang Wang.

"I'm so glad I spent some time with you here," Jack said. "It was an unexpected, but most welcome, surprise."

"I like being able to surprise you, Jack Gold," she said. "Because you seem like the sort of person who is not easily surprised. Oh yeah, I almost forgot—Are you available this Friday evening? I'm having a small get together at my place."

"I'd love to," he said. "I'm already looking forward to it."

"Excellent. I think it's going to be a fun evening."

He waited to see if she was going to give him a hug before she departed; he wanted to hug her goodbye, but not if she was uncomfortable with the public display of affection. But then she stepped closer and wrapped her arms around him and he returned the hug, kissed the top of her head, caught the faint sweet scent of the botanical shampoo she used. She looked up at him, lips parted slightly, and he leaned down and kissed her. A quick kiss, but he felt electrified by it nonetheless.

"I hope you have a good rest of your visit," he told her. "I'll see you soon."

She smiled. "Yes, you will. Have a good flight back."

CHAPTER 22

The day after Jack returned to Shanghai, he received a text message on his black phone, stating there was a discrepancy with his passport. *Incorrect data input by the stateside issuing office.* He was requested to come into the U.S. Consulate in Shanghai at his earliest convenience.

Jack re-read the message, then went online and scheduled his appointment, which he was able to do later that day. He was glad there wasn't a wait time, as he had a feeling that the passport wasn't the issue.

He tried to keep his mind focused on other things. He sent Jojo a message and said he hoped she was enjoying her visit and that he was looking forward to her return. He answered an email from Andrew and then sent a few more work-related emails out. Read his reply from Jojo, who said she was having a good time and would be back tomorrow.

Can't wait, he wrote back. She had asked what he was up to for the day, and he started to write out that he was going to the consulate, but then stopped and deleted it. Yes, he could say he was going to the consulate and leave it at that, but what if she asked more questions? He'd be forced to lie to her, and he already felt uncomfortable with his deception.

Being with Jojo made him feel so good, there was no way he could be convinced that there was anything wrong with them being together.

But being involved with something bigger than himself, something that would make a difference in lives of countless people—he could not be convinced that was wrong, either.

He sighed. The best he could do was hope that the outcome for both situations would be optimal.

*   *   *

The consular services of the American embassy were located in an unglamorous high-rise. Upon entering, Jack had to relinquish all his electronic devices and then go through a metal detector. Then, he went over to a window and informed the man at the desk that he was there for an appointment regarding his passport. The man directed him to a room down the hallway to wait for assistance. There were half a dozen chairs and a coffee table with magazines, but no other people in the room. Jack took a seat and waited.

A red-haired woman came to the window and asked him for his passport, which he gave to her. She thanked him and left through a door in back, and Jack resumed waiting. His mind drifted to Jojo. His girlfriend. He smiled a little at the thought.

When the door opened again, Jack expected to see the red-haired woman, but it was a different woman, and she motioned him to follow her into a smaller room right next door. There she slid the phone under the glass to him.

"Mr. Gold, someone would like to speak with you."

He took the phone. "Hello?"

"Hi Jack," came the familiar voice. "It's Officer Cooper. How are you?"

"Doing all right," Jack said.

"Listen, sorry for having you come down to the consulate, but I needed to speak with you on a secure line."

"I understand."

"They're tracking you via your iPhone and the microchip in your passport, which we suspected all along."

Jack shouldn't have felt surprised by this, but he did. It was also a significant invasion of his privacy.

"They've just heightened their observation activity," Cooper continued. "Things are going to speed up pretty soon, so I want you to be prepared."

"I appreciate the head's up." Jack paused, thinking about the strange man he'd seen twice now, the one with the scar. "Now, when you say 'heightened their observation activity' does that include being followed?"

"Followed? Do you think someone's following you?"

"Well . . . I'm not sure. It might be nothing."

"Everything we know indicates only heightened observation activity via tracking devices, but I would encourage you to be diligent about anything unusual you notice, and to be in touch about it immediately. As I know you're aware, we want this to go seamlessly. Expect Joshua to send you a WeChat message about visiting his friends. You are going to put four or five drops—no more than that—of the neurotoxin on your right hand just before you get there. Also—be sure you don't compliment the design of the CCTV headquarters building. They're not proud of it."

"Got it."

"So you'll need to make sure to ask for a tour," Cooper said. "It should happen within three to four days, not sooner. The neurotoxin will need time to spread. Tell them that you and your friends are fascinated by the idea of seeing inside. We need to make sure you, Ari, Joshua, and Tony Woo are on the list to get in. We'll arrange for you to meet Tony very soon. All three of these men are essential. And you, too."

Jack silently repeated what Cooper said, making sure he committed to memory, even though he was certain that Joshua would also be well aware of just what steps needed to be taken.

"Tony Woo has been fully briefed," Cooper said. "He'll be the one being broadcast to the entire Chinese population."

"What will he be saying?"

Cooper exhaled. "He'll be talking about how the communist party has changed, about the president and corruption, how we are trying to provide information to everyone, so they are aware. This is just a synopsis; he'll put it much more eloquently. But you don't need to worry about that; there are factions of the military and the party who support this change and a few select people will be assisting us." He paused. "We're doing it because they are too scared to do it. They need outside assistance or nothing would ever happen. President Zhao has too much power. Anyway, Jack, I have to go, but I'll be in touch. Like I said, things are going to start speeding up now, so be ready. I know you will be."

Immediately after the call ended, the door opened and the red-haired woman came back in. She took the phone and slid Jack his new passport. "This is a temporary passport. Good for one year."

"Great, thank you."

"That'll be one hundred and forty-five dollars, please."

Of course, Jack thought, giving her a slightly chagrinned smile as he stood and reached for his wallet, *I would have to pay for the "incorrect data input."* He started to hand her renminbi but she shook her head.

"I'm sorry; American cash or credit cards only."

His chagrined smile enlarged a little. "Sure," he said. "Here you go."

Once the payment was processed and he had his card back, Jack was free to go. He picked up his two phones and then quickly left the building, eager to be out of there. He looked at his new passport before he slipped it into his pocket; no chip. He did feel relief knowing that he wasn't being tracked, at least not until they figured out another way to do so.

CHAPTER 23

Jack was amazed when he entered Jojo's loft that Friday evening. Gone were all the statues and the pedestals, the piano had been pushed forward and behind it were two room dividers—beautiful gold leaf screens with bamboo flowers—and several young men were setting up tables and chairs. They glanced at Jack but then went back to their work.

"Jojo?" Jack called.

"Up here!" she yelled, peeking her head over the loft railing. "Come on up."

"I thought you were just having a few friends over," he said as he made his way up the stairs. She smiled and came over to him and they embraced, kissed.

"Just a few," she said. "Thirty-five at most."

He gave her another kiss. "If that's just *a few* then I'm not sure I want to see what *a lot* is. You have a way better social life than I do."

"Well, that's all going to change tonight, because you're going to get to meet my friends and I know they'll think you're as great as I do. I've told a few of them about you and they're certainly eager to meet you."

"Uh-oh," Jack said. "I hope I live up to everyone's expectations. What can I do to help?"

"I think things are pretty good at the moment. My Ayi is in the kitchen making the appetizers. They're almost done getting the tables and chairs set up and someone's coming to serve drinks. I just have to finish getting dressed and then I bet people will start showing up; I have a few friends that always show up early."

He waited until Jojo finished getting dressed. She wore a strapless black maxi dress that showed off her collarbone, which Jack was suddenly overcome with the desire to run his finger along. He could wait, though—it was time to go down for the party.

Things were almost finished being set up. He saw the bartender near the front door, stationed behind two tables covered in a black cloth. Wine, beer, and small bottles of Evian water sat on the tables, and there were two ice chests with several jugs of what looked like orange juice and watermelon juice. The set up was simple but elegant.

Jack wandered over to the kitchen and introduced himself to Jojo's Ayi, who was busy arranging little sandwiches on a tray, crusts cut off. He smiled at the sight of it.

People had started to arrive, and as they came into the loft and greeted Jojo, Jack saw that everyone was dressed impeccably—the women wore fancy dresses, the men were in suits. Jojo hugged each guest and many kissed both of her cheeks. To Jack, it looked like a family reunion, and one that the attendees were actually excited to go to.

As he looked around, he realized he knew no one else except Jojo, and that he was the only Caucasian in the room. He was used to this, but he wasn't used to not knowing anyone else, and felt a little out of place.

He went over to the bartender and picked up a glass of white wine. A few people introduced themselves, and he could tell they were curious about him, though he did not mention that he was Jojo's boyfriend—he wanted to give her the choice whether or not to let her friends know.

"Are you an artist?" a woman, whose name he already forgot, asked. She was with a young man who wore black glasses and had slicked back hair.

"Unfortunately, no," he said. "Though I have a great appreciation for it."

"Excellent!" the man said, pushing his glasses up the bridge of his nose. "We need more people like you at these things."

"Like me?" Jack asked. "What does that mean?"

"Oh, it's a compliment," the man said quickly. "We can't all be artists. If we were—who would there be left to *appreciate* the art?"

The woman pursed her lips. "So are you saying that artists are incapable of appreciating other artists' work?"

"Of course not. But it seems that in our group of friends . . ."

Jack sipped his wine and half-listened to the two argue about whether or not an artist could truly appreciate another's work in the same way a non-artist would. Clearly a topic they had discussed many times.

By now, the loft had filled up with people. Jack looked for Jojo and saw that she was making her way to the grand piano. Instead of sitting at it, though, she turned and stood in front of it.

"Hello, friends," she said, pausing to let the chatter die down. "We'll get started in a few minutes, but I just wanted to welcome everyone and thank you for making it tonight. Please get something to drink and a grab a seat."

Jack refilled his drink and found a seat at an empty table, away from the couple who were still in the middle of their argument about artists versus non-artists. He smiled as some other people came over and sat down at the table with him, and then he turned to look for Jojo again, wondering if she might sit with him.

She was still at the piano, though, and now she had sat down in front of it. "Before Dàgē comes up, I'd like to play a piece. There's someone special in the audience this evening who likes the song I'll be playing. I thought it would be nice to share my version of it with him, and the rest of you."

Jack set his drink down and kept his gaze focused on Jojo. He had never heard her play the piano. He recognized the song immediately: "Variations on the Kanon" by Pachelbel. And she was perfect. She started by playing exactly as George Winston had on the version she'd listened to with Jack. But then she began to include a more complex rhythm in the background, which gave the music more depth, making it sound both more modern and more intense. Much to his surprise, his eyes filled with tears as she finished. He had never felt so moved by a piece of music.

Everyone stood and clapped, and Jack wiped at his eyes with the back of his hand before he joined in. When he sat back down, the man next to him leaned over. "I assume you're the special someone that Jojo mentioned?" he asked in English.

Jack smiled. "I sure hope so," he said in Chinese. "My name's Jack," he added. The man was short and lean and Jack could've sworn he knew him from somewhere.

"I'm Zhu Wei." He looked at Jack closely. "You okay there?"

"Yeah, yeah, I'm fine." Jack wiped at his eyes again. "I wasn't expecting to have such a strong reaction to the song. I've never heard Jojo play before, either—she's incredible."

Zhu Wei laughed. "You're in love. Good luck; I've always lost those battles."

"How'd you know I was the special someone?"

"Lucky guess. Well, not really. You're the only person here tonight I don't recognize."

Before Jack could respond, Jojo clapped her hands together to get everyone's attention. "I know you didn't come here to hear me play the piano, but I needed to prove to Dàgē that I'm still playing. But I don't want to take up any more of your time, so, Dàgē, will you now please play something for us?"

Across the loft, at another table, a man stood to a roar of applause, and made his way to the piano. Jack realized that Jojo had been referring to him as Dàgē—*older brother*—the same term of endearment that Andrew San had used with him.

Next to him, Zhu Wei let out a whistle. "You recognize him?"

Jack shook his head. "No."

"It's Ping Ping. He's one of the best pianists in the world—he's played with all the major orchestras. He played a sold-out performance at Carnegie Hall."

Of course Jack knew who Ping Ping was—he was just having a hard time believing that the man was actually *here*. That he was sitting down at the grand piano in Jojo's loft, and he was about to play for them.

Jojo made her way over to Jack's table. There were no more empty chairs, so he stood up.

"Please," he said, gesturing to the seat.

She smiled, held his gaze for a moment, as if she were communicating something with her eyes. She did not touch him but said, "Thank you" and then sat down, giving Zhu Wei a playful swat on the upper arm, which sent them both into a fit of giggles.

Ping Ping played three songs, all different in their composition and style. After the third song, he stopped. Jojo turned in her chair to look at Jack. "He may play more later."

She stood up and went over to Ping Ping, giving him a hug as everyone cheered. "So," Jojo said, addressing the party goers, "there's no denying we have many talented people in this room. Who would like to go next?"

A guy who looked to be in his thirties, with long hair and his dress shirt sleeves pushed back to reveal forearms covered in tattoos, raised his hand and stood up.

"Great, Bobby!" Jojo exclaimed. "Come on up."

Bobby was joined by a young woman Jack assumed was his girlfriend, or at least a very close friend. Jack enjoyed the theatrics; Bobby sat at the piano and, with zero hesitation began playing, a Maroon 5 song, Jack thought it was, and Bobby sang along with gusto while his girlfriend also sang and did her best Cardi B dance moves. Jack sensed that those listening did not know how lewd Cardi B's lyrics were, nor did they know of her socialist values that would turn America into a China.

After their turn, another couple stood up and did "I'll Never Love Again," the duet by Bradley Cooper and Lady Gaga. The performances kept coming, including renditions of Mick Jagger's "Beast of Burden," Rod Stewart's "Maggie May."

"When's it going to be your turn?" Zhu Wei asked Jack. He was smiling when he said it, as if he was asking a rhetorical question, and Jack knew the man thought he wouldn't actually get up and do something like that.

Jack reached out and finished the rest of his wine. "Right now, I think," he said, and he gave Zhu Wei a grin, noting the surprised look on his face. Jack went over to Ping Ping's table. "I'm a big fan of your music," he said. Ping Ping smiled. "If I sing 'One Night in Shanghai' will you play the piano?"

"Which version?"

Jack pulled his phone out of his pocket and showed Ping Ping the iTunes version of the song he had in mind. Ping Ping raised his eyebrows—this version of the song involved singing very high. Ping Ping looked at him another second, as if giving Jack the opportunity to back out, but when Jack said nothing, he nodded.

"I can do that. Who's going to sing with you?"

It seemed only logical that Jack ask Jojo to sing the female role, so he went over to the next table, where she was sitting, and asked if she would.

"Ping Ping has agreed to play, but he's concerned about me not having someone else to sing with."

"Do you have the lyrics?" she asked.

"I do on my phone." He handed his phone to her.

"You know all the lyrics in Chinese?" She looked at him skeptically.

"I do. I wanted to make sure I knew at least one song if I ever had to go with clients to do karaoke."

"Well then . . ." Jojo grinned. "Sure, why not?"

Jack followed Jojo and Ping Ping over to the piano. "Hello, everyone," Jack said in Chinese. Silence abruptly descended; everyone turned to look at him curiously. "Ping Ping and Jojo have kindly agreed to help with this song, which has a nice piano solo in the middle of it. After that point, I will leave it up to all of you whether or not I should continue singing."

There was some laughter. Ping Ping sat down at the piano and began to play. Jack looked at Jojo and smiled, any nerves he felt dissipated. She had an incredible effect on him.

He began to sing:

> One night in Shanghai, I came from the West
>> and fell in love with a northern wàdìrén.
> I drank too much and paid too much
>> for love that I thought was real.
> Never mind that I sat with a hundred monks,
>> I'm in that den wishing and my worries have vanished.
> I didn't ask for directions for fear I'd end up
>> in the place of a thousand gates.

And then it was Jojo's turn. She held Jack's phone up to read the lyrics.

> Lovers never know each other when they meet.
> Thousands of flowers never know their bees.
> For every sad woman there is an elderly lady
>> remembering her past.
> Everyone has a long ago journey of opium-like love
>> where the pain never goes away.

As they continued to sing, Jack felt himself relax even further—he was quite enjoying this, despite a few people in the audience who had their phones out and were recording them. Ping Ping played beautifully, and Jojo sang in a clear, melodic soprano that coalesced perfectly with Jack's baritone. After Ping Ping completed the piano solo, there was clapping and cheering and whooping for Jack and Jojo to continue, so they did. Their eyes met, and as they finished out the song, they seemed to reach out at the same time to hold each other's hands.

> I know you are there but I cannot find you.
>> My eyes are weak and my heart beats softly.
> Every breath I take is for you and hoping
>> that one day we will be united.
> I raise my head, I search, and I eat to live
>> waiting here by myself for you.

They received a standing ovation as they finished the song, and then Ping Ping stood up from the piano and the three of them faced the audience, smiling. Jack gave Jojo a hug, then Ping Ping, and was about to return to his seat but felt Jojo reach out and touch his arm.

"Hold on a sec," she whispered.

She waited until Ping Ping had sat back down. "Encore!" someone shouted, and Jojo laughed.

"No, there's not going to be an encore," she said. "Though I'm touched that you guys want one. I actually have some exciting news that I wanted to share—I realize that making a big announcement like this is—perhaps—a little over the top, but it's important and I wanted to let everyone know." She paused and looked at Jack. "Earlier, I referred to Jack here as a 'special someone' which is true—since we've gotten to know each other better, we have decided to take our relationship to the next level. So, Jack is not only someone special to me, but also my boyfriend."

Raucous applause, louder and more enthusiastic than it had been all night, and Jack flushed. This was not exactly how he imagined letting Jojo's friends know that they were a couple, and yet, it seemed oddly fitting, particularly because he could feel just how happy her friends were for her. Still, he was glad when the applause finally died down and he was able to make his way back to his table.

Zhu Wei grinned when Jack sat back down. "Congratulations," he said. "I know I don't need to tell you what an incredible person Jojo is."

"No, you don't," Jack said. "I figured that one out pretty much right away."

"You guys have good energy together. I was going to be disappointed if you were not the 'someone special' she had referred to." Zhu Wei shook his head. "She deserves a good relationship after everything she's been through." He said this last part almost to himself, before looking at Jack. "So I hope you treat her well."

Jack let his gaze travel around the loft until he found Jojo, who was chatting with the couple who had been arguing about artists earlier. "Of course I will," he said. "And . . . not to pry or anything, but . . . what exactly has she been through? You make it sound like it's a great deal."

Zhu Wei puffed out his cheeks and exhaled loudly. "It was more than any one person should have to go through with someone else. But . . . I'm not going to dish on Jojo's past relationships—it's her call whether to get into all that. She's worked hard to put it all behind her."

Jack nodded, wanting to be respectful of Jojo's past history and her privacy. He also found himself wanting to know more about whatever it was that Zhu Wei was alluding to.

"I'll say this," Zhu Wei said. "When Jojo's last relationship ended, she swore that she was done with relationships. Yes, it was that bad," he quickly added when Jack raised his eyebrows. "And for a while, she seemed to be holding steady to that assertion. It certainly wasn't because no one was interested—I'm sure it will come as little surprise that there are plenty of men who would be thrilled to date someone like Jojo."

"They'd be fools not to want to."

Perhaps Zhu Wei had thought he was giving Jack a little something to sate his curiosity, but honestly, he was only making it worse. How bad did a relationship have to be if the end result was swearing off dating forever?

"But forget all that," Zhu Wei said. "That performance you and Jojo just did? Ping Ping on piano? It was brilliant!"

"It really was!" echoed one of the women sitting at their table. The other people at the table nodded in agreement.

"That's a tricky song!" someone else said.

"And you didn't mess up a single tone!"

It seemed the whole table went around, praising Jack's effort, and he smiled, felt a sort of camaraderie with everyone there. And he realized how everything changed when you sang or shared something with people. You made yourself—or at least, some facet of yourself—familiar, and that familiarity allowed you to become both unique and unified with others. That was why karaoke was so popular here—it was a great way to bring people together.

By the time the evening was starting to wind down and people were taking off, Jack felt flushed and happy. He said goodbye to Ping Ping and thanked him again for playing while he sang; he said goodbye to Zhu Wei; he said goodbye and even received a few hugs from some of Jojo's other friends.

And then, it was just Jojo and Jack, alone in the loft, empty chairs, empty piano stool, plenty to clean up.

"That'll all get taken care of tomorrow," Jojo said as Jack pulled her into his arm. She wrapped her arms around his neck and looked up at him. "You were wonderful tonight. You made quite an impression, which isn't always an easy thing to do with this crowd! Zhu Wei says you're in love with me but that it's okay since you have good energy and are strong."

"He said that, did he," Jack said, and he leaned toward Jojo until their foreheads were touching. "He also told me that he thought we had good energy together."

"Which we do."

"We do. And I'm glad he noticed. I liked him; he seems like a good guy."

Jojo pulled back a little so she could look Jack in the eye. "You don't recognize him?"

"You know, he looked familiar, like I had definitely seen him somewhere, but . . . I can't quite recall where."

"You'll probably recognize his professional name—Tom Zhu."

It clicked the second the name was out of her mouth. "That's it!" Jack said. "Yeah, Tom Zhu, the martial arts actor!"

"Zhu Wei is his Chinese name."

"I can't believe I didn't recognize him."

"Trust me—he prefers that. And he's doing fewer movies nowadays because of a few health issues, and he's been trying to spend more time with his daughters in Singapore."

"Well, I won't ask him for his autograph, but I did like him. It'd be nice to get together with him again."

"We can make that happen. But right now, the only thing I want to do is take a shower and then go to bed."

"That's the best offer I've had all night."

Jojo raised an eyebrow. "Is that so."

"You know me, having to fend off droves of them."

She looked up at him, a half-smile on her face. "I hope you didn't get anyone's WeChat."

"I did not. Because I already have the WeChat of the one and only person that I want." He kissed her forehead. "Well, I guess I wouldn't have minded getting Zhu Wei's."

She laughed, a sound as beautiful to Jack's ears as Ping Ping's piano playing earlier had been.

"Let's go take that shower," she said. "I want to get out of this dress."

She grabbed his hand and he followed her up into the loft. They undressed and entered the shower. The water was hot and felt good; what felt even better was soaping up Jojo's hair, then her back, massaging her shoulders.

"Oooh, that feels good," she said, stretching her neck from one side to the other. Slowly, he reached around, cupping her firm breasts. She groaned. "That feels even better." He kissed her neck, felt himself get even harder. She stood on her toes and pushed back against him, gyrating her pelvis, her breathing getting heavier. It was clear she wanted what he did, and he held still, gently guiding her back until he felt himself slide into her. He gasped as he did so, and she pressed her hands against the tiled wall as he gripped her hips. The hot water cascaded down on them as they moved together, in perfect synchronicity.

*   *   *

Later, they were lying in Jojo's bed together, limbs entwined. Jack ran his fingers through Jojo's hair, her arm was draped across his chest.

"How do you know Ping Ping?" he asked.

"We used to take private piano lessons together," Jojo said. "In Beijing. And we stayed friends after his career skyrocketed. He gave me the Steinway downstairs."

"It's a beautiful piano."

"He works closely with Steinway; they designed a piano for him. He said he gave me the piano so I would keep practicing, which . . . obviously I haven't."

"Could've fooled me. You played incredibly tonight. I could practice for a hundred years and not come close to sounding as good as you did."

"Well, I don't believe that for a second, but, it's sweet of you to say. Ping Ping said his favorite song tonight was the one he played for us; he said it was an unexpected challenge."

"Sounds like it was a challenge for all around. But I had a great time. You have some interesting friends, and I'm glad you included me."

"Of course I would—you're my boyfriend after all." Jojo laughed. "I wasn't planning to announce it like that, just so you know . . . I figured I'd let people know throughout the night, but then it just sort of seemed like the right time to go for it. And my friends all liked you, I can tell."

Jojo's phone chimed on the bedside table. She reached over and looked at it for a moment before setting it back down. "Bobby's girl-friend recorded us singing with Ping Ping, and guess what? She posted it to Weibo and it's now trending number one."

Jack did not have a Weibo account, China's equivalent to Facebook (nor did he have Facebook), and the idea that anything involving him would be trending number one anywhere was strange.

"I don't know whether that's good or bad?" he said as Jojo snuggled back up against him.

Jojo yawned. "It's just kind of funny; it doesn't matter."

But it did matter, except Jack couldn't convey this to Jojo. He lay awake long after her breathing slowed and she began to snore gently, thinking about this video. If it was trending number one, then a huge number of people had seen it. Being recognized now would be bad, but what was also bad was the fact that he couldn't tell Jojo anything about this. Only after he told himself several times that the video was out there and there was nothing he could do about it was he able to drift off to sleep.

CHAPTER 24

Jack woke up to a message alert on his black phone, from Cooper, saying that Tony Woo would be visiting Shanghai and to get in touch with Ari to arrange a get together at 158 Julu Road.

158 Julu Road was a fairly new open-air space featuring numerous bars, western restaurants, a German brewery, and plenty of live music. What made it interesting, though, was that it was in the middle of a park-like area, situated one level below ground. Previously located on a nearby street the Shanghai government had closed many of these establishments in the past because they were loud and the neighbors complained. Moving things below street level helped mightily in taming the noise problem.

Jack texted Ari, who replied right away and they arranged to meet for drinks that evening. Jack saw no reason to wait, and was, in fact, rather eager to meet the man who had been selected to speak to the 1.4 billion people in China.

He and Jojo had breakfast together, and he was relieved when she informed him that their video was no longer trending number one. That was the good thing about these sorts of things; people had short attention spans.

"I would love to hang out with you all day," Jojo said, "but I have to get more work done on this sculpture. Are you available tonight?"

Jack paused, wondering if it would be at all possible to include Jojo in his plans this evening. He wanted to, yet he knew it wasn't a wise idea.

"I'm actually busy tonight," he said. "'I' have to meet up with some . . . colleagues from out of town."

"Well, I can survive not seeing you for the night," she said. "Though I must warn you, I am busy all day tomorrow and I'm working at the bar tomorrow night."

"You're starting to make it sound like I'm never going to see you again. If I'm busy tonight, and you're busy tomorrow night, why don't we plan on me taking you out to dinner the next night that we're both free? I'll take you wherever you want."

She set her coffee cup down and intertwined her fingers with his. Just the feel of her skin against his own sent a jolt of electricity through his body. "You know what I've been wanting? A steak. I'd like to go somewhere where I could get a good steak."

Jack gave her hand a squeeze. "That," he said, "can most certainly be arranged."

*　*　*

He met Ari and Tony at a Mexican restaurant called El Santo, where they ordered beer and burritos. Jack liked Tony immediately—he was friendly, laid back, and easy to talk to. He also had a very pleasant, smooth baritone of a voice, radio-quality material right there.

"Tony works at Credit Suisse in New York," Ari said. "Investment banking. He obtained an MBA at Wharton and emigrated to America from Beijing."

"I heard you did something of the opposite," Tony said.

Jack nodded. "It sounds like it."

"And yet, here we all are." Ari smiled. "Tony's in Beijing for a few months to work and is here visiting Shanghai for a few days."

"Welcome to the most western place in all of Shanghai," Jack said. "How old were you when you emigrated?"

"Ten," Tony said. "I don't remember anything of the Cultural Revolution since it was over by then. My parents were sent to the countryside though."

Ten, Jack thought. "How was it, coming to America at that age?"

"It was hard at first. I didn't feel like I fit in, until I was around sixteen, I'd say. Then, two things happened—first, my English improved, and second, I began to understand American humor."

"What do you mean?" Ari asked with a grin. "I'm still trying to figure that one out."

"Let's see," Tony said. "In heaven, the food is Chinese, the women are Japanese, and the houses are American. In hell, the houses are Chinese, the food is Japanese, and the women are American."

Jack and Ari both laughed. "That's a good one," Jack said. "Do you have anymore?"

Tony looked at him solemnly. "I had a near-death experience once," he said. "I walked past a graveyard." He grinned. "A Chinese guy told that one and pioneered Chinese telling jokes in America. Then, CCTV noticed him and gave him his own show. A loss for America."

"Have you ever been to the CCTV headquarters building?" Jack asked.

"No," Tony said. "I always wanted to, though. I majored in broadcast journalism."

"Where?"

"NYU."

No wonder they picked this guy, Jack thought. *He's perfect.*

He took another sip of his beer and gazed around, noticed a number of police officers in their black uniforms, several CCTV cameras. 158 Julu seemed to have more security than any other venue in Shanghai, mostly due to the area's popularity with foreigners. The police were aggressive in their efforts to stop trouble before it started.

As the evening continued, Jack saw many parallels between himself and Tony. It was interesting that they would now, all these years later, find themselves coming together for this mission. Tony did seem to have thoroughly assimilated into America and its values, and Jack knew that most Americans would consider Tony one of them—because he was. Jack also knew that it didn't matter how long he lived in China for—or how well he spoke Chinese—he would always be viewed as a foreigner.

Jack watched as a few children tried to navigate the courtyard on scooters, their parents hovering, or doing their best to hover, as the children played. This was common with overprotective Chinese parents, which was a stark contrast to the white parents Jack had observed living here, who seemed much more willing to just let their kids go and have fun.

His Didi showed up. He got in, his thoughts still on Tony, and how this whole mission was going to work out. Understanding Chinese psychology would be essential when it came to speaking to the entire population of China, and Jack hoped whoever was responsible had done their due diligence when it came to choosing Tony. There were many variables and there was simply too much at stake.

CHAPTER 25

The next morning, Jack headed out early and took a Didi to the URBN Garden, a boutique hotel with a nice restaurant and an outside seating area. He knew the owners of the hotel and would sometimes go use one of the restaurant's private rooms to work. As he got into the car, he noticed someone on a scooter. Seeing people on scooters was nothing unusual, but there was something about this particular person that caught Jack's eye, though he wasn't exactly sure what it was.

Jack glanced out the back window as the car drove off, and was both annoyed and unsurprised to see the person on the scooter following.

Maybe it›s just a coincidence.

There were, after all, plenty of people going in the same direction that Jack was, and that certainly didn't mean they were following him. The person on the scooter stayed back far enough that Jack couldn't make out any discerning features, but he knew, in his gut, this person was tailing him.

But he had disappeared when Jack arrived at the hotel—maybe he'd been too paranoid. He went into the hotel, walked through the lobby, continued into the restaurant. He went into one of the private rooms that looked out onto the street.

As Jack sat down at the table, he saw the guy on the scooter pull up. From his closer vantage point at the window, Jack was almost certain it was the same guy he'd seen before, though he wasn't close enough to see if he had the telltale scar on the side of his face.

Jack sat there for a moment, watching the man pretend that he was looking through the menu. Every so often, he'd glance Jack's way, but when he saw that Jack was looking at him, he'd quickly look away.

Something was going on. A little burst of adrenaline began coursing its way through Jack's veins, though he remained at the table, calm exterior. He couldn't just ignore this, no, he needed to do something.

He stood up, pulling his phone out of his pocket as he exited the restaurant and went over to the table where the man was sitting.

"Hi," Jack said in Chinese, in a friendly tone. "Where are you from?"

The man lifted his head, and Jack saw the thin scar on the side of his face.

"I'm from Beijing," he said, in Beijing Mandarin.

"And why have you been following me? Do I know you? What do you want?" Jack asked, switching back to English. "I've seen you before, you're here now, so . . . what is it?"

The man stared at him, a sour expression on his face, as if he were weighing the pros and cons of telling Jack who he was and what he wanted.

Jack gave him another couple of seconds, but when it became clear that he was not going to respond, Jack quickly held his phone up and took the man's picture.

The man blinked. "You can't do that."

"But I just did. I'll delete it if you tell me who you are and what you want and why you're following me around. If not, I'll—"

The man jumped up and hurried off before Jack could finish his sentence, glancing over his shoulder a few times before he turned the corner and disappeared. Jack stood there, confused and frustrated, though glad that he had the guy's picture now, at the very least.

He went back inside and sent the photo, along with a brief message asking if Cooper had any idea who this person was. He looked at the photo for a while, as if staring at it long enough would suddenly make it clear to Jack who it was.

The reply from Cooper came on the black phone: *Don't know him.*

Jack put both of his phones away and turned his attention back to his laptop. He could spend all day thinking about the identity of this person, which he knew would not lead anywhere, so instead he tried to distract himself. He navigated to SCMP and read the headline: *President Zhao Lihong sends message to U.S. and West that China is committed to opening up.*

Yeah right, Jack thought. *Trade negotiations shouldn't even be taking place. China's been cheating on their World Trade Organization agreements since 2003.*

If it were up to Jack, he'd null and void the $1.1 trillion in U.S. treasury securities China had purchased from America. In essence, China had loaned America $1.2 trillion and now America could not pay it back. Along with voiding the $1.2 trillion, America could then calculate how much of China's IP stealing and violations of the WTO agreement had cost everyone, and afterward, the U.S. could send China a bill for unpaid fees, or a check if there was money left over.

The challenge was that other countries might lose faith in American treasuries, which could cause a massive sell-off. There were things the U.S. could do to mitigate it, such as rapidly issuing new certificates, indicating that countries significantly violating agreements with the U.S. would forfeit their treasuries if there was a violation over $100 billion.

All these ideas swirled through Jack's mind as he read the article, but so did a few stubborn thoughts about the identity of the man following him. If he saw him again, Jack would be more aggressive about finding out just who he was.

But he also needed to remind himself that there was more at stake here than just his own personal wants and needs. Infecting the Chinese leadership with a non-lethal neurotoxin and then sharing information with the Chinese people could be life-changing for so many. It would bring all sorts of benefits to ordinary citizens, rather than just create economic and political chaos.

He tried to keep this thought at the front of his mind, and not the potential danger, though he knew there was a good chance something could go wrong. He *hoped* that would not be the case, but he knew it was naïve to just assume things would go exactly according to plan. And if something did go wrong, there was the very real chance that he could be imprisoned for a very long time, maybe even indefinitely.

No more freedom.

No more Jojo.

No more life as he knew it.

It was a huge risk, and he had everything to lose, yet Jack could not imagine backing out at this point and not being a part of this.

CHAPTER 26

That Friday, Jack took Jojo out to Ruth's Chris Steak House, where they'd be able to get U.S. prime beef, which had previously been banned from being imported into China. When their food arrived, Jojo's eyes lit up.

"You going to be able to eat all of that?" Jack asked, unable to contain his smile. He thought she had been joking when she said she was going to order the Cowboy Ribeye, a twenty-two-ounce bone-in cut of beef.

"I'm going to try," she said. "But if I can't, I'm happy to take home the leftovers."

Before digging in, though, they held up their glasses of Cabernet and gently clinked them together.

Jack had ordered the filet, which was perfectly cooked and so tender he didn't even need to use a knife. For several moments, neither of them said anything while they let their taste buds indulge in all the flavors.

"Can you cook a steak that tastes this good?" Jojo asked as she dipped another piece in the butter sauce on her plate. "Because this is *incredible*. I don't know if there's going to be any leftovers."

"I would certainly give it my best effort," he said. How was it possible that someone as slender as Jojo could eat that much steak? Jack couldn't help but be impressed.

"Oh, I wanted to tell you before I forget, a friend of mine is having a gallery opening on Monday night, and I told her we'd go. She wasn't at the party, but she'd like to meet you. Does that sound okay?"

"Yeah, that'd be great." Jack paused. "Shoot, actually it won't. I'll be in Beijing on Monday." He'd received a WeChat message that morning from Joshua, about meeting in Beijing at the Jianguo Hotel. "Otherwise, I'd be more than happy to go. Is there another night? I know it's not the same as opening night, but I'm sure it would still be a good time."

"Yeah, we could definitely go when you get back. Is it a work meeting?"

He hated not being completely upfront with her, but it was for a good reason. "Um, yeah. It's a work thing," he finally said.

"Tell me about it."

"Well . . ." He smiled, stalling. It was hard to tell from the expression on her face if she was asking because she was genuinely interested or if she was asking because she didn't believe him when he said it was for work. "I'm not entirely sure about everything we're going to discuss, but it has to do with a venture I'm going to be a part of, and I'm just going up there to get some more things finalized."

That was as close to the truth as he could give her, for now, anyway.

"Maybe I'll go with you," she said.

"But . . . what about your friend's art opening?"

She gave him a withering look. Then she set her fork down and took a long sip of wine. "Are you being purposefully vague?" she asked as she set the empty glass down. "Because I have to admit, I'm finding this whole thing a little strange."

"What do you mean?"

"Well, you were just in Beijing not that long ago. And now you're going back there. You obviously don't want me to go with you."

"It's not that I don't want you to go with me, it's just that I'm going there for an extremely brief visit, just for this meeting, and that's it. Unfortunately, it's not a meeting that you can sit in on. You wouldn't want to anyway, trust me, it'll be boring as hell."

"So now you're telling me what I will and will not find boring." Jojo nodded. "Right."

For a second he thought she was joking, that she'd smile and say *just kidding*, but that didn't happen and he realized she was serious.

"Jojo," he said. "Please. It has nothing to do with me not wanting you to go, believe me." He took a deep breath. He had been trying so hard to skirt the issue and not outright lie to her, but he realized he had to if he wanted to give her peace of mind. "And the reason I can't go into more detail about it right now is because I don't know any more. I have to meet with some potential clients who are interested in investing in America. It's going to be a quick trip and then I'll be back. I'm not trying to be vague—I just honestly didn't think you'd be interested in hearing about my boring work stuff."

"I just think it's a little strange, is all," she said. "I'm not trying to be . . ." Her voice trailed off and she shook her head. "You know what? Never mind. It's fine. I don't know what I'm saying."

But Jack could tell that it wasn't fine, and he didn't want their evening to end up ruined. "I'd really appreciate it if you would tell me what's bothering you," he said. "Because if there's anything I can do to fix it, I will."

She gave him a small smile, which seemed a little forced. "There's nothing to fix. I just realized how I probably sound—like a possessive girlfriend, and I'm not trying to be like that. I'm also not trying to make excuses for myself or anything, but . . . sometimes I feel like there's something more going on with you then you're letting on. I realize how crazy that sounds, it's just hard for me to trust people, especially someone I'm in a relationship with." She rubbed her index finger over a spot on the white linen tablecloth. "I know we haven't talked about it much, but I want you to know that I've only had one other serious relationship. You know, I had boyfriends before, but I've only been in one other long-term, serious relationship, and it didn't end so well. 'Disaster' would be putting it mildly."

"I'm sorry to hear that," Jack said. "Sounds like we might have similar histories."

"It's not something I like to talk about. But, I also want you to understand where I'm coming from, so I think it might be best if I talked about it a little bit."

"I'm happy to listen to whatever it is you need to say."

And he meant it. He sat and listened as Jojo detailed what sounded like a happy and intense relationship to start: two artists—he worked in mixed media, she did sculpture—inspiring and engaging each other, at least in the beginning. At some point, things changed, though even after all this time, Jojo still wasn't sure where or why it happened.

"He started getting more withdrawn and secretive," she said. "But at the same time, he'd want to know where I was at every moment of the day. Like he didn't believe me when I said I was going to meet up with some friends or make a delivery to a client. It was like he turned into a different person. I finally broke it off, but . . . Things were pretty messed up for a little while. He didn't want to end the relationship, thought that if we just tried harder that everything would be okay. Things got a little scary, actually." She sighed. "I can stop if you want, if this is too much. I know you didn't take me out tonight to be regaled with my dating history."

"No," Jack said. "I mean, if you want to stop, you can, but I told you I'm more than happy to listen and I meant it."

"I won't get into all the details, but at the very lowest point, he ended up slicing the side of his own face with his X-acto knife. Right in front of me, he said he was going to carve up his entire face—and he probably would have—but luckily Zhu Wei was there and managed to stop him before he went too far, but . . ." She shuddered. "I can still see the way he sliced the blade through the side of his face, the way there was this pause between the skin splitting open and the blood gushing out. Sorry, that's probably way more detail than you wanted to know."

"Why did he do that?"

"I don't know. He was always into shock value, and I remember exactly what he said before he did it: *If you're going to leave me forever, I'm at least going to give myself something to remember you by, and you're going to bear witness to me doing it.* I've tried to block the whole thing from my mind, but obviously it's not something you can just forget about."

"That is intense," Jack said. "I'm glad Zhu Wei was there and able to stop things before it got worse. I can't imagine why anyone would do that to themselves."

"So you can understand why it's not exactly my favorite topic of conversation. And I know you guys are two completely different people, so I shouldn't be letting it affect me like this . . . But I guess it still does, in that sometimes I have a hard time with trust. Even though you've given me no reason not to trust you."

Jack reached across the table and took Jojo's hand. He appreciated her willingness to be open, to share this piece of her history with him, because it did help him understand her better. At the same time, he wasn't being upfront, and, perhaps, one might even say gaslighting her. Because she was picking up on his deception, yet he was trying to convince her it was nothing.

It's for her own good, he reminded himself, though he supposed her ex-boyfriend was probably telling himself the very same thing before he sliced the side of his face open—

Realization suddenly clicked into place.

The strange man following him, the person he'd seen that night outside of Jojo's, the thin scar on the side of his face . . .

What had he said the first time Jack ran into him, after he'd left the store? *Leave Wang Min alone.*

At the time, he hadn't known who Wang Min was. But now he had a feeling he did.

And he was holding her hand.

He'd be willing to bet money that Jojo Wang's Chinese name was Wang Min, and that the man who had been following him was not part of the Chinese government but rather, Jojo's ex-boyfriend. This both reassured him and filled him with a different sense of unease, which was a strange sensation.

So, the government isn't sending people out to follow me—it's Jojo's mentally ill ex.

"I'm actually glad you told me," Jack said. "And now I have something to tell you."

"I'm not sure I like the sound of that. But I guess it's only fair."

"No, it's nothing bad. Well, it might freak you out a little bit, but . . ."

She frowned. "What is it?"

"I didn't mention this to you previously, because, well, why would I? I was followed a few times, by someone I didn't know. But I realize now who it was."

"Who?"

"Your ex."

Jojo's mouth fell open. "What? He's *following* you?"

"Not all the time. But we've had a few run-ins. He's been rather reticent, but one thing he did say was to 'Leave Wang Min alone.'"

Jojo's face dropped. "I can't believe it," she said. "What the hell, I thought we were *done* with this, Jack I'm so sorry, I wish you told me sooner—"

"Hey, hey, it's okay," Jack said. "I can take care of myself, and I didn't put two and two together until just now, when you told me the story about how he cut his face. Because that's one of the things that stood out, was this scar he had on the side of his face."

Jojo let go of Jack's hand and reached for her phone. "Excuse me one moment," she said. "I need to make a phone call."

Even if he wanted to eavesdrop, he wouldn't have been able to because Jojo began speaking in Suzhou dialect. She spoke in hushed tones, though he could tell whoever she was speaking to was calming her down, because when she was off the phone, she seemed calmer.

"Okay," she said. "Sorry about that. But it's taken care of."

"Taken care of? Who was that?"

"My father."

Jack raised his eyebrows. "And he's able to just 'take care of it'?"

"The local police will. But my father will see to it that it happens. I'm sorry, Jack, that you got caught up in all of this."

"Listen," he said, reaching over to take her hand again. "You don't have to apologize. We all have our own baggage. No one is perfect."

"I can't believe he was following you. I mean, that's extraordinary." She shuddered. "He did a lot of damage and made me feel like I could never trust anyone again. Until I met you, I thought it would just be easier to be on my own, because then I wouldn't have to worry about putting my trust in someone else. But you changed that." She picked up her hand, still enclosed in his, and kissed the end of his fingers. "Just promise me we'll always be truthful with each other."

"I promise," he said, without missing a beat, though there was a sinking feeling in his chest because his promise was in fact a lie. But what was he supposed to do? He couldn't tell her about it; it could endanger her life, the life of her friends, her family.

He only hoped that if she were ever to find out, she would understand.

CHAPTER 27

Before Jack left for Beijing, he received a text from Cooper, instructing him to bring the vial of neurotoxin with him when he went to meet with Joshua. He made sure it was tucked safely in his bag, which he kept close to him on the train to Beijing.

He arrived at the Jianguo Hotel a few minutes before five; he didn't see Joshua in the lobby. He took a seat to wait, but only waited a few more minutes before Joshua came through the entrance, carrying a few books, looking clean and wholesome. Jack stood to greet him. "How are you?"

"I'm great. Sorry if I kept you waiting. You ready for tonight?"

"Um . . . maybe? I'm not sure what to expect."

"Let's get a Didi and I'll tell you on the way."

Once they were in the back of the car, Joshua leaned toward Jack and began to speak in a low voice. "I've been working with the children of some senior government officials, practicing English with them. The parents will often come back early to spend some time with us before taking their kids home. And because the parents are senior government officials, you'll see some security around." He gave Jack a reassuring look. "But there's nothing to be worried about."

Jack appreciated his words but still couldn't help feeling anxious about the whole thing. He tried to push that out of his mind as he discreetly reached into his bag and took out the vial of neurotoxin. He squeezed exactly four drops onto his right palm and then put the bottle back.

"Here we are," Joshua said a few minutes later when the car pulled up in front of a nondescript complex with high walls. They walked over and stood in front of the door.

"Come closer so you can be seen on camera," Joshua said, looking up. Jack looked up, too, and saw a security camera, pointed toward the door, giving perfect view of anyone entering or exiting. Jack took a few steps closer to Joshua, who was leaning forward toward the intercom next to the door.

"It's me, Joshua," he said. "And my friend, Jack Gold."

A sturdy Chinese man wearing a bulletproof vest opened the door. He held a submachine gun. Strapped to his chest was a handgun. Though Jack had heard about China's Central Security Bureau, who were trained special forces to protect China's leadership, seeing one of their members up close was still unnerving.

The guard stepped back to let them in. They had to walk past several more guards, all armed, all wearing the high-quality dark green and gray combat fatigues of those trained by the Central Security Bureau. Jack's heart felt as if were galloping in his chest, beating so loudly that surely these guards could hear it, surely Joshua and anyone within a half-mile radius could hear it and would know exactly what he was up to. He tried to keep his breathing normal as he followed Joshua to the entrance of the house.

An older woman was there, wearing an apron, her dark hair pulled back. She smiled when she saw them. "Hi, Joshua."

"Hi, Auntie." Joshua looked at Jack. "Auntie, I'd like to introduce you to my friend, Mr. Gold."

Jack returned her smile. "It's so nice to meet you, Auntie," he said in Chinese.

Her eyes lit up, her smile widened. "Come in, come in."

They walked along a cobblestone path, surrounded by trees, then up three steps to the large, two-story cottage, reminiscent of something you might see in the English countryside. As they stepped into the entranceway, Jack could smell food cooking, hear the faint sound of children talking, laughing. They continued to follow Auntie farther into the house, until they reached a large, open room.

Three women sat on a sofa, drinking tea. They were casually dressed and appeared, to Jack, to be very good friends, judging by how closely they sat next to each other. On the floor in front of them five children played a board game. Jack guessed the youngest of the group to be around eight; the oldest looked to be thirteen or so. The three boys were dressed in jeans and t-shirts while the girls wore short-sleeved, white dresses.

The women looked up as they approached. "Hello," Joshua called. "Mrs. Li, Mrs. Chen, and Mrs. Zhao—May I introduce you to Jack Gold?"

He shook each of their hands. And just like that, he had poisoned them, these women he had never met, who all looked like they were pleased to meet him.

"It's a pleasure to meet you," he said in Chinese.

Mrs. Chen looked at him curiously. "Where are you from?"

"Originally Los Angeles, but I lived in Beijing for a while and now Shanghai."

The women exchanged glances. "You speak Chinese like you're from Beijing," Mrs. Li said. The other two nodded. "That's unusual."

"I hope our children can learn to speak English as well as you speak Chinese!" Mrs. Zhao exclaimed.

Joshua was talking with the kids, greeting each of them in English. They responded likewise. Jack stepped back, not wanting to inadvertently infect one of the children, and continued his conversation with the three women, who wanted to know all about who he was, what he did, where he lived, did he have a girlfriend? It was like they'd never spoken with a foreigner before.

When their inquiries finally began to taper off, Joshua asked if Jack had any questions he wanted to ask the group.

"Hmm," Jack said, this time in English. "I could probably come up with a couple."

The children sat on the floor, looking up at him eagerly. Out of the corner of his eye, he could also see the three women watching him closely. He wanted to be engaging, but he also needed to be careful. He smiled at the children.

"If you were Chinese and born in America, but now lived in France, what would you call yourself in Chinese and English?"

"Ooh, starting them off with a hard one," Joshua said. "Actually, I think I need to think about that one, too."

Jack watched as the kids frowned, looked at each other, then frowned some more, trying to figure out the right answer. He'd been expecting this—the Chinese always confused such things.

"We don't know," one of the girls finally said. "What's the answer?"

"Well," Jack said, "the fact is, you could be born in one place, grow up in another, and live in yet another. That would make you an American-born

Chinese who lives in France. Where you're born can be separate from where you grew up, and that can also be different from where you live. In America, this is common. In China, the reverse is true."

The children nodded. "Ask us another!"

"Okay. If a Chinese man marries a white woman, are their children Chinese?"

The oldest boy raised his hand. "Yes."

One of the younger boys shook his head and said, "No," right as one of the girls said, "Half."

"If the man is Chinese, then his children are Chinese," the older of the two girls said.

They all looked at Jack. "I'd say it depends on where the child grows up and how they view themselves," he said.

The children blinked. "Wait," the older girl said, looking at him in confusion. "You're saying the *kid* decides?"

"Well." Jack smiled. "It's not how the government views things, but it is interesting, isn't it?"

"Ask us more!"

"How about this—I'll read you something in English and you tell me what it means."

They nodded enthusiastically.

He took out his phone and went online to find what he had in mind. He read:

The little prince asked, "What does 'tame' mean?"

The fox replies, "It is to establish ties ... to me, you are nothing more than a little boy who is just like a hundred thousand other little boys and I do not need you. And you do not need me either. I am only a fox to you like a hundred thousand foxes. But if you tame me, we shall need each other. To me, you will be unique in the world. To you, I shall be unique in the world.

"That's a great quote."

Jack looked up at the sound of this new voice, a man who had come into the room as Jack had been reading.

"*The Little Prince*," the man said, before Jack could register who he was seeing.

Joshua stood. "Jack, I'd like to introduce you to President Zhao Lihong."

Zhao was shorter than Jack and a little overweight. He wore a suit and tie and had a grin on his face as he came over to shake Jack's hand.

"It's a pleasure to meet you," Jack said in precise Mandarin as he gripped Zhao's hand. He was the only leader that the vast majority of Chinese knew. Jack wondered what that must be like; he hoped they would be receptive to someone new.

"Nice to meet you, Mr. Gold," President Zhao said. "Your Chinese is excellent. Do you have any more quotes you could read to us? That first one was quite good."

"Yes, of course," Jack said, his mind reeling. Everything had happened so quickly, the way Zhao had suddenly appeared, and now, with the handshake out of the way and the neurotoxin passed on, Jack had to scramble to come up with another quote. He focused on the children.

"This one is a little trickier, so listen carefully. I'll read it slowly; first in English and then in Chinese."

Watch your thoughts for they become your words. Watch your words for they become your actions. Watch your actions for they become your habits. Watch your habits for they become your character. And, watch your character for it becomes your destiny.

"Brilliant," President Zhao said, beaming.

"Who said that?" Joshua asked.

Jack smiled, a little sheepishly. "I don't know. But they used the quote in a movie about Margaret Thatcher."

"It's still brilliant, whether or not you know who to attribute it to," President Zhao said. "Why don't we take a break in the lesson and you two join me for a cup of tea."

He pointed to a table near the back corner of the room. Auntie appeared a moment later with a tray of tea and cups.

"What type of tea is this?" Jack asked, watching her pour.

"Raw Pu'er," President Zhao replied.

Jack picked up his cup and inhaled. "From Yunnan Province?"

"Yes. Though not all tea is of the same quality. This tea is compressed and aged for decades. That's what gives it such a good fragrance and its rich texture."

Jack took a slow sip. "It's delicious."

"But never mind the tea," President Zhao said. "Tell me a little about yourself, Mr. Gold."

Jack felt guilty for sickening the man. He tried to remind himself that Zhao might be the nicest person on the face of the planet, but his policies and ideas for the country he was in charge of were hurting most of its citizens.

He had just started to tell Zhao a censored version of why he had come to China when another man entered the room. Unlike Zhao, this man was tall and lean, and there was something strangely familiar about his face. President Zhao grinned and waved him over.

"Wang Yang, I'd like you to meet Mr. Gold."

Jack stood up and shook the man's hand, guilt again flaring as he infected another person.

You're doing the right thing, he told himself. *This is for the greater good.*

"Very nice to meet you," Jack said.

Wang Yang gripped his hand firmly, smiling. "Where are you from?"

"I'm from America, but I don't represent America," Jack said quickly.

The adults all laughed. It was common for people in China to assume you represented or were responsible for your country's actions.

"Interesting," Wang Yang said. He looked at President Zhao. "It's funny, President Zhao, this American speaks Chinese with a Beijing accent. My Chinese daughter speaks English with a French accent."

When spoken in Chinese, the words were repetitive and rhymed, which made the statement sound funny. Everyone laughed again, though this time, Jack had to force it.

Did he just say his Chinese daughter who speaks English with a French accent?

"Is there a restroom I could use?" Jack asked.

Joshua nodded. "Right down the hallway to the left."

Jack excused himself and hurried into the bathroom. He took a deep breath once the door was shut, tried to tell himself that everything was fine, everything was going according to plan—because it was, except for the part where he met Jojo's father.

Maybe it's not.

But how many other Chinese women were out there who spoke English with a French accent?

There could be one or two more.

He looked at himself in the mirror. Yes, of course there was the possibility that Jojo was not, out of 1.4 billion people, the *only* woman who spoke English with a French accent, but there was no denying the fact that she was Wang Yang's daughter. The man whose hand Jack had just shook was the same man in the photograph that had fallen out of Jojo's copy of *Le Petit Prince*; older, yes, but the same, Jack was certain of it.

He washed his hands thoroughly, hoping the hot water and soap would remove what was left of the neurotoxin. He liked everyone he had met today, which made the fact that he had just poisoned them even harder to take. Never mind the fact that Jojo's father could now be counted as one of those people.

What are the chances, Jack thought as he left the bathroom.

But now it was beginning to make a little more sense to him, Jojo's desire to not talk about her father. He was a powerful man with a prominent position in the Chinese government. While there were some people who would use such a prominent familial connection to their advantage, he understood why Jojo might want to keep her father's true identity to herself—living in the shadow of a well-known parent was difficult.

Jack's unease only grew as he returned to the room, saw the way everyone was talking amicably. President Zhao was deep in conversation with Wang Yang, and as Jack looked at the taller man, all he could see was how much he looked like his daughter.

"Jack, would you like to come over here and say goodbye to the kids before we go?" Joshua asked.

"Of course," Jack said, welcoming the distraction. The children clamored around him, asking him for another quote, another question.

"When we visit next time," Jack said.

"So you're coming back?" the youngest boy asked.

"Yes, I'll definitely come back. I had a great time, and you guys are doing great with your English."

He then said his goodbyes to the three women, before going over to President Zhao and Wang Yang.

"If I had a daughter who spoke English with a French accent," he said to Wang Yang, "I would speak Chinese to her."

Wang Yang smiled. "You know, Mr. Gold, you could be a broadcaster on CCTV news. You just have one of those voices."

"Oh, I don't know about that," Jack said. "But thank you. I must admit, I am fascinated by the CCTV headquarters. Do they give tours? My friends and I were hoping to visit it." He looked at President Zhao as he said this.

President Zhao frowned, his gaze going to Wang Yang, then back to Jack as he shrugged. "You know, I'm not sure. But why not? When would you like to go?"

"Within the next few days would be great; one of the people interested will be traveling abroad next week."

"Then consider it done. Just write down the names of the people going and we'll let them know you'll be stopping by for a tour within the week. I do have a favor to ask of you, though, in return."

"Absolutely."

"Send me the quote, the one used in the Thatcher movie. Give it to Joshua and he can pass it along."

Jack smiled. "Not a problem."

He wrote down the four names—Jack, Joshua, Ari, Tony—on a piece of paper that one of the kids gave to him, and then he gave it to President Zhao.

"It was an honor to meet you," Jack said, shaking the man's hand once more. He then shook Wang Yang's hand again, wondering if and when the man would find out about who his daughter was dating.

"So good to meet you," Wang Yang said. "I'm certain my daughter will be interested to hear that I met an American who speaks fluent Mandarin. Did you ever live in France?"

"Unfortunately, no," Jack said. "Though I have visited."

"It's a beautiful place. My daughter enjoyed it there very much."

Jack was relieved when they finally left; the situation was getting more surreal by the minute. He tried to keep a cool exterior as they walked past the guards.

"I booked us a Didi," Joshua said as they stepped outside. "Should be here in about a minute."

When they were in the car and driving away, Joshua turned to Jack. "I'm sorry for not telling you earlier, that they were going to be there. I figured it would have made you more nervous if you knew ahead of time."

"You're probably right. That was entirely not what I was expecting, for more reasons than one. But I think you made the right choice. What I need now is a stiff drink."

"Then let's get that for you. David would be interested in meeting up with us, if you'd like."

"Sure," Jack said. David would certainly be able to provide a distraction and some much-needed comic relief. "That would be great."

CHAPTER 28

Jack was happy to be back in Shanghai, and even happier to be heading over to Jojo's. He had wine with him and had ordered Thai takeout on his way over, but the only thing he wanted was her.

He knocked and then took a step back. The door opened. She wore a long-sleeve, scoop-neck black t-shirt that showed off her collarbones and a pair of jeans. Her hair was down, and she ran a hand through it once before giving him a quick hug.

No sooner did he settle into the feeling than her arms were releasing him and she was pulling him inside.

"Come on in," she said.

"The food should be here in about forty-five minutes." he said as he followed her inside. "They sounded pretty busy."

"That's perfect. Here, let me take those from you." She took the two wine bottles from him and set them on the counter. Then she walked right up to Jack, a slow smile on her face. She wrapped her arms around him. "Now for a more proper greeting."

"I missed you," he said, breathing in the scent from her hair. Her arms wrapped tightly around him left him with an overwhelming sense of well-being, like this was exactly where he was supposed to be.

"I missed you, too," she said. "More than I thought I would, to be honest."

"Well, if we're being honest then, I was counting down the minutes until I could get back here and see you. It's all I wanted."

She loosened her grip around him enough that she could lean back, look up at him. "I hope that means you can spend the night."

"There is nothing I would rather do. Especially because I have to go back to Beijing in a few days."

"You do?"

"Yes. It was unexpected, but I have to go back in a few days. I won't be staying long, though."

"More work stuff?"

"Yes." He couldn't quite read her tone; was she going to be upset? "Trust me when I say I'd much rather spend the time here with you."

"Then I guess it's good you're going to spend the night."

He leaned down and kissed her, relieved she wasn't upset. "We'll have a great time tonight," he whispered in her ear.

"I know we will. So . . . how was your trip?"

"It was good. I actually ended up meeting some interesting people." He paused. He hadn't necessarily been planning on bringing this up now, but it seemed like a natural segue, and he did want to confirm what he was already mostly certain was true. "And I actually had a question for you."

Jojo raised her eyebrows. "Yes?"

"Is your dad's name Wang Yang?"

The color drained from her face. "How did you find out?"

"One of my friends introduced me to some kids and their parents, and President Zhao and your father wound up being there, too. Your dad commented about having a daughter who spoke English with a French accent. And . . . you two look alike."

"Please don't tell anyone," Jojo said immediately.

"I won't," he said, "though I'm not entirely sure why it needs to be a huge secret."

"I don't want to be known as my father's daughter. I mean, I'm proud of my dad and I love him and he's a great person. But I want to be taken seriously on my own merits, and it's harder when people know you're the daughter of a standing committee member."

"I hear you," Jack said. "But who your parents are or are not would never factor into my feelings for you."

"I know that *now*," Jojo said. "And it's not like I'd hide my dad's identity from you forever, it's just . . ." Her voice trailed off and she shrugged. "I'm sorry for keeping that from you. I wouldn't want you hiding something like that from me."

"Well, I guess I know who to go to now if I ever need a favor," he said with a smirk. "It makes sense to me now, when you said that you'd have your dad see to it that your ex didn't bother you anymore." He tried to ignore the pang of guilt he felt—*I wouldn't want you hiding something like that from me*—by reminding himself that coming clean about this would only serve to put Jojo in danger. He'd rather have her be upset with him after the fact than potentially in harm's way now.

"He just sent the local police over. But yes, don't worry, neither of us will be bothered by him anymore."

"That's good. Seriously, though," he said, "you're vastly more interesting and talented in your own right."

Jojo grinned. "Ooh, you're good. Keep the compliments coming."

"But you should also know that China monitors WeChat communications, and can overhear our conversations."

"That's not a compliment." She frowned. "They monitor phones? I did know about WeChat."

"Think about it. It's in the government's best interest if they monitor foreigners and important people associated with the country's leadership. And from a technical point of view, it's easy to overhear conversations, even when cell phones are turned off."

Jack pulled his iPhone out of his pocket and then held his hand out for Jojo's phone, which she gave to him. He put both of them in a small pot, covered it with a lid, and put the pot in the refrigerator. He kept the black phone safe in his pocket.

"So I don't have to worry now about being overheard?" Jojo asked. "I know all that stuff is happening, but I never think about it."

"Most people don't."

"Do you think putting the phones in the refrigerator is going to work?"

"It'll help, I would think. Or maybe not, but I'm guessing your dad already knows about us."

"You're probably right. I'm sorry."

"You have nothing to be sorry about. I was glad to meet your father. To be honest, he seems the most open-minded of all the leadership. That's important."

Jojo nodded as she opened one of the wine bottles. "I love my dad, but that doesn't mean our relationship has always been free from conflict. He didn't want me to go to France, but I went, in part, because I wanted to put some distance between us, to sort of have the chance to stand on my own two feet. I know he thinks I'm isolated, and I also know he wants me to get married soon and have kids. Which has not been high on the priority list, that is until I—"

There was a knock at the door.

"That must be the food," Jojo said.

She hurried to the door, as though relieved she'd been interrupted, leaving Jack to wonder just what it was she'd been planning to say. He had his guesses, of course, but also didn't want to be presumptuous.

He thought she might bring it back up while they were eating, but she did not. Instead, she told him about what she was working on, and that some of her friends were hoping she'd host another get together, because they wanted to get to know him better.

"They like you," she said. "They're curious. That's good."

"Interesting," Jack said. "I've become an object of curiosity."

"From some of my friends? That's a compliment of the highest order."

"Sounds like the pressure is on me now . . . I mean, I wouldn't want to let your friends down."

"You just be yourself, then, and how could they not be impressed?" Her tone was light, joking, but her eyes reflected a seriousness and he knew she meant what she was saying.

After he'd cleared their plates away, he went into the bathroom. A message had come through on his black phone. Three short sentences:

Take phones out. Go home. They are worried.

He went out to the kitchen and removed the pot from the fridge, took the phones out.

"I think it's best if I spend tonight at my place," he said, handing Jojo her phone back.

She looked at him in surprise. "Really? But . . . I thought you were going to stay here."

"I know, it's just . . ." His mind spun, trying to come up with some reason that wouldn't sound completely ridiculous. "I'm not sure if it was something with the food or what, but I'm feeling a little . . . unwell. And if it's not the food and I'm coming down with something, I don't want to get you sick."

She fixed him with a long look, and he wanted to scream or hit something in frustration—he didn't want to be lying to her.

"Fine," she said, her tone chilly. "If you need to leave—go ahead."

"Please don't be upset, Jojo. I'm sorry. We'll be able to do this soon, okay?"

She said nothing for several seconds. "Like I already said—it's fine."

But she did not give him a hug, did not walk him to the door, and as Jack let himself out, he couldn't help but think back just a few short hours ago, how he'd stood in this very spot, his whole body alight with anticipation that he was about to, finally, see Jojo.

How quickly things can change, he thought sadly. He walked a few blocks and then hailed a taxi, which dropped him off at his apartment, alone—not the evening he'd had in mind.

CHAPTER 29

He did not see Jojo again before he left for Beijing.

This was not because he didn't want to, but he wanted to give her some space, though he also wanted her to know that he was there for her. So he sent her a message and let her know he was still feeling a little down (which was true), and that the only thing he wanted to do when he arrived back from his trip this time was spend the night with her.

I'm sorry I got upset about the other night, she wrote back. *I was disappointed, yes, but it was stupid to let it affect me like that. I can't wait to see you when you get back.*

Jack smiled, refusing to allow himself to entertain the notion that things might not go according to plan, that he might not come back.

* * *

He took the train again to Beijing, not wanting to have to deal with the chaos of the airport. He gazed out the window at the countryside passing by, thought of Jojo. Eventually, he couldn't hold off any longer and he sent her a text, letting her know he missed her and how were things going?

Her reply came almost immediately: *I'm worried. I haven't heard from my dad in a few days.*

He asked if there was anything he could do, the words ringing hollow as he typed them, knowing he was the reason she hadn't heard from her dad.

Was he that sick he can't return a phone call?

That wasn't good.

He tried to tell himself that it was for the greater good, that Jojo's father would be better in a few days. That *everyone* he had infected would be better in a few days. But Cooper's words echoed in his mind, the unlikely possibility of a fatality from the neurotoxin. And what if it turned out to be Jojo's father?

The thoughts continued to swirl, though he knew the futility of it. It was out of his control. He could only hope that everything was going to work out.

*　*　*

It was a relief to finally get off the train and make his way to his hotel in Beijing. As he finished checking in, he saw the hotel's long-time manager, Veronica. She saw him too and came over, smiling.

"Hello, Mr. Gold," she said in English. "We're glad you're staying with us; it's been a while."

Jack returned her smile. "Hi Veronica. I'm glad I ran into you; I'd like to ask your help with something," he replied, also in English. He found it useful when speaking about important matters to use English—people were often so absorbed that a non-Chinese person was speaking Chinese that they didn't listen to what he was saying.

"Certainly," Veronica said.

"Tomorrow some friends and I are taking a tour of the CCTV Headquarters Building."

She frowned. "They don't give tours of the CCTV Headquarters Building. It's closed to the public. You can view the outside, though. Or do you mean the CCTV Tower?"

"I know it sounds odd," Jack said, "but we *are* taking a tour of the inside of the building. Tomorrow afternoon. Could you please call them and confirm that I'll be there at about five pm with three of my important foreign friends?"

He could tell she was still skeptical, but she nodded.

"Tell them President Zhao's office made the arrangements," Jack continued. "And then can you please call my room when it's been confirmed?"

"Absolutely," Veronica said, not batting an eyelash at the mention of President Zhao.

Jack thanked her and then made his way across the lobby to the elevators. He had just shut the door to his room when the phone rang.

"Hello, Mr. Gold, I've confirmed your visit for tomorrow. They said you should use the Tower 1 entrance and ask for Tingting. She'll be your tour guide."

"Thank you, Veronica," Jack said. "I appreciate your help."

"My pleasure. Have a nice stay and enjoy the tour."

Jack hung up the phone and then lay back on the bed. He felt strangely calm, all things considered. There was no going back now.

CHAPTER 30

Jack was eating breakfast in his room the next morning when he received a text on his black phone:

Get inside the main news broadcasting Control Center in Tower Two. Joshua and Ari will know what to do from there. Make sure Tony Woo gets there to speak. Several fire trucks with hazmat suits will evacuate the building. If things go wrong, leave like nothing happened. Violence only if absolutely essential.

Take both phones with you.

Jack read the message once more, now understanding how it was they might be left alone in the building. He wrote back, asking if there was any way they could send him a picture of the Control Center and a map of the facility.

Cooper's reply came immediately:

No. There are zero public photos. It's on the 39th floor. We never thought we'd need access. Have your tour guide escort you there.

Afterward, leave your iPhone there and walk to the China World Hotel lobby.

Jack swallowed. It suddenly seemed like far too simple a plan, though he knew sometimes, simple plans worked. But had he just been willfully naïve this whole time, was he about to walk into what would surely be life imprisonment if they were caught?

He took a deep breath. The Chinese were, in many respects, highly predictable. They listened to authority figures and did what they were told, largely without ever taking initiative. Why? Because initiative meant taking a risk, and most citizens of China feared retribution.

So long as the government wasn't expecting such a plan, there was good chance it could succeed.

He couldn't let himself think of what would happen if they didn't.

*   *   *

At four, Jack took a taxi to the Jianguo Hotel. He waited in the lounge and at four-thirty, Ari and Tony arrived, both dressed in casual clothes, like tourists. Jack waved as they headed over.

Joshua showed up a few minutes later, and they headed over to the CCTV headquarters. They decided to walk, as it would take them about twenty minutes to get there on foot, putting them there right at five.

They kept the conversation light and informal; anyone who happened to overhear them would think they were just four tourists eager to see the sights of Beijing. Jack waited until there was no one within earshot to quietly tell them, "If things go south, we walk out."

Jack could see the building in the distance, which to him, looked like a chair. In Chinese it was nicknamed "big boxer shorts." He had heard others joke that it looked like a naked woman on her hands and knees. Clearly, it was not the pinnacle of aesthetic achievement.

They walked southeast, crossed a few streets, then came to the East 3rd Ring Middle Road, a massive raised highway. Jack looked up, feeling small in comparison to the large concrete pillars supporting the road above them. You couldn't hear the cars because they were too high up, but underneath it was plenty busy with traffic coming from both sides.

They crossed the busy intersection and then the CCTV building loomed in front of them. The building was surrounded by a lawn that was flanked with trees and bamboo. The four men made their way to the entrance, which was around back.

Ari looked at him before they entered. Neither said anything, but they exchanged a glance and briefly nodded at each other. It seemed like so long ago now that Jack had gone on that date that didn't work out, only to start up a conversation with Ari. And now here he was, embarking on what could have life-changing effects for over a billion people.

Upon entering the tower, they were in a large lobby which Jack knew stretched three floors underground and three floors up. Above ground, there were massive windows that let in an abundance of natural light.

Jack took a deep breath. The air was dry and clean, which meant powerful air purifiers were hard at work. This was unusual in Beijing, given the cost of purchasing and then operating the purifiers, but it also seemed appropriate: It wasn't just the air that was purified, it was also the content of the broadcasts. The government had banned foreign content during the prime time hours of seven to ten. The rest of the time, foreign content was limited to about a third of total daily broadcasts on any given channel. Online streaming platforms were also limited to no more than about a third of foreign content, which had to clear censorship before it would be broadcast.

They approached a long silver counter where two men and two women sat, all four dressed in smart black suits.

"Hi," Jack said. "My name is Jack Gold. I'm looking for Tingting."

"Yes," one of the women said. "Hello, Mr. Gold. Tingting will be out in a minute. Would you like to take a seat?" She gestured behind them to a sofa and several chairs.

"Sure," Jack said, relieved that they had indeed been expecting them.

No sooner had they sat down when a tall woman in an elegant white dress approached them.

"Hello," she said in perfect English. "Who is Mr. Gold?"

"That would be me," Jack said, standing up. He went over to her and they shook hands.

"My name is Tingting. Welcome to CCTV Headquarters. I look forward to showing you around."

"We're very much looking forward to it." Jack felt the black phone in his pocket vibrate. He pulled it out and looked at it discreetly.

Go to the main broadcasting control room in Tower 2 first. Try to remain around there.

"Is this the first time you've visited?" Tingting asked.

"No," Jack said. "I've been here a few times and wanted to arrange a visit for my friends." He gave Tingting his most convincing look, hoping she'd believe his lie and assume he was very familiar with the place.

"That's excellent. Let's get started then. If you'll please follow me this way, we can begin the tour in Tower 1."

Jack coughed. "Actually, the main reason for our visit was so my friends could see the main broadcasting room and the Control Center in Tower 2. Would it be possible to start there first?"

Tingting frowned, clearly thrown off by this request. "The best way to see the architectural and cultural significance of the structure is to follow the route I'm about to take you on." The frown shifted back to a smile and she looked over Jack's shoulder at Ari, Joshua, and Tony.

"We'd like to go directly to the Control Center. We can come by another day after we have someone call with more specific instructions, if you prefer." He spoke calmly, kept his tone friendly, but also with a barely discernible indignation at the idea that she might not placate guests from the president's office.

This is the moment it could all go wrong, Jack thought, the air seeming to thicken around them. His mind began to race, playing out possible scenarios. If she pushed back against starting in Tower 2, perhaps he could backpedal and they could follow the route she wanted them to go. He just had no idea how long that would take, but he didn't want to jeopardize the entire mission over a disagreement about where to begin the tour.

But then Tingting nodded. "Certainly, Mr. Gold," she said, and she turned and began to walk in the opposite direction.

Jack let out a breath and exchanged another look with Ari. But they were on their way, and in the right direction.

"There are two towers," Tingting said as they entered into an elevator. "Fifty-one floors, and seventy-five elevators."

"Wow," Joshua said. "Seventy-five?"

"Yes. It was designed through a collaborative effort between the Chinese and the Europeans."

The elevator began to ascend. Jack didn't understand how it was possible to commission and build a structure that had seventy-five elevators, though he knew, because of the way the building was designed—with the two towers connected by a third—that different elevators were needed to get to the different areas within the buildings. This meant some people likely had to take two different elevators each time they had to get to and from their offices.

"We'll be going directly to the thirty-ninth floor, where the main Control Center is. Fortunately, we'll only have to take one elevator." She looked at Jack as though she could hear his thoughts.

Jack gave her a brisk smile and hoped this wasn't true.

They exited at the thirty-ninth floor. Thick beams of steel criss-crossed like lattice work from the floor to the ceiling in front of the large windows. The gleaming hardwood floor stretched in front of them; at the end of the long hallway Jack could make out double doors, shut tight.

"Right this way," Tingting said.

"How many channels does CCTV have?" Joshua asked, quickening his stride to fall in step next to her.

"Twenty-four public television channels and seventeen pay channels. But the facility has the capacity to manage two hundred channels."

"Interesting," Joshua said. "That's so many channels that could be used but aren't."

Tingting slowed as they approached the Control Center. She turned to face the four of them, a serious expression on her face. "The Control Center is a restricted access area. It's open to authorized staff only. But, Mr. Gold, I know you are a privileged guest. Management has agreed you can walk in silently, but only for a minute or two. No photographs are allowed."

She turned, arm outstretched to swipe her access card. Before she was able to, though, a fire alarm went off. Though Jack knew to expect it, the blaring noise jarred him and made his heart race.

"Is it a false alarm?" he yelled to Tingting. "Should we just ignore it?"

She paused. "No. We should leave."

"I don't smell smoke," Jack yelled. "It would be a shame that we came out here for the tour and it wasn't able to happen because of a false alarm."

She was wavering. "We'll make it quick," he said. "And then we won't have to come back here again."

That sealed the deal. "Fine," she said. "But no more than a minute, two at the most." She swiped her card and unlocked the door. Ari and Joshua hurried in. From his vantage point, Jack looked down upon the Control Center. At three stories high it was massive and unlike anything he had ever seen before. TV monitors in various sizes bordered the room, hundreds of them, they had to be at least three stories high and all broadcasting different things. The largest screen was in the center of the room, and was, in Jack's estimation, sixty-five feet across, broadcasting a news program. In the middle of the room, two curved desks, each with four work stations, formed a circle that was flanked by two rows of desks equipped with about twenty work areas each. From this vantage point, the configuration looked exactly like any eye.

This isn't just a place to broadcast, Jack thought. *It looks like the whole world is being monitored.*

A voice came over the loudspeakers. *"There is a biohazard in the building. Everyone must evacuate immediately. This is not a drill. Repeat, this is not a drill. Evacuate immediately."*

All the workers in the Control Center were on the move, heeding the wail of the fire alarm. Jack looked over his shoulder, where Tingting stood in the threshold, blocking Tony's path. She looked at Jack.

"Mr. Gold, they just announced that this is not a drill, and we must leave immediately. They say it's a biohazard. Please, follow me." She motioned with her arm for the three of them to step out of the Control Room.

Tingting was a problem, and now Jack was going to have to figure out a way to deal with her. It would be possible to incapacitate her without causing too much damage, which was not what he wanted to do. Ideally, it should look like an accident.

But before he was able to do anything, a security guard in a blue uniform and hat strode down the hallway directly toward them. Jack tried to look confused, or at the very least disoriented—which wasn't entirely false, as the alarms were still blaring around them—as he looked at Tingting. "I'm sorry," he said, hoping that Tony would take the opportunity to nudge his way into the room. "I don't understand you."

"You have to leave!" the security guard shouted. "All of you! Immediately!"

"Mr. Gold," Tingting said, "it's a biohazard, not a fire. We need to leave right now!"

The guard had reached them, and he looked in disbelief that they would still be standing there. "NOW!" he shouted. "You need to leave now."

Tony looked at Jack, clearly unsure of what his next move should be. Everything seemed to fall away, even the sound of the alarm. *This is it,* Jack thought, pins and needles shooting up his spine. *It's all over. It's all going to fall apart unless I think of something . . .*

The guard reached for Tony's arm. Before he was able to make contact, though, Tony clenched his fist and drew it back. Jack watched as if it were happening in slow motion. The guard ducked and the force of Tony's missed punch spun him around, allowing the guard time to reach out and shove Tony into a metal railing by the entrance. The crack as Tony's head made contact was unmistakable, and when he slid to the ground, Jack knew he wasn't going to be getting up any time soon.

Shit, Jack thought as he looked at Tony, motionless on the floor. He shifted his focus to the guard, who took a step toward him like Jack was going to be next. That's exactly what was going to happen, unless

Jack had more success against the guy than Tony did. No sooner had he stepped into his fighting stance than five individuals dressed in full hazmat suits appeared. They converged on them before Jack could do anything, and from the look on the guard's face, he seemed as surprised to see them as Jack was. Jack watched as the guard and Tingting were guided away. One of the people picked up Tony and threw him over their shoulder as if Tony weighed nothing at all. Jack's muscles tensed, ready to react if he was the next one they tried to drag off, but they didn't. Instead, moving like a pack, the group turned and left.

Jack let the door close and turned and looked at Ari and Joshua.

It was just the three of them.

There was no one sitting at any of the terminals in the Control Center, though the TV monitors still glowed as they continued to broadcast their programs.

"What happened to Tony?" Ari asked.

"He tried to hit the guard, and the guard pushed him into the railing. He hit his head. Those guys in the hazmat suits took him. Along with the guard and Tingting. Tony will be a little sore, but he's going to be okay."

"Shit," Ari said. "I mean, glad to hear he'll be all right but . . . he was our guy. He was the one who was going to tell everyone what we've found out, tell them about the facts we learned about the leadership and how the internet is now opened up." He rubbed his eyes. "And the documents that will be released."

"We have to go through with it," Joshua said, eyes wide. "We made it this far—we can't just give up."

"You're right," Ari said. "We have no choice."

They both looked at Jack.

"You have to do it, Jack," Ari said after a moment. "Like I said—we have no choice."

Joshua nodded. "You can definitely do this."

"Hold on," Jack said. *What* were they saying to him? "I can't speak to 1.4 *billion* people."

"Yes, you can," Ari said firmly. "You know more than just the basics of what's been going on. You believe it. Your Chinese is impeccable. You're perfect. Let's get going."

"You have this, Jack," Joshua said, nodding enthusiastically. "Please. We can't waste any more time."

Jack nodded. The pins and needles sensation in his spine seemed to have migrated to his entire body. This was happening. If they were to succeed, Jack would have to address an entire nation. No pre-planned speech, no notes, nothing. He would have to improvise.

"How long do I have to speak for?" Jack asked.

Ari looked at him. "Five to seven minutes. Max."

"Okay." What was he going to say for *five minutes*?

"Follow me," Joshua said. "We're going to go into the main broadcasting room."

Jack followed Joshua out of the Control Center and next door, to the main broadcasting room.

The alarms had finally stopped. Jack wasn't sure when that happened—just a second ago or several minutes? Was he in the right state of mind to address a billion people if he hadn't even noticed when the alarms had stopped?

"Sit down and get ready," Joshua said, nodding to the main broadcasting desk. Jack took a seat. He pulled the microphone closer. Never had anything in his life felt more unreal, yet here he was.

An image of Jojo flashed through his mind. He was about to be broadcast to an entire nation—he didn't know where she was at this very moment, but chances were good she would see him. What would she think? Obviously she would know that he hadn't been completely forthright with her—he could only hope that she would understand the reason for his need to keep her in the dark.

He took a deep, shaky breath, his palms were sweating, and he was almost certain that if he were standing, not sitting, his legs would be trembling.

But he had to do this.

And he had to do so in a way that would be effective, that would make their efforts not be in vain. Because he only had this one chance.

His broadcast would take the place of Xinwen Lianbo, the evening news. Since its first broadcast began in 1978, Jack knew that it was a national ritual to watch it while at the dinner table. It was the mouthpiece for the party and the state, and it was used to influence the masses, by showing how busy the leaders were, how rapidly the motherland was developing, and how all other countries were in chaos.

"How long do I have before I go on?" Jack asked. He adjusted his black polo shirt, tried to sit up straight in the chair. It would've been better if he had a tie on, but nothing could be done about that now.

"Two minutes and counting."

It was almost six o'clock on a Friday evening, when everyone was off work. The broadcast would be aired, and then repeated at seven, maximizing viewership. Jack took another deep breath.

"One minute," Joshua yelled. He had a look of concentration on his face as he flipped some switches and made a few final adjustments. Then he looked up at Jack. "You can start when you're ready. We can edit the front and the end."

Jack nodded.

"You're going to be fine," Joshua said, and he gave Jack a big smile, like he believed this was all going to work out.

Jack turned the microphone on. He took one more deep breath and then in slow, formal Chinese, he began to speak. If he focused just on the camera, it wasn't so bad—it wasn't like he had a billion people's faces staring back at him.

"Ladies and gentlemen, hello. My name is Jack Gold. I'm an American, but tonight I represent other countries too—including the UK, France, South Korea, and Israel."

He paused. Joshua gave him an enthusiastic thumbs up.

"I'd like to share some information with you," Jack continued. "Some simple but important facts that you can verify." He paused again. It was imperative he said the right thing, or people would stop listening. "I want you to know how much I love China and that I'm only here reluctantly. China's leaders have been infected by a neurotoxin. But don't worry—they'll be well in a few days." He had no idea what sort of rumors might be flying around right now pertaining to the high-level officials that were all suddenly sick. He wanted to sound calm and encourage everyone else to remain calm, too.

But in the back of his mind, a movie reel unspooled, playing the myriad of different scenarios that might be occurring all over the country at this very moment: a family gathered around the dinner table, food untouched as they stared at the foreigner on their TV screen; an elderly couple who had perhaps grown so accustomed to the same news broadcast every night they were seldom even paid full attention anymore was suddenly riveted; an exhausted, still dusty construction worker as he ate his dinner at a small noodle restaurant; college students in their dorm room lounge who had seldom paid attention to the news but were now; and, Jojo.

"This is not a coup or invasion. You have nothing to fear." And here he offered the camera a small, but reassuring smile, the sort of smile you might give to a young child who was lost. "It's in the best interest of the Chinese people to have open access to news and information. A network of satellites has been deployed and you now have open internet access to information from any country—the BBC, CNN, FOX. The free press serves as a check against the government officials. Why is this necessary? Because if you control the information, you control the citizens. You. I am addressing you as a whole, but I am speaking to each and every one of you—the government has used censorship and its vice-like grip on the dissemination of information to control you. To shape how you think and the values you hold dear.

"We will be downloading verifiable information on China's leadership and key officials. It's useful for people to know more about their leaders. Have you ever wondered where they get their money? How they pay for things? How it is, for example, that President Zhao Lihong's daughter is able to go to Harvard? Where did he get the money to pay an annual tuition of seventy-seven thousand dollars when his salary is only twenty-two thousand dollars a year? How is it that he's worth over one point five billion dollars?"

Jack paused to let the numbers sink in.

"We've also uncovered documents that outline the intent of the Communist Party. They are putting the party's interests above those of the Chinese people. Let me give you an example—the One Belt One Road initiative. What should be more important: infrastructure projects or enhancing the country's educational system? Is this project the best way to grow China and enhance the lives of the people who live here?"

He paused again, as if he had an audience there in front of him, answering these rhetorical questions. He didn't want to rush what he was saying, even though his time was starting to dwindle. But his nervousness had abated and he felt fully present, engaged, like he was doing the right thing, not just for himself but for an entire nation. He knew there was still ample opportunity for things to go wrong, but he had at least given it his best effort. His father would be proud.

"State-owned enterprises benefit from things like the One Belt One Road initiative, not everyday citizens. Big business plays a disproportionate role—an inappropriate role—in leadership selection. And this happens at your expense. At your children's expense. It's a form of corruption. Four thousand people die in this country every day due to pollution-related illnesses. *Four thousand every day.* Yet the pollution continues. Who benefits from it?"

He leaned forward a little, looking straight into the camera, as if he were about to impart a secret. He could imagine the viewers at home leaning a little closer, too. At least, he hoped.

"Everyone I've met in China feels oppressed by the government. There are no laws to control officials, and no one to redress wrongs. How can this be fixed? It often feels like a hopeless situation. Which is why, I believe, so many of you emigrate to America, or make sure your children are born in other countries. How many of you send your children overseas to be educated? Those of you with the money to do so will go abroad for medical treatments, or leave to get what you want because you can't find it here. But the majority of you cannot afford this luxury. And so you remain, and are continued to be fed lies by the government, all in an attempt to keep the masses under control."

Jack was aware of Joshua in his periphery, standing there watching him, nodding along. "These are symptoms of a deep problem," Jack said. "Someone in China earns only *sixteen percent* of what someone in the United States makes in the same occupation. Do you think something like this is going to be resolved by giving the state more control?

"China's private sector contributes sixty percent of GDP and eighty percent of employment. Why haven't state-owned enterprises done better?" He could only hope people were still listening. That they were taking seriously what he was saying.

"And now the Communist Party is starting to put its members in private companies, alleging it's because they're in *positions of authority.* They used to control where you live, where you work, who you married, and how many children you had. Yes, things have changed, but what has this meant for China? China's population is aging. There are far more old people than young. There are one hundred and eighteen men for every one hundred women. Centralized planning has resulted in unintended consequences. And the government has been lying about economic growth data. The economy has been growing by at least two percent less than reported over the past ten years. That is a fact."

Jack cast his gaze downward for a moment, before resuming eye contact with the camera. Emotion surged through him, though his exterior remained impassive. It was as if he could feel the presence of every single set of eyes taking in his broadcast. Some would listen to what he had to say. Some would not. And one person in particular, he hoped, would see him now and be able to forgive him for his deception.

Jack gave the camera what might have looked like a closed-mouth, resigned smile. The sort of expression that said *I am just telling it to you straight. I'm leveling with you, because I have no reason not to.*

"One of the people I most admire won a Nobel prize in economics—Dr. Milton Friedman. I've been fortunate enough to meet him twice. And I'd like to share with you something he said: *The greatest advances of civilization, whether in architecture or painting, in science and literature, in industry or agriculture, have never come from centralized government.* In China, seventy percent of technological innovation comes from the private sector. Friedman wrote an important book called *Free to Choose.* We're making a copy, in Chinese, available to everyone. I think you'll find it to be the starting point for many great debates.

"And the final thing I wanted to mention is that it is you, the people of China, who will need to decide how to select government officials. You need to decide on what sort of economic policies you want. But you need full information to be able to make that decision if you want to avoid *tiāngāohuángdìyuǎn*. This is a fact."

Joshua held a hand up and made a twirling motion with his index finger—time to start wrapping it up. Jack spread his palms on the desk and looked with earnest at the camera. "We're not here to change China. But this is an important message, and one in which we felt *had* to be communicated to each and every one of you. So you could make your own informed choice—something that many of my compatriots in the U.S. have come to take for granted. But for you—the citizens of this great country—this will be an experience you've not had before. I believe you will find it to be most empowering, but you do not have to take my word for it. You can try it yourselves." He gave a brief, crisp nod, as if this was the last glimpse of someone he was fond of but would never see again. "Thank you. And goodnight."

CHAPTER 31

Jack switched his microphone off and looked around. "Was that okay? Are we done?"

"Yes," Joshua said. "Let's not hang around. We need to find Ari." His expression was focused, but he flashed Jack a quick smile. "That was impressive. Good job."

"Thank you," Jack said with a nod. As he stood, a wave of exhaustion steamrolled him. Not just physical exhaustion, but mental and emotional as well. He tried to think back to what he'd just said and couldn't recall a single word. And what now? He looked toward the door, half-expecting a security official to come in and shoot them.

It was time to go.

He followed Joshua up the stairs and then back down into the Control Center, which was eerily quiet, except for Ari, who was feverishly at work.

"Give him a minute," Joshua whispered.

Jack pulled his phone out of his pocket. No reception. His black phone, however, did have reception, and he used it to systematically take pictures of all aspects of the Control Center, including a panoramic shot, followed by a video. He walked back downstairs and stood behind Ari, who was deftly navigating through an array of icons and text, all in Chinese, on one of the computer screens.

I didn't realize his Chinese was so good, Jack thought.

Ari looked over his shoulder at Jack. "We have a problem," he said. "I can only upload the broadcast to channels 1 and 13. For some reason, I can't upload to Channel 4."

"Ari, leave it," Joshua pleaded. "We have to go. People know they can switch channels and it'll be on a loop anyway. We have to get out of here."

Ari locked eyes with Jack. He didn't want to leave until he was able to upload it to channel 4, Jack could see that on his friend's face, but each moment they stayed made their capture all the more likely. He gave Ari a tiny nod. They had done, to the best of their ability, what they had come to do. It would have to be good enough.

"Fine," Ari said, a note of exasperation in his voice. "Let's go."

Before they were able to make their way out, Jack's black phone vibrated. It was a message from Cooper, telling them all to leave their phones behind except for the black one, and to walk to China World Hotel. Just hearing from Cooper reassured Jack.

"We should leave our phones here," he said. "Otherwise they might be able to track us." Ari and Joshua nodded and left their phones next to Jack's.

They retraced their steps and hurried down the corridor to the elevators. They took it down to the lobby and as they approached the main door, Jack took a deep breath, knew this would be the moment of truth: What would be awaiting them when they stepped outside? A wall of soldiers, weapons pointed directly at them? Considering the magnitude of what they'd just done, there was a good chance they'd shoot first and ask questions . . . well, never.

As Ari gripped the handle and pushed the door open, Jack fought against the urge to squeeze his eyes shut. An image of Jojo appeared in his mind, and he wished more than anything that he had a chance to say goodbye, to tell her how much he loved her, how happy she had made him–

The door opened all the way. There was no one there.

Jack blinked. It was almost impossible to believe he was in China, because not only were there no people, there were no cars, no motor-bikes, the fire trucks had left. It was like they were on a movie set, if the movie were about a civilization that had been completely wiped out.

"Okay," Jack said. "Let's head over to the China World Hotel."

"I bet it's happy hour by now," Joshua said.

Ari nodded. "Sounds good to me."

They said little as they walked, eager to get to the hotel. Upon arrival, they went to the bar and ordered beers. It wasn't until they started in on their second round that they began to relax enough to be able to talk.

"So it's done," Ari said, inspecting the neck of his beer bottle. "And despite things not going exactly according to plan, I think it went well."

"I don't even remember what I said," Jack confessed. "Was it all right?"

"What's done is done," Ari said. "For someone who basically had to improvise–I think you did great."

"Yeah," Joshua said. "I never would've been able to come up with that on the spot. I'm sure whatever Tony had planned to say would've been good, too, but everything you said, Jack . . . I don't think there's anything I would have changed."

As Jack was lifting his beer bottle to his lips, he saw three men enter the bar. The men were Caucasian and dressed in formal suits. They stood there for a moment, looking around, and then walked over to Jack. The man in the middle was older than the two flanking him; he had salt and pepper hair and fine lines etching his face.

"Mr. Gold," he said. "My name is Davis. I'm from the U.S. Embassy." He opened his jacket and pulled his government ID from his pocket. "For your safety, please come with me. There's a flight out of China you need to be on."

"Got it," Jack said, taking one more swig of his beer.

"Gentlemen," Davis said, looking first at Ari, then Joshua, "there are flights waiting for you as well. You'll be taking separate cars."

One of the men went over to Ari and escorted him out; the other did the same to Joshua.

"But . . ." Jack said to their retreating figures. Davis had also started to leave, and Jack reluctantly followed. There were three black SUVs waiting outside, and they each entered into a different one. Ari turned and caught Jack's eye as he was getting in the vehicle; they exchanged a brief nod and a tiny smile, and Jack wondered if this was, perhaps, the last time he was going to see his friend.

CHAPTER 32

He flew in a Gulfstream private jet the eighteen hours back to DC. The majority of the journey, Jack slept; Davis had assured him it was the comedown from all the adrenaline that had been coursing through his body, and what better way was there to spend a flight that took nearly an entire day? Jack had to agree.

An identical-looking black SUV was there at the hangar to pick Jack up when the plane landed. He got right into the vehicle and didn't need to bother with customs. Just seeing the familiar sights, knowing he was on safe ground, filled Jack with relief. As they drove, he reached into his pocket and pulled out his iPhone, which had been recovered from the Control Center, as a precaution, Davis had explained when he'd given the phone back. He hadn't gone into further detail, and Jack hadn't bothered to ask—he was just glad to have his phone back.

The gratitude quickly evaporated when he opened WeChat and saw the message from Jojo:

You fucking liar!

His blood ran cold. He resisted the urge to call her immediately and explain himself. Now that the Control Center mission had been success-fully completed, he realized how badly this could mess things up with Jojo. Though she'd only written those three words to him, he knew what she was thinking. That he was a spy. That he had used her. That, perhaps, he didn't even have feelings for her.

He took several deep breaths.

"It's pretty incredible, huh," Davis said, eyes straight ahead as he drove. "And all because of what you did."

"Huh?" Jack said.

Davis glanced at him for a second. "You're reading about what's going on over there now, aren't you? Zhao's been replaced. It worked. Some people had their doubts as to whether something like this could be pulled off successfully, but it *worked!*"

Jack opened his news app and began to scroll. Davis was correct—Zhao had been replaced by . . . *Wang Yang*. Jack blinked and read the headline again. Scrolled down a little further and there was a photo of the man—Jojo's father.

Jojo's father was now the president of China.

He continued to read:

"There have been street protests in Beijing and Changchun, about one hundred injuries have been reported. Some protesters were objecting to colonial influences on China. Others were in support of President Zhao. There was little coordination amongst protestors. Despite the use of water cannons, it was only after shops and automobiles began to get destroyed that the police subdued protestors."

His eyes scanned the words again. "That's incredible," he said, and he thought of Ari and Joshua, and hoped they had made it safely wherever it was they were going, that they were also proud of what they had managed to pull off.

*   *   *

Davis took Jack to the W Hotel, where he had a room waiting for him. He also had two Secret Service agents, Tom and Denis, who would be accompanying Jack wherever he went.

"For your protection," Davis said.

Jack nodded, stifling a yawn. "Well, gentlemen, I think the most I'm going to be doing tonight is taking a shower and then going to bed. I'm wiped."

They both gave him crisp nods. Davis told Jack he'd pick him up tomorrow at eight for several debriefing meetings he needed to attend.

"I'll be a little more alert by then," Jack said.

He retired to his room and recognized his suitcase at the foot of the bed. Someone must have gone into his apartment and packed some clothes for him, along with some of his stuff from the bathroom—toothbrush, razor, hairbrush. The familiar sight of his belongings comforted him, even though it was a little weird to think of someone entering his home and going through his stuff.

He undressed and took the hottest shower he could stand, methodically cleansing himself of the Beijing pollution. When he got out of the shower, he changed into a clean t-shirt and his pair of flannel lounge pants and crawled into bed. Thoughts of Jojo swirled through his mind, and then he thought of Ari and Joshua. He hoped that they were somewhere safe. He would wait a little while and then try to contact Ari. He couldn't imagine never hearing from his friend again.

*   *   *

Jack woke early the next morning, before the sun had risen, disoriented at first, but then he remembered he was here at the W in DC. In a way, everything that had happened the past few days felt like a dream—except for the fact that Jojo was probably ready to end their relationship. Though he had several meetings this morning, the only thing he wanted to focus on was how to win her back.

Since there was still some time until Davis would be here to pick him up, Jack decided to go down to the hotel's restaurant to get some breakfast.

"Good morning, gentlemen," he said to Tom and Denis when he stepped out of his room. It felt strange to have these two men with him, but, as he made his way through the lobby, he realized that a few people were looking at him curiously, like they recognized him from somewhere.

He kept his gaze down and made his way into the restaurant. He ordered coffee, Eggs Benedict, and a banana mango smoothie, and was vaguely aware of Tom and Denis, seated at the table next to him. After his coffee arrived, Jack took his phone out and re-read Jojo's last three words to him. His silence probably wasn't helping, but he wanted to say the right thing when he finally spoke to her.

If she would talk to him.

Would Jojo accept his explanation? Was he prepared to accept it if she never wanted to talk to him again?

Well, of course he would be—what could he do about it?

Jack sighed as he worked through his food, which he was vaguely aware was good, but he barely tasted, he was so distracted. If Jojo felt he had betrayed her, if she felt that she could never trust him again, then yes, their relationship would have to end. And hadn't he been aware that this could be a potential consequence, if he undertook this mission when Ari had first proposed it? It wasn't as if he'd been forced into it—he'd been given a choice. Which he'd made, and now had to deal with the potential fallout.

When he was finished eating, he refilled his coffee. He took a sip and looked around the restaurant. Two young Chinese women were at a corner table, whispering and looking his way. One of the women held up her iPhone, and it appeared she was taking his picture. No doubt she would share the photo on her WeChat account.

But when the girls stood up and appeared to be making their way toward him, Tom and Denis were on their feet immediately.

"It's almost eight," Denis said. "Why don't we get going."

Tom stood several feet in front of Jack, blocking the women from getting any farther. They tried to peer around him, and Jack gave them a little smile and a wave as he stood and allowed himself to be escorted out.

They went out a back entrance, where Davis was waiting in a black SUV. Denis and Tom would wait back at the hotel for Jack's return, and though Jack knew it was for his own good, he couldn't help but feel a bit like a child who required constant supervision by an approved chaperone.

"Who are we seeing first?" Jack asked.

"Mogul."

Davis did not elaborate, leaving Jack to assume that "Mogul" must be the Secret Service's code name for the president. He was glad he decided to wear his dark blue suit.

When they arrived at the White House, the lobby was abuzz with action, people going in every direction, it seemed.

"I didn't get to go on the tour last time I was here," he mused. After he'd relinquished his phones and went through the metal detector, one of the attendants gave him a ticket so he could retrieve his phones when he left.

Jack followed Davis down a narrow corridor which opened into a small alcove where there were two mahogany desks. He recognized the woman sitting behind one of them—the president's secretary. She smiled.

"Go right on in, Mr. Gold," she said, gesturing to the door, which was not flush with the wall, like a regular door, but instead was at a slight angle. Because the room that it opened in on was not a room with right angles—Jack swallowed. He was about to enter the Oval Office.

He glanced at Davis, who nodded and extended his arm, gesturing for Jack to walk past him. He did so, hesitating only for a moment before he turned the doorknob and pushed.

President Sutton was right there to greet him, a big smile on his face.

"Jack," he said, extending his hand. "How are you doing?"

Jack returned the handshake, still having a hard time believing he was *here*. Shaking the president's hand.

"It's a pleasure to see you again, sir," Jack said. "I have to admit—I'm a little surprised to be here; I got on an airplane, went to a hotel, and now I find myself here."

"Why don't we sit down for a few minutes," Sutton said, motioning for Jack to follow him over to the middle of the room where there was a sitting area. Sutton took a seat in one of the wingback chairs; Jack sat on the sofa. To his right was the Resolute Desk, behind it the three large, south-facing windows.

"So," Sutton said. "It sounds like you've had a rather unusual couple of days. Have you heard what's happened?"

"I heard Wang Yang is now president. That's a good a choice, I think he'll do well. I met him a few days ago."

"You are correct," Sutton said. He rubbed his palms together and gave Jack a big smile. "I want you to understand the magnitude of what you have done. You've turned a negative into a positive. China is now a friend instead of an enemy. You've galvanized and educated *both* sides on what socialism is and the dangers of it." Jack hoped his face wasn't flushing. Regardless of whether what Sutton was now telling him was true or not, he couldn't help but feel slightly uncomfortable that the President of the United States of America was heaping all this praise on him.

And Sutton wasn't done. He looked Jack right in the eye. "You have impacted not just Eastern civilization, but Western, also. And very few people were hurt. There was no loss of life. It's incredible!"

"Thank you," Jack said. "But it wasn't just me."

"I know, but from everything I've heard, things would've gone disastrously in the opposite direction if it hadn't been for your quick-thinking. Because of you, they've replaced Zhao Lihong with Wang Yang. If they'd selected Li Keqiang, things would've been horrible. The man's a bowling ball looking for pins."

Li Keqiang had been China's number two after Zhao Lihong, and Jack nodded at Sutton's assessment—he was absolutely right.

"He's great at finding problems but wouldn't know how to get himself out of a wet paper bag."

"I know about Li Keqiang," Jack said. "He substituted unreliable official GDP data by looking at railway cargo volume, electricity consumption, and total loans disbursed by banks. He's a hunting dog, but he can't shoot."

"A hunting dog," Sutton said. "I like that. You know what I also like? The fact that you were the one to deliver the message to all the citizens of China. My guys tell me there was nothing rehearsed about it, and I think that went a long way. People can tell when you're simply reciting words or when you're authentically speaking the truth. It would've been a vastly different outcome if Tony Woo had been the one to deliver the message. It wouldn't have gone over nearly as well." Sutton paused. "While China isn't mad at us, there are obviously still some bad actors out there that don't like what you've done. I've talked with Wang Yang and you'll have protection from both of us for as long as you need it."

"I appreciate it," Jack said, though he hoped he wasn't going to need protection for much longer.

"We might want to have a ceremony or something in the future. How do you feel about that? I imagine you could go on a speaking tour if you wanted."

"Certainly," Jack said. "Except . . . I think I'm going to decline the speaking tour, for now." He didn't like the idea of cashing in on what he'd done; that hadn't been his reason for doing it, and he could only imagine what Jojo's reaction would be.

"Of course, of course," Sutton said. "Now—is there anything I can do for you?"

Jack hesitated. "Yes," he said finally. "I'd like to get a passport for Jojo Wang. Wang Yang's daughter," he added, when Sutton's brow creased in confusion.

"Ah," he said, his brow smoothing. "A passport for Wang Yang's daughter?"

"I'm in love with her." The words were out of his mouth before it occurred to him that he was confessing his romantic feelings to the president.

"We can get that for you. She must be very proud."

"Uh . . . no, not really. There's actually a good chance she's never going to speak to me again—she thinks I'm an American spy. And that I lied to her. Which, I guess is true, but it was only because I didn't want her to be in danger." Jack sighed. "When do you think it'll be safe for me to travel back to China?"

Sutton gave him a surprised look. "When?" he asked. "Why, it's safe for you to go to China right now, considering you have Wang Yang's protection. You're responsible for putting him in office."

"Well," Jack said, "I don't know if I'd go *that* far."

"You might not, but I will. If it hadn't been for you, Jack, Wang Yang would not be in power right now. That's a fact. Just let us know when you plan to leave and we'll inform him. Actually, he wanted me to tell you he'd like you to visit. And we can arrange private transportation."

Sutton stood and walked over to the Resolute Desk and picked up his phone. "I need a passport for Jojo Wang, daughter of Wang Yang," he said. "Diplomatic, full citizenship. Yes, that's right. Yes . . . Yes . . . Please get it to Mr. Gold as soon as possible. And while we're at it, let's get one for him, too. Yes. Thank you."

He hung up. "I figured you should have one, too," he said as he came and sat back down. "You deserve that—and much more. What do you think you'll do now?"

"Thank you, Mr. President," Jack said. "Well . . . now that things seem settled, I'd like to head back to China and see if I can fix things with Jojo."

"I hope it all works out for you, Jack. You have the gratitude of two nations behind you. Let me know if you need anything. We can create a position for you here any time you want."

"Thank you, sir," Jack said, a part of him wishing that his father were here to witness what was happening right now.

"We'll plan on speaking again in about a week or so, when things have calmed down a little more."

"That sounds good," Jack said. "Is there going to be anymore debriefing?"

"Usually there would be, but these are unusual circumstances. They've already interviewed Ari and Joshua, and we have the audio from your phones. Everything is very clear."

"Great." Jack exhaled, relieved that Ari and Joshua were also safe.

"Before you go, though," Sutton said, "I want you to tell me something. I saw the pictures of the Control Center, but . . . what was it like inside?"

Jack thought for a moment, trying to find the right words. He was one of the few outsiders to ever set foot in the place.

"It felt exactly like what its name is—a malevolent, high-tech center that only wanted one thing: to control a civilization. Futuristic and at the same time, completely out of date. It wasn't any sort of place I wanted to be any longer than I had to."

"The stuff out of a science fiction movie," Sutton said. He stood, and Jack did the same. "I can't thank you enough, Jack. You should come to Camp David some time."

"That would be an honor, sir." The two men shook hands.

"Would you mind if we had our photo taken before you left?"

"Not at all," Jack said. "But would you give me twenty-four hours before you release the photo, please?"

"Of course." Sutton went back to his desk and picked up the phone. "Send him in."

A moment later, the door that Jack had entered through opened and a man who looked similar to Joshua appeared with his camera. Jack stood next to Sutton in front of the Resolute Desk and smiled as the photographer snapped photos from several angles. Jack and Sutton shook hands once more, and then he exited the Oval Office.

Davis was waiting for him. "They'll have the passports sent over to your hotel later today," he said, as they walked down the corridor. "And . . . I'm breaking formal protocol, but there are some people who would like to say hello. Is that okay?"

"Absolutely." As he followed Davis through another corridor, he wondered who it was that wanted to say hi. Ari? Joshua? He doubted they were here, but that would be great, he'd love to see them.

Davis had led him into a good-sized office, full of people. At first, Jack didn't see anyone he recognized, but then there was Cooper, getting up from his chair and hurrying over.

"Jack!" he exclaimed, and his enthusiasm made him seem almost like a different person. "You did amazing! It was incredible, just incredible." He gave him a hug, and then turned and yelled, "Hey, everyone, it's Jack!" Those who had not already turned to look at him did so, and a moment later, the entire room broke into applause and cheers. He was lauded with praise—all by people he'd never seen before. But he knew these people were the ones working behind the scenes, the ones who helped ensure things would go down as smoothly as possible.

"I just wanted to thank you all," Jack said. "I know things didn't go exactly according to plan, but because of you all, we succeeded in doing what we wanted to do. Thank you for your remarkable support and trust. I look at you guys as family."

And he did—these people had kept him from harm, had heard every word he'd spoken and read every text on his phone. In a way, they knew everything about him, and Jack felt a gratitude for these people he didn't even know about until now, the way they had all worked together to pull this off successfully.

*   *   *

After Davis dropped him off back at the hotel, Jack decided it was time to reach out to Jojo. He opened WeChat and again looked at her last message. He had about a novel's worth of words he wanted to write to her, but he decided it was best to keep it succinct.

I'm not a spy. I was called upon to help my country, and yours. I love you.

He sent the message. Now he needed to be patient. He didn't want to obsess over it, but he felt actual physical pain thinking this might be it for him and Jojo. If that's what she chose, then of course he would have to accept it, as a consequence of his actions. And seeing as things had gone successfully, he couldn't regret those actions. The lives of countless people would be changed.

And possibly, so would his—just not in the way he hoped.

His phone began to vibrate, and his heart leaped—Jojo! This was better than he thought it would be—she was calling him, not just replying to his message on WeChat.

But it wasn't Jojo.

It was his father.

He took a deep breath and picked up the phone. "Hi, Dad."

"Jack," his father said. "I couldn't believe it when I first saw it online. That was you, wasn't it?"

"That was me, Dad."

There was a pause. Was his father going to admonish him for doing something that could've gotten him locked up for the rest of his life, something for citizens of another country?

"Jack, I . . . I'm at a loss for words. I couldn't be prouder of you is the only thing I can think of to say. I mean, it takes my breath away to think about the amount of trouble you could've gotten into, to put yourself in a position like that. To undertake something of such magnitude. It's hard to wrap your head around it!"

"I know, Dad," Jack said. "And I'm sorry you had to find out through the internet, but I couldn't—"

"You can just stop right there," his dad interjected. "No need to explain, Jack. I understand. I understand and I am just so proud of you, and so grateful that it worked out. It's unbelievable. Good job, son."

Jack smiled, his cheeks flushing. Why, he almost felt a little teary-eyed. This was exactly what he had always hoped to hear from his father, because if he did, it meant that he had done something.

"Have you talked to your brother?"

"Not yet, no. It's been a while, actually. I should give him a call."

"Well, he might not even realize what's been going on, he went on some meditation retreat, no phones or other technology, allegedly."

"Allegedly?"

"If I recall correctly, he went on something like this before yet somehow still managed to text me a few pictures of the yurt he was staying in."

Jack laughed. "I'm sure I'll talk to him at some point and we can both entertain each other with everything we've been up to lately."

"What do you have planned now? You're back in the U.S., I assume."

"Yes. For now. But I'm going to be heading back to China shortly."

There was a pause. "You are? Why?"

"There's someone I need to see about."

"Is that a wise idea? A *safe* idea?"

"It is. I know Wang Yang, the new president. It's actually . . . it's his daughter that I need to go back for."

And because it felt like it had been so long since Jack had talked to Jojo, he found himself talking about her, at length, to his father.

"I can understand why she might think you deceived her," his father said. "And why she'd be upset about that sort of thing. But I can hear in your voice, plain as day, how much you care for this woman. Perhaps, if the feelings are mutual, she'll be able to set aside her anger toward you, and the two of you will be able to work it out. Regardless of how that turns out, though, Jack, I hope you know that what you've done is something that not everyone would've been capable of doing. I wouldn't have."

"Oh, sure you would have, Dad."

"Do I speak Chinese? Have I ever *been* to China? No. And I admit, I thought you were squandering your considerable talents over there, but I was wrong. And I'm proud of you."

The words he had always wanted to hear. And it did feel good, and for a few moments, Jack's mind was not on Jojo and the fact that she hadn't responded yet; he basked in the feeling of his father's pride, he let himself enjoy how good it truly felt.

They talked for a few more minutes, and then Jack said goodbye. Still nothing from Jojo. He decided, right then and there, if he hadn't heard back from her by tomorrow, he'd get on a plane to Beijing then back to Shanghai.

Some explanations could only be made in person.

Please leave a review
and if you have any inquiries visit
www.bradleygood.com

THE TRADE EXPERIMENT

THE CHINA AFFAIRS

BOOK 2

CHAPTER 1

It was strange to feel like a celebrity, but that was exactly how Jack Gold felt now that he was back in China.

Davis had informed him on the private jet back to Beijing that Jack would not be staying at the Marriott; rather, Wang Yang had insisted Jack stay at a hotel closer to him, which turned out to be a high-end boutique hotel light years more decadent than the business-styled Marriott.

The hotel's manager, a man named Jim, had escorted him to an opulent suite with huge picture windows overlooking a garden and a pool. Jack had heard about these hotels before—there were hundreds of them throughout the country, meant for senior Party members, who had the best of everything, no expense spared. And Jack found this to bc true, even in the shower, where the soap was L'Occitane, from Provence, in Southern France.

It had surprised him, though, when he went downstairs, freshly showered and in a clean pair of clothes, to find Jim the only other person in the hotel.

"The hotel was emptied for you, for this visit," Jim said. He gestured to his left. "And here is our cigar lounge."

Jack nodded at each amenity Jim pointed out, though he couldn't help but feel strange, being the sole occupant of this hotel.

"We have a chef on staff twenty-four hours a day, so any time you feel hungry, you can come down here or call for room service. Order whatever you'd like. It's an honor to have you as our guest."

"Thank you," Jack said. What he wanted right now, more than anything, were some eggs and hashbrowns. No matter how talented the chef employed here was, Jack was willing to bet he wouldn't be able to properly cook that American breakfast classic.

"If there's anything you need, just let us know. We want to make your stay here as comfortable as possible."

"I appreciate it."

Jim excused himself after that, leaving Jack to wonder what he was supposed to do now, alone in a hotel. An entire hotel, all to himself! Not necessarily a scenario he ever dreamed of being in, yet here he was. He wandered around, peeked into the cigar lounge, walked past the heated pool, his restlessness growing. He made his way toward the empty lobby, where two of his security detail agents were standing near the front door. Though they were only here because they had to work, seeing familiar faces helped a little in quelling the feeling that he was trapped in a cage.

"I wasn't expecting the entire place to be cleared out," Jack said.

Tom smiled. "Well, it certainly makes our job easier."

"Not a bad place to have all to yourself," Denis said.

Jack's phone beeped, and he eagerly pulled it out of his pocket, knowing it wasn't going to be Jojo, but hoping anyway. "Excuse me one moment."

It was Andrew San.

Hey dàgē! his message read. *How are you? WHERE are you? I couldn't believe my eyes when I saw you broadcast on TV!*

Jack sighed as he looked around the empty hotel. It'd be great to see Andrew, but it wasn't like he was about to hop on a train from Shanghai to come up here. *I was surprised to find myself on TV too. Maybe we can get together when I get back to Shanghai, in Beijing right now.*

Andrew's reply was instant. *Me too, what are the chances? Want to meet up for a drink?*

Jack was so pleased at the strange coincidence he didn't bother to think twice about it as he wrote back an enthusiastic *Yes!* Andrew suggested the Jianguo Hotel, and Jack was more than happy to be on his way.

"That was a friend of mine who would like to meet at the Jianguo Hotel," he told Tom and Denis.

It was close enough that he could walk, and a wave of relief washed over him as he stepped out of the hotel, Tom and Denis following a few yards behind.

As he approached the hotel, he recalled the last time he was here—when he met with the three men—Ari, Joshua, and Tony—who would accompany him to the Control Center. How were they doing? He'd have to try to get in touch with them soon.

But first—Andrew. Jack smiled at the sight of his friend strolling up, smoking. Andrew waved, took one last drag, then put the cigarette out.

"Dàgē!" he said. He eyed Tom and Denis for a moment, but then returned his attention to Jack. "I haven't been able to stop thinking about you since I saw your face on the news! What are the chances we'd both be in Beijing at the same time? I'm glad it all worked out! Let me buy you a drink."

They went inside and took a seat at the bar. After they ordered and had their beers in front of them, Andrew turned and looked at Jack. He didn't say anything, but instead spent several seconds just looking at him, until Jack finally smiled.

"What?" he said. "Do I have something on my face?"

"Your face," Andrew repeated, returning Jack's smile. "Jack, I almost didn't believe it at first when I saw you on TV. How long had you been planning that? Was that your intention all along? I thought you came to China for the excellent business opportunities."

It was hard to read Andrew's tone—he sounded a bit incredulous and perhaps a little in awe. But Jack had a feeling there was also a fair measure of disapproval there too, though his friend was doing a good job at keeping it in check.

"I did," Jack said. "And obviously, I can't get into all the details. It was just one of those situations that I ended up involved in. But not the reason why I came to China at all." He shook his head. "You know that."

"Do I?" Andrew raised his eyebrows. "I couldn't believe it. There I was, just got home, cracking open a beer, wondering what I was going to do that evening, and wait a second, I recognize that voice on the TV. I was in the kitchen and the TV was on in the other room, I heard you before I saw you. But I *knew*, I just knew, that it was you, even before I went out there to look."

"It must've been a shock."

"*That's* putting it mildly! And then Stanley starts messaging me and wants to know if this is something I knew about. Can you believe that! As if I'd be part of something like this." He took a sip of his beer and shook his head.

"It's for the good of everyone," Jack said. "We did it because we wanted to improve things for everyday people here. They deserve it. They deserve to have the freedom to make their own choices based on uncensored, factual information. Don't you agree? Isn't that what you'd want for yourself?"

"Of course I want what's best for myself," Andrew said, grinning. The smile turned into a laugh. "Seriously, though, I hear what you're saying Jack. And I still think you're a good guy. I just didn't realize you were also a TV personality." He glanced over his shoulder and then back at Jack. "You do realize that you're something of a celebrity. You have your own security. Obviously you're now someone important. Have you noticed the way people are looking at you?"

"I'm trying not to," Jack said. "I don't like being recognized every time I go out in public." Yet it was certainly something he'd have to deal with now, he was realizing. Yes, people's attention spans seemed shorter these days, but what had just happened was a very big deal—the sort of thing that children would be reading about in history books decades from now.

"Seems like maybe you should have thought about that before you decided to get in front of that camera," Andrew said. He tapped the neck of his beer bottle with his index finger, frowning. Jack thought he sounded a little sad, or maybe disappointed that Jack would have decided to go such a route.

"Look," Jack said. "I know it was probably a big shock to see me on TV like that. Trust me—it wasn't my plan to be the one sitting there. And we did this because we truly believe that it's the best thing for the regular, everyday citizens of this country."

Andrew's eyebrows shot up. "Is that what you told yourself?"

"Of course," Jack said. "Because we believe it. People should have free access to information, to facts, whether or not they paint a particular leader or government in a rosy light. How are people supposed to think for themselves and make informed choices if they're only being given one side of the story?"

Andrew looked at him incredulously. "Because it's worked out so well in other parts of the world? In America? You Americans and your liberties—sure, it all *sounds* well and good, but your country is a mess. People shooting each other up in schools, at churches. Your healthcare system is a disaster. People only care about wealth. And themselves. Let's say something big happens, some sort of pandemic that requires people to put the good of the whole ahead of their own selfish wants and needs.

Citizens of China can do that. But Americans? Europeans?" Andrew shook his head. "That's the problem when you place more emphasis on individualism. It'll just screw you over in the end."

Jack regarded his friend, nicely dressed in an expensive-looking gray button-down shirt and a pair of designer jeans, black leather shoes. "People in America care about more than just wealth," he said, "though I won't argue that it is an important component of the American Dream. But it's not even wealth, really—it's the freedom to be able to live life on your own terms. And yes, for many that means cultivating a successful career and enjoying the liberties that money can afford."

"But this is China, not America," Andrew said. "How can one country claim to know what is in the best interest of another? America certainly has a penchant for that sort of thinking."

Jack took a long sip of his beer. Out of the corner of his eye, he could see a couple seated at table nearby looking at him, then looking down at their phones, then back to him. They whispered to each other. He had a feeling that, at any moment, one or both would be lifting the phone to take his picture.

"I think I better get going," he said.

"But you haven't even finished that drink."

Jack picked up the bottle and drained the final sip. "I'm sorry I can't stay out longer. I'm sure you can understand that it feels a little strange to be back, especially considering some people actually recognize me."

"Of course they do. You're the most recognizable man in China right now. How come you're so surprised? Surely you knew that would happen."

Jack paid for their drinks, then patted Andrew on the shoulder. He wasn't going to be able to put it into words that Andrew understood— why he had done it, why he had risked so much for so many people he would never meet in person. "I'm glad we met up," he said. "Thanks for getting in touch. And we'll get together soon, and hang out for longer next time, I promise. Things are still settling down. They're not going to be like this forever."

"I guess you're right," Andrew said. "I just wish you had thought about things a little more before you went and did it."

"Maybe," Jack said, "but if I spent too much time thinking about it, I probably wouldn't have done anything. Action was needed in this situation, not endless pontification."

The expression on Andrew's face was hard to read. He just needed to wait and see how things were going to improve. The changes that would come for people because of it. Jack was certain his friend would eventually come to realize that the right thing had been done.

*   *   *

The next morning, for his meeting with Wang Yang, Jack chose a bright yellow tie to go with his navy-blue suit, and at eight-thirty exactly, he made his way downstairs. Davis was waiting in the lobby with Tom and Denis.

"Good morning," he said as they exited the hotel. "Our vehicles aren't allowed to enter the compound, so they'll take you in their car." He pointed to a dark gray Audi parked in front of their SUV. "But don't worry—we'll be nearby."

A few minutes after they started driving, Jack's black phone beeped. He pulled it out of his pocket and read the message: *Turn off this phone before you give it to them at Zhongnanhai.*

They were going to Zhongnanhai, the Communist Party's base? Most of the Politburo Standing Committee lived on the twenty-two-acre property, which had formerly been the imperial garden in the Imperial City, located next to the Forbidden City and closed to outsiders.

As they turned, Jack stared out the window and saw they were entering the Xinhuamen, the "Gate of New China." He could see two slogans on the side of the entrance; one read "Long live the great Communist Party of China" and the other said "Long live the invisible Mao Zedong Thought." He could not help but feel humbled by the history of this place, and at the same time in awe of the traditional Chinese architecture.

Once within the compound, they continued down a road toward the more modern-looking office buildings. The car slowed to a stop where a man and a woman waited for him near the entrance.

"Hello, Mr. Gold," the woman said as he approached. "We are here to guide you to your meeting." He followed them through one set of double doors, where he relinquished his phones to a gentleman who was waiting right inside. He continued on his way through an extensive set of corridors, passing by offices, some with their doors open, others closed. They went through a door and Jack found himself outside; to his right was a lake, and they walked along a path toward another building, which they entered, wove through some more corridors, and then exited to the outside again. There was a pool house and an elegant pagoda, under which were two tables and several chairs, partially hidden by willow trees and bamboo.

Wang Yang sat at one of the tables, smoking, a stack of paperwork in front of him. He looked up as they approached, a broad smile on his face. He stood. "Hello, Mr. Gold," he said. "I'm so glad to see you again so soon."

"Likewise," Jack said. He smiled at his two guides, who had turned and were starting to walk back the direction they had just come. "Thank you," he said.

"Have a seat. Have a smoke." Wang Yang pushed the pack of cigarettes toward him as they sat down. "Would you like a drink?"

"I'll try any tea you recommend," Jack said as he pulled a cigarette from the pack.

An attendant appeared, and Jack lit his cigarette while Wang Yang told them what type of tea to bring out. Then, he took another cigarette from the pack and lit it, leaned back in his chair. "Jack, I just have to ask– do you know what you've done?"

Jack exhaled a plume of smoke. "To be honest, I haven't gone online much. I haven't even watched the news. So, yes, I know what I've done, but I haven't been paying much attention to what other people are saying about it."

Wang Yang nodded. "One of the things you said: tiāngāohuángdìyuǎn. Which literally means *heaven is high and the emperor is far away–there's no help for it.* When you said that, you got people's attention. Everyone knows that saying and believes it, but they never talk about it. You helped elevate the consciousness of a nation. You were humble and honest. You didn't try to hurt anyone. You were truly acting in the interest of others."

The attendant returned with a tray with their tea. "Oolong," Wang Yang said. Jack watched as he put some of the tea in the tea pot and then added the hot water. He swished the water around the pot several times and then poured it out. Because the tea leaves were handpicked and then left outside to dry, it was a custom in China to wash the tea before it was consumed to clean it and "wake up the tea." Wang Yang added new water to the pot and let it steep for a few moments before pouring a cup for Jack.

"I must ask," Wang Yang said, "how long did you practice that speech?"

Jack set his teacup down. "Let me first say I'll never speak to the Chinese people uninvited again. And, as you probably heard, I wasn't even supposed to be the person up there talking. Tony Woo was, and I'm sure he had something great prepared. I had a few minutes to prepare, but honestly, I think it was better that way."

Wang Yang regarded him. "A few minutes," he said slowly. "Incredible. But I think you're right—that's why it sounded from the heart. Not rehearsed."

"I truly love China." Jack paused. He hadn't been sure when and if he would bring this up, but now seemed as good a time as any. "And . . . more importantly . . . I'm in love with your daughter." Wang Yang nodded and took a drag off his cigarette. "She thinks I'm a spy," Jack continued. "Which I'm not. But she's very upset with me, and I do understand why. I want to make amends and to continue our relationship. I'd like nothing more than to marry her. If she agreed, would we have your blessing?" He was certainly putting the cart before the horse, but he had to ask, even if Jojo never spoke to him again. Perhaps she had said something to her father, something that Wang Yang might pass along to him now that would let Jack know if reconciliation was even possible.

"If Jojo wants to marry you, then yes, you have my blessing. But not for at least three months; things need to settle down."

"Of course," Jack said. "And if I know Jojo at all, *she'll* be the one who decides when she gets married."

"I do control when she gets married," Wang Yang said. "Here, the father has the Hukou Bar. You can't get married without that."

"That's true," Jack said. In China you had to go to the town where the bride's family is formally registered and use the family documents, called the "Hukou Bar" when getting married. "She could travel to the United States and get married there."

"That would be difficult without a passport," Wang Yang said. "China confiscates the passports of its leaders and their relatives. They can't travel unless approved."

Jack pulled Jojo's new US passport out of his pocket and slid it across the table. Wang Yang gave him a quizzical look before picking it up.

"I met with Sutton and asked him for it," Jack said. "And if Jojo is willing to give me a second chance, I'd like to ask her to take a brief trip with me to the US. If that's okay with you."

Wang Yang closed the passport and handed it back to Jack. "As we both know, Jojo's an independent person. And Chinese law says that if she has another passport, it's up to her whether she wants to travel. It's not my place to approve or not." He paused. "If you get married, will you promise to do so in China?"

"Only if you have better Maotai here than we can get in America," Jack said with a smile. *Maotaijiu*, an aromatic and very strong, clear alcohol, was China's national liquor. It was so renowned that Henry Kissinger had once said, "I think if we drink enough Maotai we can solve anything."

Perhaps, Jack thought, he should imbibe some of the stuff before trying to solve the issue of Jojo never wanting to see him again.

"Do you know Maotai?" Wang Yang asked.

"I love it. It's just hard to find."

"Let's see what we can do about that." Wang Yang gestured for one of the attendants to come over, and he spoke to him in a Suzhou dialect. The attendant nodded several times and then disappeared.

Jack was considering whether or not to indulge in another cigarette when he saw a man approach. As he came closer, Jack thought he looked familiar. He wore tan slacks and a navy blue shirt, and he walked casually, not in a rush. Jack blinked. Was that . . .? No, it couldn't be . . .

But it was.

It was Zhao Lihong, and he was smiling.

Jack stood immediately, and the former president of China went right over to him, took Jack's hand in both of his, shook it warmly.

"I . . . I didn't mean to cause any difficulty for you . . ." Jack stammered. What was going on? Zhao Lihong was probably the last person he expected to see here.

"You did me a big favor," Zhao said. "No need to get into it all now, but let's just say I was being pressured to do things I would not normally do. I should be thanking *you*."

Zhao took a seat and helped himself to a cigarette, so Jack did the same.

"Jack's in love with my daughter," Wang Yang said, looking at Zhao. "Look what he got when he met with Sutton." He nodded to the passport, and Jack handed it over for Zhao to look at.

"I was in his office and he asked if I needed anything," Jack said, as Zhao flipped through the pages.

He gave an approving nod as he handed the passport back. "Can you get me one of these, too?"

The three men laughed. They had some more tea and finished their cigarettes, and then Wang Yang asked if they could take some pictures. Four photographers rushed out, as if they'd been waiting in the wings for this very moment. They stood with the lake in the background, their pictures being taken from every angle—first, the three of them, then just Jack and Wang Yang.

After they were done with pictures, the current president and the former president walked with Jack back the way he came. The man Jack had surrendered his phones to gave them back, and Jack said goodbye to Zhao Lihong.

"I'll walk you out to the car," Wang Yang said as they stepped outside. "What's next for you?"

"I have to go to Shanghai," Jack said. "See if Jojo will even talk to me. I guess it's going to be difficult to explain myself if she doesn't even want to see me."

"She's independent and stubborn," Wang Yang said, "but she is also compassionate and forgiving."

"I hope she'll be able to extend some of that forgiveness to me."

"You have the passport?"

Jack felt his pocket, even though he knew it was already there. "I do."

Wang Yang smiled. "Well, if the passport and your apologies don't work, try a dog."

"Huh?"

"A dog. Jojo's always loved animals, and recently she was talking about getting a dog. The topic comes up every few years, and she always decides that it's just not the right time. But when is it ever going to be the right time?"

Jack thought back to their very first date, the picnic they went on and the dog that had run over to visit. He wouldn't mind having a dog, and he certainly wouldn't mind having one with Jojo, but he wasn't sure if showing up on her doorstep with a dog would be the best way to begin making amends.

"Things will work out for you, Jack," Wang Yang said. He shook Jack's hand and then opened the car door. He gestured to a bag Jack did not recognize. "Two bottles of Maotai. Jojo likes that brand. Good luck."

"Thank you," Jack said. He slid into the backseat and shut the door. A passport, her favorite drink, and possibly a dog. He hoped that would be enough to win Jojo back, but there was only one way to find out.

Made in the USA
Las Vegas, NV
02 November 2022

58630538R00132